# Make Me Stay

## Safe Harbor
### Book 2

## Annabeth Albert

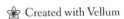

# Author's Note/Content Advisory

Safe Harbor is a made-up town somewhere between Astoria and Portland, Oregon, and any resemblance to real towns, persons, places, businesses, and situations is entirely coincidental. The series does center around a town secret, but the criminal case takes a big backseat to the stand-alone love stories in each book. No gruesome details and happy endings are absolutely guaranteed!

*Make Me Stay* touches on grief, loss, military-related PTSD, disability and chronic illness, and the realities of modern military service.

*To Annabeth's Angels, my reader fan group that is so much more. You have accompanied me on my grief journey, and it is only because of your support that I'm able to bring you a story like Cal's, where love triumphs over grief. You remind me daily that love wins.*

*To Super-Angel, Louise Auty, who beta read an early version of this book and always pushes me to bring the most authenticity possible to my work.*

# Chapter One

*Holden*

"Come on, come on. I have a case to solve." Fingers drumming on the steering wheel, I glared at the ancient, plodding RV in front of me. This country road led into the state park that surrounded the nearby lake. Tourists were a given, even in early spring, but I had no patience that morning. The sun was out after a long, long winter, and it was exactly warm enough to crack the windows and blast one of my favorite classic rock songs. My zippy Mustang was itching to take these curves at something other than tortoise pace. The curves, however, meant I had to wait for a passing lane to open up. *Torture.*

"Move. Faster. At least go forty," I bargained with the RV, which predictably went slower, not faster. I shook my head, mentally cursing the driver to a damp campsite and poor hookups. "Tourists."

Finally, a passing lane opened, and the second it was safe to do so, I zoomed around the RV. However, as I prepared to slide in front of the RV, a squirrel darted out from the dense green foliage, and I had to swerve far sharper than I'd intended. As a result, I nearly cut the RV off and undoubtedly looked like an asshole trying to make a point rather than a dude who preferred not to flatten a squirrel.

The RV honked twice as if to show how doubly perturbed the senior citizen driver was. At least, I presumed it was someone older, out on a scenic drive. It was hard to tell from a fast glance at the driver's side. A dusty and battered ball cap pulled low was the main thing I'd noted.

"Whatever." Eager to leave the irritating RV behind, I sped to the lake. The dense foliage continued as the road narrowed past tiny clapboard cabins ringing the eastern shore of the lake and huge hills of evergreen trees behind the row of little houses. The skinny, barely maintained road led past the public swimming area and several docks that would see far more use in the summer months. The eastern side of the lake—complete with cabins, a community center, Adirondack chairs, and volleyball courts—was a popular family retreat despite being in Middle of Nowhere, Oregon. The nearest town, Safe Harbor, was over a half-hour away, and we were hardly a metropolis.

Past a grove of haphazardly laid out picnic tables, warning signs started cropping up about deep water and steep drop-offs. The way more dangerous western side of the lake had an irresistible pull over local daredevil teens drawn to legends about the old timber railroad and wrecked train engine under this portion of the lake. Safety concerns about the dam that had created the lake in the fifties further added to the intrigue. And even the limited parking along the western shoreline wasn't enough to discourage thrill seekers.

But I was forty, not sixteen, and despite my need for

speed, I wasn't out to catch an adrenaline rush. I was here in pursuit of answers for a twenty-year-old cold case surrounding the disappearance of the mother of one of my high school friends. My friend Monroe and I had traced a serial killer to one of these very idyllic lake cabins that fateful summer, long before his first known victim. Both of us were professional investigators, but our personal interest in this case had driven us to spend long hours analyzing interviews with the killer, who spoke almost exclusively in movie quotes.

All signs pointed to the possibility of answers being under the lake, so here I was, impatient and ready to find out if our hunches were correct. I found the most level place to park near the designated meeting spot, but getting my chair set was tricky. The mix of gravel, dirt, and old asphalt was hell on my tires and made me glad I'd packed my wheelchair gloves for better grip.

"Sorry." Monroe hurried over, looking flawless as ever in a polo and pressed khakis. "I should have thought more about accessibility issues here at the lake. Maybe—"

"I'm fine." I waved his concern off with a flick of my wrist. "And I love the smell of potential evidence in the morning. Wouldn't miss this."

"Ha." Monroe shook his head at me. "Don't you ever run out of bad jokes?"

*All the damn time.* "Nope."

And if it kept Monroe and others from dwelling on accessibility issues and limitations, well, I'd keep right on rolling with the same class-clown routine that had served me well for over thirty years now. I'd discovered laughter hurt less if you laughed first yourself.

But this time, I must not have smiled widely enough or something because Monroe narrowed his eyes, gaze going sharp, exposing all his years as an NCIS investigator.

"Maybe Knox is right." His tone was thoughtful. Too thoughtful.

"He generally is." I kept my tone jovial, complimentary even, about Monroe's boyfriend. No sense letting on how my neck prickled under his careful concern.

"There's an...edge of sorts to you lately. Knox thinks you're lonely."

"I'm not," I shot back, then softened my voice. "I'm an extrovert. We're always lonely unless there's a party of two hundred of our besties."

"Exactly." Monroe smiled like I'd rolled right into the center of a trap he'd laid. Damn it. "Knox thinks you should get a roommate. You said it yourself. You're an extrovert. Maybe you simply need more people around."

"I don't need a roommate." What I needed was fewer meddling friends and a solution to this case. Neither thing seemed forthcoming. Pity. We were the first on the scene, with no rescue from Monroe's good intentions. "No roommate means no one to care when I leave my grading on the dining table or when I want to record an emergency podcast episode."

"Don't be so quick to dismiss the idea. Knox said you likely miss having your sister living with you."

"And my brother before that, but I launched the kids." I grinned, hopefully wide enough this time. "I'm okay with extra rooms at my place. Still debating whether to turn Marley's old room into a home theater or sex gym. I'm coping fine."

"No one said anything about coping. You always cope." Monroe said this like it was a bad thing. "But if you're lonely, you could try putting an ad up on the bulletin board at Blessed Bean."

"And get a ton of responses from college kids I've had in criminal justice classes? Pass. I'm too old for a roommate."

"Or too stubborn." Monroe exhaled as an engine rumbled behind us. "Oh look. Here's Phillips now."

I carefully swiveled in time to see the same ancient, rusty, and battle-scarred RV I'd pissed off pull up behind Monroe's compact.

"Seriously? This is the famous SEAL rescue diver you recruited?"

"Yep. I offered him a ride this morning, but he said his gear was all in the RV. He got in late yesterday and was super grateful for the dinner Knox saved him and the chance to get a better shower than the one in his old RV. Real polite guy. You'll like him."

*Doubt that.* But I made myself nod as a slim man exited the RV. No more a senior citizen than I was. Maybe late thirties. Hard to tell with the hat and unshaven jaw disguising one of those timeless faces, like an old western sheriff. He carried himself like one too. The classic military bearing made it so I could always spot a fellow first responder. He walked toward us with long strides, though he wasn't particularly tall. He did have surprisingly broad shoulders, given his narrow waist and hips.

Well, at least he looked the part of a legendary diver.

"You made it." Monroe waved him over.

"Yeah, a few minutes behind my ETA, thanks to this idiot who tried to run me off the road." The guy had a small hint of country to his voice, southern perhaps, but not Deep South.

"It's me." I held up a hand. He'd spot my car soon

enough. Might as well own up to it with a smile. "I'm the idiot who was trying to save a squirrel."

"More like the idiot who couldn't deal with going under forty-five." This Phillips guy didn't even crack a hint of a grin.

"Holden." Monroe and I were roughly the same age, which made his tendency to act all paternal to me frustrating as fuck. "You should try slowing down sometimes. Might do you good."

"Hey, I'm a safe driver." My declaration earned pointed looks from both men. "I am. Trust me, I spent enough customizing my Mustang. I'm not going to take stupid risks."

"You're a good guy." Monroe's tone was the verbal equivalent of a head pat. Good thing I loved my friends. He gestured at Phillips. "Holden, this is Chief Callum Phillips."

"Just Cal is fine." The guy continued his flat delivery, no smile as he shook the hand I offered.

"When does the rest of your team arrive?" I asked.

"I am the team." Chiseled jaw firm, Cal pursed his lips as if his dry tone hurt his full mouth. "Director, assistant director, employee of the year, and intern, that's me."

"Seriously?" As usual, I hadn't thought before I spoke, so I quickly backpedaled. "I mean, I was under the impression from Monroe that multiple people were coming."

"Whenever I do a recovery dive, I find local volunteers from the dive and veteran communities to help with logistics. They should be along any time now. But I dive solo."

"Is that smart?" All I could picture was Cal struggling on the dive and me helpless on the shore. I didn't even know the guy, so the vision shouldn't have hit me on such a visceral level. Yet, my chest ached and my breath caught. I knew diving, knew how indispensable dive buddies were, knew procedure, and damn well knew the value of a good team. "I'm not sure we should allow—"

Cal made a disgusted noise. "You need to see my stack of certifications? Discharge papers? Medals and commendations? My last five years of solo recovery dives?"

"No. Sorry. I'm sure you know what you're doing." I offered a smile but wasn't surprised when he didn't return it.

"I do."

"Cal comes highly recommended." Ever the peace-maker, Monroe had a too-bright tone. "We've been discussing the case and evidence for months, waiting for the right timing to do the dive. I'm excited to see what we find."

"Me too. And I'm here to help." I kept smiling even as Cal raised his eyebrows. "Put me to work."

"Good to know." He nodded sharply, but the brush-off couldn't have been clearer. "I better start assembling my gear. Back in a few."

With that, he strode back to the RV, leaving Monroe to glare at me. "Well, that could have gone better."

"Hey, it's not my fault the guy has the personality of a weathered fence post. Probably doesn't know how to smile." An uninvited urge to see Cal smile took hold. I wanted to know how a grin transformed his grim features, and more-over, I wanted to be who put it there.

"Not everyone is the life of the party." Monroe put a hand on my shoulder. "And I know you're trying. But give Cal a chance to impress you. He doesn't need a sparkling personality to crack this case for us."

Oh, he'd impressed me all right, not that I'd confess that to Monroe. Instead, I nodded. "Let's see what he can do."

# Chapter Two

*Cal*

I wasn't kidding about diving alone. Simply organizing the ragtag group of volunteers was an effort, much as sending emails and fielding questions had been in the lead-up to this dive. Having some volunteers was necessary, and whenever I did a recovery dive, there were generally locals eager to get involved. Which was good, but their presence could also easily be a problem. Every Joe and Jane with a dry suit thought they could help. It took diplomacy, something I was woefully short on, to find appropriate jobs for people, teach them how to run equipment when necessary, and explain the basics of the mission and the plan for the day. A lot of damn talking.

And I'd talked enough already, sniping with Monroe's impatient civilian friend who had an endless stream of opinions. Monroe was nice enough, but I could already tell Holden would be one of those civilian problems.

"Hey, Cal." The more reasonable Monroe strode over to where I was laying out my gear. A good-looking guy with brown hair and aristocratic features, he was a preppy dresser who still carried a lot of lieutenant energy. "Anything I can do to help?"

"No." *Manners, Cal. Manners*, a distant voice echoed in my eardrums. "Thank you, but I've got it."

"Good. I know you two didn't get off to the best start, but Holden really is a good guy." Monroe's too-serious expression was a dead giveaway that this was the real reason he'd come over. "And he and I have both been looking forward to you doing his podcast while you're in town like you said you could."

"Holden's the podcast guy?" I blinked. I'd conveniently forgotten about agreeing to be on the podcast. I was hardly media savvy, but when Monroe had called about the case a few months back, I'd recently finished a ten-hour drive listening to episodes of Holden's podcast. Being asked had made all my stiff muscles from the long drive fade away. Ego. Always getting me in trouble. And I should have recognized Holden's deep, melodic radio voice, but I'd been a bit preoccupied with my irritation. "He's Professor Justice?"

I glanced over to where Holden was reviewing something on a tablet. Unlike Monroe and his preppy tastes, Holden was dressed simply in black cargo-style pants, heavy hiking boots, and a sweatshirt making a joke about nineties music I didn't quite get. Not sure why, but I'd expected Professor Justice to be all suits and shiny shoes.

"Yep. It's his real last name. And a fitting one too. He jokes around, but he's on my short list of people I'd call in a pinch and trust to come through." Monroe was so earnest he might as well be Holden's spokesperson. "And the podcast is popular for a reason. He's a nationally recognized expert on procedure, and his podcast has led to a number of cold case breakthroughs."

"I'm sure he's smart." Smartass, more like, but I could at least try for civility. Try. "And I've heard the podcast a time or two." Or twenty, but who was counting?

"It's great, isn't it?" Monroe's tone was almost too enthusiastic, like he was trying too hard to get me to change my mind about Holden. "He's a former cop as well. Injured on the job in Portland."

"Huh." I made an inarticulate sound. So he wasn't entirely a civilian, but that didn't make him less irritating.

"Plus, he has extensive experience volunteering at the command post for various search efforts locally. Put him to work. Please?"

Damn it. Monroe was a man who knew the power of a well-placed *please.* I couldn't exactly turn down the guy who'd brought me here, was giving me a place to stay, and whom I probably still owed a favor from our navy days. Glancing at Holden, I considered various tasks, searching for something that wouldn't require too much maneuvering of his chair on the uneven ground.

"Okay. I suppose I can use help wrangling volunteers when they get here. Maybe he can check people in?"

"Excellent." Monroe beamed as I dug out my clipboard. I'd stopped in Boise a couple of days prior, found a chain shipping store, and printed off a roster and a few other papers.

Naturally, Holden—Professor Justice—ended up being great with the volunteers, many of whom seemed to know him. Hard to tell because he greeted everyone with the same enthusiasm: fist bumps, handshakes, and back-slapping hugs all around. He answered all the basic questions, like where to park, which usually took me out of my pre-dive prep. As I continued checking over my equipment, he assigned tasks and checked in volunteers with the ease of a natural-born extrovert. His ever-smiling, always-joking demeanor made it hard to stay mad, but somehow, I managed. I had no idea why he got to me so much, but he did.

Monroe did a commendable job as well, coordinating with local law enforcement and state parks reps who arrived on the scene. He gave all those assembled a quick review of what we already knew about the case and what evidence pointed to the lake.

"We believe the serial killer known as the Multi-level Marketing Murderer rented a lake cabin here the summer Melanie Stapleton disappeared. He'd dropped out of a nearby college sometime prior and become involved in recruitment and marketing for Kitchen Kingdom. We've recently learned that Melanie became a popular party host-ess, and the same landlord who verified the rental occasion-ally saw other cars at the cabin, including a green sedan similar to the one Melanie drove." This revelation made a murmur pass through the group before Monroe continued, "The suspect had a fishing license, and the landlord remem-bers repeatedly warning him to avoid the western shore of the lake."

"Then why not start the search on the eastern shore? Near the popular fishing piers?" One of the younger, more-eager volunteers raised her hand. She was a fresh-faced woman who'd introduced herself as Heidi from Washing-ton. She had a limited number of dive hours under her belt and a bottomless supply of questions. I made a mental note to pair Heidi with Holden for volunteer command.

Monroe gave the young woman a patient nod. "A couple of reasons. First, the suspect repeatedly references west, treacherous waters, pits of despair, underwater tracks, and buried trains in his cryptic statements using movie quotes. Second, the suspect's cabin was the one closest to this shore. We have some reports that the suspect may have even joined local search parties. Third, when the original searches took place after Melanie's disappearance, search dogs were used all along the lakeshore. Two of them pawed at the water near this area, but heavy early autumn rains delayed getting a police dive team out here. Their eventual dive didn't reveal evidence, but technology has advanced significantly over the last twenty years. Experts, like Cal here, have reviewed their data and believe it's worth another look."

"Yep." I nodded when Monroe glanced over at me. This was my chance to reassure the masses. "I've charted out the most likely areas based on what we know and what I've learned on other recovery dives. After twenty years of chilly lake water and silt, evidence may be in short supply, but if it's there, I'll find it."

And I kept that same attitude as we started work. Long experience and hours reviewing footage from prior dives at this lake had me homing in on a few specific spots before I ever ventured below the surface. I relied on the volunteers to help me set the jackstay search pattern using surface buoys, down weights, and lines.

To maximize my dive time, I preferred to use a small ROV, driving the underwater camera to scout and do a recon of specific sites before I dove. Some volunteers with older and civilian-grade ROVs had done earlier work at my request, and reviewing their footage helped, but I still always did my own recon. The ROV didn't search the area as much as give me valuable information about what I might encounter and where. Once we'd collected the necessary footage, I returned to shore to review and prep for actual diving.

"What are you seeing?" Holden wheeled over to where I was working on my laptop. *Intently* working, not that he seemed to pick up on that.

I inhaled sharply to quench the impulse to snap back with "*Water.*"

"Oops. Sorry. Guess you were deep in concentration." Holden didn't wait for me to find my way to a civil response. At this point in my life, I ran on black coffee and bitter determination, but if I were a nicer guy, I could appreciate how damn likable Monroe's friend was. And it wasn't simply the radio-perfect deep voice or his relentless enthusiasm. He had a rugged, friendly face with a closely trimmed dark beard, tussled dark hair with a distinctive peak, and hypnotic eyes so hazel they were practically bronze. "I just noticed you were using a Pro 4 Plus BASE, and we don't yet have a team in the state with that capability. Saw one demoed in Colorado at a conference. Impressive, especially with the forward-looking sonar."

"Yep." I loosened my shoulders and my grip on my laptop. Clearly, Monroe had been right, and Holden knew his way around search and rescue. "Getting my hands on one took every bit of funding I could drum up, but it's worth every penny."

"Yep. Dive equipment costs add up fast. In Portland, we were always short something. Just getting access to side-scan sonar was huge for us."

"You've got dive experience?" I couldn't keep the surprise out of my voice.

"Yep. I worked for the missing persons detail, which meant I also did my share of search and rescue for the PD. Most of my dive experience was recreational though. Pleasure dove all over the state and also some pretty sweet tropical spots. The Maldives, man." His voice took on the wistful tone of divers everywhere. "Best vacation ever. Miss it."

"I bet." I'd tried for a gentle tone, but my voice still sounded a bit clipped. Empathy wasn't my strong suit. "Maybe you still could dive? I've known other mobility-impaired divers. Got two amputee friends from the service who dive all the time."

"Oh, I know it's possible. The challenge is finding a dive buddy or operator willing to take me on." He patted the rim of one of the tires on his chair, which was red like his blasted Mustang. Probably a custom job too, given his large frame with broad shoulders and chest, and I could see where certain dive operators might doubt their ability to keep him safe in the water. "Did some fun diving in Hawaii to celebrate my little sister's graduation from nursing school, but it took her a fair bit of searching to find an operator open to divers with disabilities."

"I'm sorry." The roof of my mouth itched from an unexpected and entirely unwelcome urge to offer to dive with Holden. To distract myself, I turned back to my monitor. "I was reviewing this area right at the limit of our tether near the buried railroad tracks. There's a steep drop and a ton of debris—old railroad ties, some sort of oil drums, and lots of trash. Low visibility as well, but I keep coming back to this shadow."

Holden peered at the screen. "Sharp right-angle sides. Decent size. Could be any number of things, but the way it's sitting isn't going to be easy to get it positioned for lift bags if it turns out to be something worth getting."

"If it's promising, I'll get it up," I assured him. "And that's where I want to start."

"Not one of the more straightforward areas in the search pattern?" He frowned, and how someone could be so by-the-book and also so easygoing was one of life's mysteries. Super smart. Super nice. Super pain in my ass.

"Nope. I trust my hunches." I shut the laptop with a decisive click, leaving Holden and his scowl behind as I prepared to dive.

# Chapter Three

*Cal*

Once I moved to preparing to dive, I tried to push Holden and his questions and his strange pull over me from my mind. I dove alone. I didn't need to be volunteering or even entertaining unfamiliar urges to be friendly. Nope, I had a job to do, and that was that.

Using the buoys and drop weights from the jackstay search pattern I'd performed with the ROV, I could precisely calibrate a put-in spot that would optimize my air supply and get the boat and winch in position if I found something worth sending up.

As always these days, keeping my pulse rate steady on the way down was a challenge. Even now, five years on, I heard Evan's voice on every descent. But I'd learned to breathe through it, to remind myself why I did this work and the utter necessity of staying methodical in my approach.

Not so much for my safety but because even a split

second of inattention could be the difference between spotting something useful and coming up empty-handed. And finding potential evidence was only the beginning. Each promising scrap had to be logged, preserved, documented through pictures and other means, and professionally handled for the chain of custody requirements. Metal items often had to be packaged in the water they were found in to prevent oxidation and potential loss of evidence.

Maintaining a high level of concentration meant being able to differentiate between random trash and relevant evidence. As I searched the area using a deliberate pattern, I encountered way more trash and debris than anything worthy of bagging as evidence. But I also knew better than to get discouraged. Disappointment meant getting sloppy, speeding up when I needed to stay slow and steady even though I could feel the restlessness from the surface volunteers.

I'd always loved how diving distanced me from the world, insulating me from others' energy and real-world problems and concerns. It allowed me to focus solely on the task at hand. But that didn't mean I was oblivious to the eager voices and tense energy of those waiting.

Carefully, I went lower into one of the steep drop-offs, murky water made worse by random railroad ties, fallen trees, and debris in the bottom of the pit. But then I saw it. Right angle. Boxy shape. Large.

*Steady. Steady.* I didn't say anything on the mic as I investigated closer. Plastic, but hard, like a shell. Oh. Wait. I encountered a protrusion that was definitely a handle. Suitcase. A large old-fashioned one with hard sides, a plastic handle, little nubby feet, and latches on either side of the handle. But the handle itself was wrapped with a cord of some kind which led to several cement blocks, the sort used in gardening projects.

I used my light to examine it further. There was something slick on the top side. Looked like half a bumper sticker with a distinctive crown on it.

"Yup. Got something." I kept my voice level on the com. Any excitement I felt would have to wait—adrenaline was the enemy in these situations and the reward later. "Suitcase. Weighed down with bricks. Documenting the scene, then coming up for evidence and lift bags. Gonna be a heavy, awkward hoist, but we'll get it done."

Of that, I was certain. I didn't do hope, but I did trust my gut, and my gut said this suitcase was key. No try. No hope. No might. I *would* get that evidence.

However, as it turned out, getting back down to the suitcase proved almost more challenging than finding the damn thing. I knew exactly the equipment I needed, a large bright-yellow, self-draining evidence bag, bridle straps, and lift bags commensurate with the expected weight of the case. I made quick, efficient work of assembling everything.

Holden rolled over to where I was double-checking connection points and carabiners. I was mentally rehearsing each maneuver, and I took my time looking up, knowing full well I wouldn't like whatever he had to say.

"Are you sure you don't want to take a team back down with you?" he asked, leaning forward, voice deceptively casual. And yep, I didn't appreciate the question.

"No need." Meeting his alarmingly intent gaze, I matched his casual tone. "I've deployed evidence bags solo many, many times, including under worse conditions. It's a steep, tight space with a lot of debris. None of the volunteers have the sort of experience needed."

"I get that. But wouldn't it be better to take a helper or

two down than to have to scramble divers to go retrieve your ass if you run into problems? Maybe just a spotter to watch?" His patient tone was that of someone who'd practiced his pitch on the way over to me.

"Did they draw straws to decide who got to try to talk sense into me?" I glanced back over at Monroe and the cluster of volunteers.

"No straws. I volunteered." He laughed lightly before sobering. "But yes, there's a lot of concern about the risk to you in retrieving this item. The weight of the case is only one factor. As you said, it's in a difficult spot."

"And I'll handle it."

Holden gave me a lengthy and considering stare that made my spine prickle. "I'm sure you will, but we're going to have a team of rescue divers suited and ready to deploy."

"Fine." I knew my rep, knew the fine line I walked between independent and difficult to work with.

"Cal." Holden breathed my name like a question. "What's with the go-it-alone insistence? I have plenty of military friends. SEALs operate in teams, right?"

"Not a SEAL anymore." And that was all I was going to say about that.

"Fair enough." He sighed like I'd let him down by not talking more. And while I got that reaction from people often, Holden's stung more than most. This was neither the time nor the place for soul-bearing conversation, but for the first time in a very long time, I had to swallow back my words as Holden continued, "But no stupid chances, okay? You coming back up safely matters a hell of a lot more than the evidence, and you know that."

Actually, no, I didn't. But I knew when to not disagree. "Yep."

I was absolutely determined not to require the three

divers waiting in the boat, one of whom was Heidi from Washington. She especially looked ready to launch at the tiniest hiccup over the mic.

I had to work damn hard not to curse as I worked the suitcase free of the ledge it was wedged on. Nothing about underwater retrieval was ever grab-and-go simple like they show on TV. The suitcase was bogged down by silt, sediment, awkward positioning, and plant life. The nearby metal debris posed a further hazard. My priority was capturing all relevant evidence, including the wire, the bricks, and any loose items. Bulky items like this were among the hardest to package. I also wanted to avoid the case unexpectedly popping open before I got it safely in the bag. There were also a ton of small calculations to make on the fly—which lift bags to use, how many, where to position them, when to deploy them.

And naturally, right as I wrestled the suitcase and bricks into the correct evidence bag, I felt an icy gush along my neck. Fuck it. Something long and jagged and metal had pierced my suit. It got me good too, cold water rushing in through my compromised neck seal, along my upper arm, and in freeing my arm, my damn sleeve ripped too. The cold was annoying, but I'd been in worse.

The main issue was that it affected my buoyancy, and while fighting that, I couldn't be sure every minuscule piece of evidence made it into the bag. I'd have to come back down and thoroughly search along the ledge and deeper on the bottom of the lake to ensure nothing was missed. But right then, I had a rapidly flooding suit and a bag to zip as quickly as possible.

I grunted from the effort to maintain my position as the suit fought against me.

"Everything okay?" a female voice chirped over the comm set.

"Fine," I said stiffly. "The suitcase was tightly wedged, but I'm getting the brindle in place now before I attach the lift bags."

That part, at least, went off without a hitch, but of course, needing to drain my suit on my ascent didn't go unnoticed.

"Dude! Your suit!" Heidi, the newbie diver, rushed over to me on the boat. "Why didn't you call for us?"

"No need." I moved so she couldn't see the extent of the rip.

"But—"

"Let's get the evidence to the team." My voice was terse, mainly because my neck and arm were starting to hurt like hell now that they were out of the frigid water, but also because I needed to get this suit off. I wanted to figure out if I had enough air for a third dive in my far less preferable backup suit. Another sweep of the area with the evidence team now that the case was up would be helpful.

As the state and local police representatives swarmed the case, I quickly initialed the chain of custody papers and made my way to my RV, only to be met by a spitting-mad Holden.

"What the fuck?" he demanded, pointing at my left arm.

"It's just a rip."

"In your skin." He pointed more emphatically, finger wavering. "You're bleeding."

"I am not." But then I put my hand to my neck, and it came away red and bloody. *Damn it to hell.* "Okay. Maybe I am."

"Don't you dare say it's just a scratch. That's going to need cleaning and stitches. Probably antibiotics too. God knows what's in the water."

"More concerned with what's in that case." I grabbed a towel and clamped it over my neck, which seemed to be the main source of the blood. Striding away from Holden, I walked over to where I could listen in on the evidence team. A female tech wearing gloves cracked the case as a hush ran through the crowd assembled around the team.

"*Bones.*" The word buzzed through the crowd. The case was shut again with a loud click.

"Off to the state lab," the tech announced. "Straight to the human-remains team. Chain of custody needs to be strictly observed."

"I need to go back down," I said to no one in particular. "I need to look for any other evidence."

"Not today, you're not." Holden remained infuriatingly at my side.

"I have a backup suit. Not as good, but it'll do."

"The hell it will. I'm taking you in." He motioned for Monroe to come over.

"You're arresting me?" I was pretty sure he didn't have that authority, but the deadly glint in his eye said otherwise.

"Into the clinic." Holden shook his head like I might have a concussion impacting my thinking, not a minor scrape. "You need an urgent care doctor, not another dive."

"Go with Holden," Monroe ordered as he arrived next to us. "I'll arrange to get your gear and RV back to town."

"I can drive."

"One-handed while keeping pressure on that gash?" Monroe shook his head. "No, Chief. You did good. Now, go get stitches before you pass out. Don't make me call for a medical rescue chopper for your ass."

"Fine." I grit my teeth. That *Chief* hadn't been a mistake either. That was a deliberate reminder that he outranked me. Accompanying Holden was a command, not an option.

Whatever. I could survive an hour or two with the guy, then get right back down to the bottom of the lake where I belonged.

# Chapter Four

*Holden*

I wheeled ahead of Cal, unlocking my car as we went. The guy looked like hell. He'd stripped out of the dry suit, which had smeared blood on his arm and neck, and the T-shirt he'd put on was already blotchy and red. He still had a towel pressed to the worst of his wounds, but his pale skin concerned me the most.

"Pray for my upholstery," I muttered as we reached the car. The Mustang's exterior was red, but I'd selected a light-gray leather for the interior, a decision I was questioning at the moment.

"This is a sweet ride." Cal hesitated at the passenger-side door. "You said it's custom?"

"Yep." Another time, I would have happily shown off all the nifty accessible bells and whistles, but right then, I was concerned about the growing red spot on the towel. "Damn it. You're really bleeding."

"Sorry. I'll pay for your cleaning." Cal made a face as he gingerly lowered himself into the seat, making a clear effort to not touch the seat leather with his shoulder or back.

"I'm not truly worried about the leather. I was joking. I do that." Probably too often, but who was counting? My mom always complained that I used jokes to cover every uncomfortable emotion, and she wasn't entirely wrong. It wasn't the upholstery I was worried about. It was Cal, but he'd been bristly from the start all day. He wasn't going to welcome my concern. But worried I was, so I transferred myself to the driver's side and stowed my chair in the back as quickly as possible. "I'm legit wondering if we should have sent for that chopper. Keep pressure on the wound, and tell me if you get lightheaded or feel faint."

"I don't faint." Cal managed the seatbelt with a decisive click.

"Next, you're going to tell me you don't do stitches either, but I guarantee you're going to need some." I put the car in drive and gave Monroe one last wave. He and several state police personnel were chatting near the other vehicles. Cal had reluctantly given Monroe the keys to the motorhome, and his gaze lingered on his RV.

I left the dive site in my rearview, not speeding, but definitely calculating the number of minutes to get to the urgent care clinic in Safe Harbor.

"Damnit." Cal slapped his thigh with his free hand. "Sorry. Not mad at you. But I want to get back down to where we found the suitcase. I need to look for trace evidence and anything I didn't see on the first pass. And if I need stitches, you know a lecture is gonna come about not getting the wound wet."

"Take it from me. If the doctor says don't dive, don't dive." I made my tone as grim as possible, using all the wisdom I had achieved in forty-one years. Cal was prickly as hell and clearly didn't like me, but for whatever reason, I felt invested in his well-being. Perhaps it was guilt over not pushing harder for him to take a buddy or team down with him. There was also this strange fluttery feeling where I *cared* what happened to someone who was little more than a stranger. "I learned the hard way to listen to people smarter than me."

"Huh." Cal made a thoughtful noise, which was better than him dismissing my advice outright. "What happened to you?"

I'd been expecting that question. New people always wanted to know why I used a wheelchair, even non-chatty stoic sorts like Cal. My chair was basically a big question mark, and everyone from little kids to senior citizens felt entitled to ask. And this time, I'd more or less invited the inquiry by referencing lessons I'd learned. Cal wasn't an idiot. He'd known what I meant. Even so, I couldn't stop my heavy sigh.

"The short story? I was a dumbass newly minted detective who thought he knew better than everyone else." I kept my tone as clipped as Cal's had been earlier. He wasn't the only one with topics he'd rather not talk about.

"Sorry. I get it. You're probably sick of sharing the longer version." His voice was surprisingly gentle, that slight southern accent more apparent. "Everyone wants a story, and people have no problem asking you to show your scars, let them poke and prod."

Now there was a level of understanding I hadn't expected. And I supposed his SEAL discharge wasn't that different from my chair. Nosy people were everywhere, myself included.

"Yup. And I'm sorry as well. I shouldn't have pressed you earlier about your service."

"Nah." He grunted the reply, then groaned. "Damn it. No idea why this hurts."

"Maybe because it's a deep gash?" I suggested blandly.

"Maybe." He groaned again and rocked slightly in his seat. "Distract me with a story. Not the one you don't like telling. Just anything."

"Nah. I'll tell you the long story." I felt he'd earned that much from me, but also, I wanted to make my point that he needed to listen to whatever advice the medical professionals gave him at the clinic. And I was too concerned about his increasingly pasty skin and pained expression to search my memory banks for some funny anecdote. "You stay awake for me though, okay?"

"Okay." After a day of being wet-cat levels uncooperative, a docile Cal was worrying.

"Any other symptoms I should know about? Nausea? Lightheaded? Vision okay?"

"Fine." He clamped his lips shut. "Story, please."

"Well, since you said please..." I gave a strained laugh. I hated this story, but maybe it would help him to hear it. "I'd finally gotten myself assigned to the crimes division of the Portland PD, and I was working with the missing persons unit. And loving it." That needed saying too. Even now, well over a decade later, I still felt the sting of loss over a job I'd loved. "We got assigned a missing kid case. The kind where every minute counts while searching a neighborhood for a toddler who'd vanished from a backyard."

"Scary." Cal's tone was distant, either because of pain or possibly limited exposure to kids. He certainly didn't strike me as a family man.

"Yep. The parents were beside themselves, and it was all hands on deck. I spotted something at a house of one of the neighbors, an older three-story craftsman with a high, steeped roof with a trellis leading up to the roof. I thought it was a kid-sized shadow, partially hidden by a dormer window. The neighbors were out searching with everyone else, so I couldn't gain access through the house. I called my suspicion in and was instructed to wait for backup."

"Let me guess. You didn't wait?" Cal half-laughed, half-groaned.

"Like I said, dumbass. I ignored the order because the shadow I saw moved. It was a sharp drop from the roof into a rock garden, and I couldn't risk the kid falling before backup arrived. I started to climb the trellis on the side of the house. I was almost at the top when the whole thing collapsed. And as I fell, my radio crackled. Kid found safe."

"Oh damn." Cal whistled. This was one of the reasons I tried not to tell the whole story. The irony was painful. "So you broke your spine, but it wasn't even the kid up there?"

"Nope. My shadow was a freaking cat. And no, not my spine. Out of everything I broke, I didn't have a complete SCI, no paralysis. I needed multiple surgeries and metal plates in my legs, hips, and pelvis. I use crutches some, especially at home, but regaining full use of my legs simply wasn't in the cards for me." I kept my tone matter-of-fact. Cal's assumption that I had paralysis was common. I always hated correcting people and tried to gloss over that the real issue wasn't a lack of feeling or sensation. Rather, I felt too much and had a never-ending struggle with chronic pain. I could walk a little, especially on better days, but exertion tended to bring on pain crises, no matter how much PT I put in, and on bad days, the chair was an absolute necessity.

"Wow. I'm..." Cal grimaced, either in pain or sympathy or both. "I'm sorry doesn't really cut it, does it?"

"No." With others, I'd be more polite, but something

about Cal made it so I was way more honest than usual. Raw too. "I still miss it. Being out there, on the scene. Heck, I even miss my rookie beat cop days. I could have taken a desk job with the department, of course, but it wouldn't have been the same. At all. When I say don't take stupid risks, I mean it. You won't know what you'll miss until it's gone."

"I get that." He released a long shuddery breath. "But sometimes it's the risks you don't take that haunt you. And for the record, I would have done the same thing."

"I'm not surprised." I wanted to follow up on what haunted him but was also wary of making him retreat. He continued to have vibes not unlike a feral cat, but I couldn't seem to help wanting to get closer to him. "You seem to run on adrenaline."

"More like black coffee, bitter regrets, and stubborn determination. I'm not a thrill seeker." Cal snorted, then groaned with pain.

"Oh?" I needed to keep him talking or, at the very least, distracted. A quick glance at the passenger side revealed he was paler, and it wasn't only his voice that was shaky. His hands trembled as he shifted restlessly in the seat. "Solo diving isn't a thrill?"

"Choosing to dive solo isn't a stupid risk. It's a calculated one. And trust me, no one wants me as a dive buddy. I'm the one who's the bad risk."

"Want to tell me about it?" I wanted to know in the worst way, but those cat-backed-into-a-corner vibes were back in a big way.

"Not...now." Which wasn't a no, so I'd take the win.

"Fair enough." As the speed limit decreased on the outskirts of Safe Harbor, I took another look at Cal. "Hanging in there? What's your pain level?"

"Swear to God, do not make me use a pain scale." He released a low, tight noise that made my gut clench.

"I hear you. I've had enough pain-rating questions over the years to want to throw a blood pressure cuff, but I need you to stay with me. We're almost there."

"I'm...awake."

"Is there someone I should call for you when we get to the clinic? Family? Partner?"

"There's no one." He didn't sound sad as much as matter-of-fact, but that straightforward tone hit me harder than a complaint would have.

"I'm sorry. I couldn't have gotten through my injuries without my friends and family. I'll wait while they stitch you up, and I'll warn Monroe and Knox that you'll likely need help tonight."

"I don't need help." The slur in his voice called him a liar and made alarm bells ding in my brain. We were behind a slow-moving line of traffic led by a school bus. I alternated between drumming my fingers and glancing over at Cal. A shudder raced through him. "Did you turn the AC up? I'm cold."

"We're almost there," I reassured both of us. As we arrived at the clinic, I bypassed the parking lot to pull even with the emergency bay doors. "Don't get out yet."

"Okay." His eyes fluttered. His lack of argument was terrifying, and I waved frantically to get the attention of the person working the information table near the door. I'd long ago made my peace with most of my limitations, but right then, my inability to bodily carry Cal in made my stomach twist.

"Help," I called as the young male clerk came to the door. "I've got a guy here with a bad gash. Happened out at Foxtail Lake."

"We've got you." The clerk motioned to a passing transport orderly, and the two of them hustled Cal into a wheelchair. The clerk turned back to me. "We're taking your friend straight back to be examined. Go park, and we'll direct you to his room."

"Okay." I wasn't Cal's friend, wasn't his anything, really, but hell if I was going to leave him alone. I'd be his temporary friend, at least, whether he wanted it or not.

# Chapter Five

## *Holden*

My assessment that angry cats had nothing on Cal was only strengthened by his demeanor in the exam room of the Safe Harbor urgent care center. In fact, my mom's old, ornery beagle had a better disposition.

"You don't have to stay," Cal said for the tenth or maybe twentieth time. I was losing track. But he was also pale enough lying on the gurney that I wasn't going anywhere. The clinic was overcrowded and understaffed, and I didn't trust Cal to ring the call button if he felt faint. Hell, I hadn't known Cal a full day, and already I could tell he could be on the brink of death, angels descending, and he wouldn't want to trouble the nurses.

I got it. I'd been that guy a time or thirty.

"I know I don't." I found the patience for a wide grin. Gesturing with the remote in my hand, I pointed at the TV in the corner. "But this is more cable channels than I have at home."

I'd made myself useful by scrolling channels for Cal,

who had an IV in one arm and heavy bandaging on the other. I clicked away from a cooking show, breezing past an international soccer game, a sports talk show, and landing on some sort of DIY competition.

"See? Here's the one remaining house-flipping show I haven't seen."

"Is everything a joke to you?" Cal snapped, then grimaced, face contorting. The triage doctor had given him a painkiller in his IV, but it clearly wasn't enough. "Sorry. That was rude."

"It's okay. You're in pain, but truthfully, you're not the first one to complain I joke too much." My mom's face flashed in my mind, followed quickly by a fleet of physical therapists, bosses, and graduate school advisers. Shifting in my chair, I flipped the channel again, this time landing on another reality show. "It serves me well in the classroom to keep my students awake, but sometimes I'm not sure when to dial it back."

More like I had no idea how to provide empathy to a prickly cactus like Cal. I'd never known someone who needed fussing over more or wanted it less.

I could have remained in the waiting room, but when I'd entered the clinic after parking, the desk attendant had been only too happy to whisk me back to Cal. And there had been this unguarded moment when relief had swept across his face, quickly replaced by his near perma-scowl. But every time he bristled, my chest went soft and tender with the memory of his relief, and I stayed put.

"There are worse afflictions than being a comedian." Cal's tone was crisp, but there might have been a touch of humor lurking in his fathoms-deep blue eyes. "And it's not that I mind jokes. More like I've forgotten how to laugh at them."

His expression shifted, wistful and distant, another hint at some past pain. I wanted his story in the worst way, but perversely, I wanted to earn it, not force all the gory details out of him.

"Or maybe I'm not that funny," I said lightly instead of demanding to know what robbed him of his smiles.

"You're funnier than this show." Cal pointed at the TV with the arm that had the IV. Wincing, he wrinkled his nose. "What the hell is this anyway? He's on a date with three women?"

"Oh, I know this show. My sister's favorite dating competition. This is from season three. And that, my friend, is Timber." On the TV, a bottle-blond guy with tan, almost plastic skin laughed manically at something one of his companions said. All three women wore nearly identical tiny black dresses and sparkly heels. "He owns an eco-tourism company. The lovely ladies are competing to be his bride. And alas, he can only pick one out of the thirty-odd contestants."

"Reality TV is just weird." Cal shook his head like a dude who'd never once tried to fill the hours of a long, lonely night with channel surfing. It wasn't simply his past story I wanted. I wanted to know how he kept busy between dives, what music he listened to on his long drives, what made that hidden pain better, and what made it worse. And I knew full well the danger of such cravings, so I laughed lightly and asked precisely none of my burning questions.

"Tell me about it. Hollywood needs to stop putting cishet men in charge of romance shows. Give me a budget. I'd come up with something way better. *Panning for Gold*, maybe?" I leered at him, my cheesiest smile, until, wonder of wonders, the corners of Cal's mouth lifted.

"Ha. Took me a minute. You're pan?"

"Yeah. Labels can be a tricky business, but yes." Unlike Monroe, who'd known he was gay back in high school, my journey had been a long, winding road of self-discovery, and there had been plenty of years when I wouldn't have dared to come out to a stranger like Cal, especially not a SEAL. But I was past forty now, settled in my own skin, and curious enough about Cal's labels that I'd purposefully tossed mine out there. "Waving the pan flag feels the most representative of my dating adventures past and future, so to speak. And now I'm one of the advisers for the queer student union on campus, and let me tell you, my students would have *thoughts* on how to do an inclusive dating show."

Cal made a noncommittal noise. "I bet."

"How about you? What sort of show would you produce?" I kept my voice casual. Idle conversation, not a fishing expedition, even if Cal likely saw through my pretense.

He snorted. "I don't think there are enough viewers for *Pining from a Distance*. These shows are all about fast hookups. *Confused About Feelings* or *Mainly Into Myself* isn't gonna sell ads."

"Sure, it would." I laughed long, pleasure at finding Cal's dry sense of humor coursing through me. "And look at you, cracking jokes. Demisexual ones at that."

"It's the pain meds." Waving a hand, he groaned. "And demi what? That's a thing?"

"Demisexual." I put on my best professor tone. "It means you need emotional connection before you experience sexual attraction. Not saying that's you, but what you described fits. And there's a lot of people who would love a show for that target audience."

"Huh. I figured I was just shy, regardless of gender."

35

Cal's mouth pursed. And certain parts of my body ran a highlighter over that *regardless*. Circled and underlined with red pen too. Not that it made a lick of difference, so I kept my expression neutral as he continued, "But yeah, I can't do the anonymous thing. Wish I could."

"No, you don't. Trust me that hookups get old after a while. I'm not demi, but I'm giving celibacy the old college try simply because I'm tired of playing the game." Huh. As I said it, I wondered if my lengthy dry spell was part of why I'd been snappy lately. Maybe Monroe and Knox had a point, but I'd long learned the hard way that one-offs were a way to feel more, not less lonely.

"You don't seem like the type to get tired of much." Cal made a noise that might have been a chuckle, and I wasn't sure whether he meant because I had so much energy or because I gave off manwhore vibes.

"I'll take that as a compliment, but even extroverts wear out." I waggled my eyebrows, not flirting but definitely trying to earn a real laugh.

"Think I saw a commercial for a med..." Trailing off, he licked his lips and reached for the mug of ice water on the table over the hospital bed. Groaning, he dropped his hand, face contorting.

"Here." I sped to the rescue before he could proclaim he didn't need a drink after all. I knew all the tricks. And I also knew the exact angle to hold the mug and straw so Cal could take a sip. "Don't strain."

"Thanks." His gaze softened as our eyes met over the rim of the hospital cup. I held still, mug and breath both, not wanting to pierce this moment. It was sweet and strange. When had I last had someone to take care of? Not gotten laid or had a date or done a favor for a friend, but when had I taken care of someone? Cal made me want to remember,

36

made me want to try, made me wonder if there was a way past all his prickles and claws.

"Mr. Phillips." A young doctor with short twists poking out of her colorful scrub hat popped our little bubble of peace as she entered, followed by two medical assistants. Coughing, Cal batted away the mug like we'd been caught making out, and the shorter of the two assistants grinned.

"I'm Dr. Washington." The doctor grabbed a rolling stool and plopped down on the other side of Cal. "Congrats on avoiding the need for surgery or a blood transfusion."

"Um. Thanks." Feet moving restlessly under the light hospital blanket, Cal seemed to have no clue what to make of Dr. Washington's chatty, cheerful energy. I liked her immediately, and not simply because she made me appear undercaffeinated and shy by comparison.

"Luckily for you, I was on call. I did a residency in plastic surgery before emergency medicine won my heart, and I was able to talk triage out of transferring you to Portland." The doctor kept up her conversational patter as the medical assistants laid out a tray of stitching implements.

"No transfer," Cal gritted out. "Don't care what the scar looks like."

"Luckily, I do." Dr. Washington laughed. "Though, I'm going to warn you that the stitching process will be uncomfortable. Not painful, but because of the location and depth of your wound, you're going to feel pressure, and I need you to hold super still."

"Fine." Cal held himself as stiffly as if she'd asked for his name, rank, and serial number.

"You might want to grab onto your...partner." The doctor jerked her head in my direction. And why my chest gave a weird pang, I had no freaking clue. So I did what I did best and laughed.

"Oh, we're not a couple, but he can squeeze my hand anyway." Mindful of Cal's IV, I took the hand on his uninjured side in mine.

"No...need." Cal didn't pull his hand away, but he did make an utterly disgusted face like we might all be about to revoke his SEAL trident if he admitted the slightest anxiety.

"It's that, or I crack more bad jokes to distract you." I had no issues threatening a SEAL, and all three women tittered at my commanding tone.

"Fine. Hold my damn hand." Cal loosely laced his fingers through mine, a frisson of electricity racing up my arm. "I've had tats. This is no biggie."

"Mm-hmm." The doctor shook her white lab coat sleeve to reveal some truly spectacular floral work along her forearm. "So have I, and I'd rather get a full-color backpiece than neck sutures any day. You have no idea how lucky you got. Wonder you made it back up to the surface."

Her cheerfully gory speech earned a mere grunt from Cal.

"Ignore him." I waved away Cal's crankiness like we were old friends. "He's just mad he won't be able to dive for a while."

"Dive? Oh, heck no." The doctor's dark eyes went wide as she looked up from cleaning and prepping the worst of Cal's wounds. "It will be a few weeks before you're back in the water. Sutures need to heal, your neck mobility will be compromised, and the antibiotics are likely to irritate your stomach. Not a combo I'd want to dive with."

"I've dived with worse." Cal tensed, fingers tightening against mine.

"Uh-huh. Don't think I missed the navy tat, sailor." She nodded at the anchor and compass near Cal's wrist. "But you're not ruining my handiwork. No, sir. No diving. That's an order." Setting aside the wipe she'd been cleaning with, she flipped over her hand, revealing a carefully lettered *Whatever It Takes* and army logo tattoo on her inner arm. "Reserves. Most folks just call me Doc, but if it keeps you on shore, you can call me Captain."

"F—sorry." Cal made a pained noise as she resumed her work. "That hurt."

I had a feeling he meant his ego at the doctor pulling rank rather than his neck and shoulder, but I took the opportunity to ask, "Can you numb him more?"

"Absolutely. Listen to your friend, sailor." She patted Cal's leg before reaching for a syringe. Moving quickly, she injected Cal before he could inevitably protest that he was plenty numb. "You're going to be sore for a good while. Take all the help we can give you. Before you leave, I'm going to give you an antibiotic prescription as well as pain meds."

"Don't need 'em." The wet, angry cat was back in Cal's eyes and tight body language. I wouldn't want to meet him in a dark alley, but hell if I didn't want to comfort him, dangerous as that might prove.

The doctor shrugged like Cal being stubborn was nothing she hadn't seen before. "Good luck finding a viable position for sleep tonight without pain meds."

"I don't sleep." Cal's voice was terse, and the doctor set her needle down to peer into his eyes.

"Wanna talk about it?"

"Nope."

She inhaled sharply, but her tone stayed as unflappable as ever. "Have you tried—"

"Yep. Trust me, whatever you're about to suggest, I've tried. Unless you've got a do-over button or a sledgehammer, it's not gonna work."

"Who manages your PTSD, sailor?" Gone was the cheerful doctor, replaced by a hardened army captain who had seen some shit. Her full lips thinned to a steely pink line, daring Cal to disagree with her assessment.

"Me." Making a frustrated noise, Cal stared down at where his hand rested in mine. "You know how it is, Doc. Sure, the VA was quick to label the insomnia PTSD. But others have it way worse."

"Mm-hmm." Resuming stitching, she didn't sound like she believed Cal any more than I did. And I'd bet money the insomnia was only the tip of the PTSD iceberg weighing down Cal.

"I've tried meds. Long list. Only thing that helps is diving."

"Therapy?" She squinted at the wound, her careful, perfect stitches slowly repairing Cal's skin. Lord, how I wished she could repair his psyche as easily.

"Navy made me try that too. I'm not much on talking."

"No kidding." I laughed, but his stubbornness was no joke.

"Well, if you ever want to try again, I know someone great in town." The doctor managed a bright tone like Cal might actually take her advice. "Former school counselor opening up a private practice. Love her. We've got ourselves a little support group of service people going too. Casual. A few times a month in a church basement."

"I'm not sticking around." Cal shook his head, and Lord, wasn't that the truth. This wasn't a guy who put down roots. No dust gathered on those boots, and I'd do well to remember that.

# Chapter Six

*Cal*

By morning I felt like pond scum, an algae bloom choking out what little life and energy I had left. As usual, I'd barely slept, but the pain in my neck, arm, and upper back was new. I'd never known how many small muscles it took to turn my head until I couldn't. Hell, I couldn't even shrug without moaning. And keeping my arm motionless was almost worse, the stiffness that had set in as painful as the wound.

"Good morning." Knox greeted me as I gingerly made my way into the B&B's dining room. He was Monroe's much-younger partner, built like a Greek god with an ever-present smile. At the moment, he was devouring a large plate of muffins and fruit at the large oak table. The room was decorated in various shades of blue with a coastal theme. White wicker baskets displaying breakfast items added to the beach retreat feel, but I had zero appetite. I wasn't even sure I could manage coffee, and if I sat next to Knox at the table, I might not get back up.

"Morning. I'll be heading out in a few." Earlier, I'd dragged my backpack out to my RV parked on the street. Whomever Monroe had asked to drive it from the lake to the B&B had at least done a decent job parallel parking. Because lifting was a literal pain in the neck, I'd made sure to get my stuff out before the rest of the house woke up. No one needed to witness my grunting and wincing.

"Are you sure you're fit to drive?" Knox gave me a searching look.

*No. Not at all.* I knew better than to express any doubts, though, and I schooled my expression. "Absolutely."

"What did the doctor say?" Knox sounded not unlike Holden's repeated bossy instructions the night before to follow all medical advice. "We've got guests coming in tonight, but I could move things around or maybe give you the daybed in my art studio on the third floor. If I were you, I'd want to lounge around all day with bad TV, not hit the road."

The absolute last thing I wanted to do was be around people, particularly helpful people who wanted to fuss over my injuries, but before I could answer, Frank, the older, barrel-chested handyman for the B&B, loped in.

"Forget TV. You should sleep it off. Body needs rest to heal." Frank had the gait of an elderly cowboy and a deep voice to match. And if he'd ever laid around a day in his life, I'd be shocked. "Leon and I have a spare room and better taste in TV than this one." He jerked his head in Knox's direction with a fond smile. "And I play a mean hand of cards if you need R&R time."

"I don't." And yet again, I'd forgotten how to human. I took a deep breath. "Sorry. Thank you for the kind offers. I really am fine."

"Well, at least take one of Leon's muffins for the road." Knox pushed a basket of berry muffins toward me.

"Sure." My stomach was ready to stage an outright revolt, pain along with the antibiotics I'd taken earlier doing me no favors.

"We'll miss you." Knox was an adept liar, all bright tone and welcoming expression, but I knew better.

"Eh. I'll be back in town to get these damn sutures out and when I'm allowed to dive again."

"Good. We'll look forward to seeing you. You'll record the podcast then? Monroe said you asked Holden for a rain check."

"Yeah. We'll try for another time." I tried to sound regretful rather than relieved. And, of course, that bit of gossip had made it back to Knox. I'd simply been too bushed after the urgent care visit, and when Holden and his infinite supply of kindness I didn't deserve offered to postpone any talk of me recording a podcast, I'd leaped at the offer.

"Holden's a good guy. He texted earlier to see how you were. And he's amazing at the podcasting thing. He'll make sure you're not uncomfortable."

"Uh-huh." I was already plenty uncomfortable. I'd do the podcast if I had to, but I couldn't say I wanted any part of a Q&A with Holden. He'd already burrowed under my skin far too deeply. He'd held my hand for the whole suture procedure, taken me to the pharmacy, insisted on seeing me into the B&B house, and pressed his phone number on me. He acted like we were friends, like I wasn't a grumpy ass, like I deserved his nice gestures. I wasn't capable of being anyone's friend, not anymore, especially not to someone as magnetic and charming as Holden. Everyone from the nursing staff to the doctor to Knox and Monroe absolutely loved Holden. He had his pick of friends. Didn't need my cranky antisocial self.

As soon as Frank wrapped up some muffins for me, I started inching toward the door, narrowly avoiding a hug from Knox. Wasn't that I hated touch. Far from it. Holden's hand in mine the day before had felt good. Too damn good, warm and secure and stable. A hug was liable to make me crumple like a used tissue, and we couldn't have that.

"See you soon. Good luck with your plans." Knox waved from the porch as I made my way to my RV. Like me, the darn thing was sluggish, taking several tries to turn over and limping its way out of Safe Harbor toward the highway.

Knox assumed I actually *had* plans beyond getting out of town before people could press more charity on me. The last thing I needed was a room to recover in or caretaking. No, I was headed to the closest campground that would accept my ancient rig. From there, I had no clue. I had no other recovery gigs lined up, which I supposed was a blessing since I was a few weeks out from being able to dive anyway. I'd used a good chunk of my rapidly dwindling funds to order a replacement dry suit the night before. The neck seal especially was too badly damaged for repair. I'd had the replacement sent to the same dive shop in Portland where I picked up my air tanks.

The outskirts of the city seemed as good an option as any, so I pointed the RV east. However, I was only a few miles out of Safe Harbor when the damn vehicle went from slow to slower, with no acceleration. It hiccupped and hesitated, revving helplessly when I tried to urge it faster. When the engine compartment gave a mighty rattle, I finally accepted my fate and pulled onto the shoulder seconds before losing power altogether.

"Fuck." I was alone with no one to hear my yell, so I

said it a few more times just for good measure. Visualizing my bank and credit card balances, I pictured all my remaining funds going up in smoke. Starting with a tow truck because my cut-rate car insurance didn't have road-side assistance. And naturally, the one place I could find with an RV-capable truck was back in Safe Harbor. Fuck me, indeed.

The big, shiny black tow truck with a yellow logo arrived in a surprisingly short amount of time. Even more surprising, however, was the truck's driver. A tall, broad-shouldered woman emerged from the truck. She was fifty or sixty with platinum hair, red lips, colorful arm tats, and blue coveralls that said Earl on the nameplate.

"Yep." She pointed at the name tag. "Call me Earl. Or Earline. Or early to dinner. I'm easy."

"And I'm screwed." I gestured at my camper.

"I'll be the judge of that." Earl gave a curt nod. "Rare is the RV I can't tinker with." She made a slow circle around the rig, likely planning out logistics for the tow. "This is a classic. Bet there's not even twenty of these from that year still on the road."

"Not helping me feel better, Earl." I groaned. For what-ever reason, I found it far easier to banter with the gravelly-voiced Earl than Holden. And there I was, thinking about him yet again. Earl was easy to talk with because ours was a clearly defined temporary business relationship. Nothing at all to do with how unsettled Holden made me.

Earl let me ride up front in the tow truck, and I tried to angle myself so my neck bandages were less obvious. Didn't work.

"Shark attack?" she asked as we started our slow trek back to Safe Harbor.

"Something like that."

45

"Yep. I already figured you for the silent type." Mercifully, she flipped on an oldies station and let me stew the rest of the way to town. Her garage was part of a larger complex at the edge of town with a gas station, mini-mart, repair shop, and automatic car wash.

She took the RV into a large garage bay and led me to a small waiting area with a view of the gas pumps. Too tired to sit, I paced. Whatever the damage was, it wasn't going to be good. I'd maxed out my last card simply paying the upfront cost of the tow. By the time Earl came back, I'd made several circuits of the waiting area, read all the informational signs twice, attempted a cup of truly terrible coffee, and rejected the plate of sugar cookies near the coffee.

"So I've got bad news and worse news." Earl's hair, lipstick, and coveralls drooped as she settled on one of the plastic chairs. "Come on, sit. You're not gonna wanna stand for this. Sorry."

"It's okay." Reluctantly, I perched on the chair next to her, trying to avoid the urge to slump to the chipped floor. "How much damage are we looking at?"

"We're not. Your rig is already held together with duct tape and baling wire. It's a wonder you've kept it on the road, let alone found places to let you camp."

"I manage." I ended up boondocking more often than I'd like, dry camping with no hookups or parking at out-of-the-way no-frills campgrounds that didn't have restrictions on age or vehicle condition. Or, on certain recovery missions, someone like Monroe would offer me a room, and I'd take the prospect of unlimited hot water and the risk of finding street parking.

"You've managed yourself right into a pickle." Earl made a clucking noise. "Transmission's shot, but so are a number of other things. And on top of being older than dirt, your rig is a limited edition. One of the parts that most needs replacing simply isn't on the market anywhere for love nor money."

"Thought you said you could tinker with it. Like, maybe there's a temporary fix?"

"Honey." She put a large hand on my knee. "I'm a mechanic, not a magician, and even a magic wand isn't saving that transmission. And even if I could get a hold of the necessary parts, you're looking at a hell of a lot more in parts and labor than this thing is worth. I can't in good conscience let you toss that kind of money at something destined for the scrap yard."

"Well, fuck." I glanced over at Earl, fully prepared to apologize for my mouth, but she gave a hearty laugh.

"Yep. You're fucked, all right." She chortled. "But you're navy, right? I saw those veteran plates. I know Bud, who runs a used lot on the other side of town. Old marine, but he'll give you a military discount. Tell him Earl sent you, and he'll get you set with some low payments."

"Thanks." I managed a weak nod. Earl had no idea how bad my credit was. A buddy's wife had helped me with the paperwork for my organization, such as it was. I had a logo and nonprofit status, but when it came to fundraising, I'd been all on my own. And more often than not, I'd used my own funds for equipment, travel, and other expenses to the point that every card I had was crying for mercy. No dealer with eyeballs would give me any sort of loan. "I'll figure something out."

"Son, you look likely to fall off this damn chair." Earl peered intently at me. "Is there someone I can call?"

An image of Holden darted through my brain. He'd asked that yesterday and meant it too. He was helpful and

47

caring and couldn't fathom a world where a person had run out of favors, where there wasn't a line of hands waiting to offer assistance. He'd have been only too happy to call someone to take me off his hands the day before, and then finding no one, he'd settled in to wait for me, another good deed to add to his ever-growing horde of them. Pity. God, how I hated pity.

"No."

"Whelp." Earl's resigned grunt echoed my own. "I can store your rig for the time being. The RV dealer is closed today on account of a show this weekend in Portland, but I can get you a ride to a motel. You can check out his stock first thing tomorrow. Reckon you need a nap anyway."

"No nap. No ride. I'll...call someone." I was lying, but I pulled out my phone, turning it over in my hand like I was trying to decide among a crowd of contacts who would get the privilege of bailing me out. Me. I'd do it.

But Earl wasn't buying. She shook her head and pointed at the phone. "Uh-huh. Go on then."

Fuck. Now I was stuck. Calling Monroe would make the most sense, but I already owed him several favors. Didn't want to add to the debit there or end up with Knox and Frank hovering over me, either one. Scrolling my phone, I landed on my most recent contact.

"Guess there's Holden."

"Yes, there's Holden now." Earl's voice was almost too encouraging. Fuck. How bad off did I look?

"I meant a phone call. No guarantee he's around." I tried to temper Earl's enthusiasm, but she was already standing.

"No need. Professor Justice just pulled in." She pointed at the pumps, where, sure enough, a familiar Mustang parked near the closest pump. "Come on, let's go tell him your dilemma." She motioned at me before yelling at the pump attendant. "Tommy, go fill Professor Justice's tank and get his windshield too."

"Howdy, Professor." Earl greeted him with the same wide smile she'd had for me before pity had softened her gaze and I'd become her pet project. "My new friend here was looking for you."

"Was he?" Holden gave me a pointed look over the rim of his sunglasses. "Thought I recognized your RV over there in Earl's garage. I needed gas anyway, so I thought I'd see if you needed a hand."

"He does," Earl answered for me. "His rig's a goner. Toast. Darn shame."

"I'm fine." I waved a hand, then had to wince from the sharp pain in my neck. "Just need a ride."

"Sure. Where to?"

I reviewed my finances in my head yet again. "Cheapest motel. Don't care about quality. All I need is a place to think. I'll come up with a plan." *Somehow*.

"Hop in." Holden pointed at the passenger seat.

"Your belongings are safe enough here for the time being, but you'll want to come collect them before too long." Earl's tone was matter-of-fact, but it still underscored how totally screwed I was. A clock was ticking, and I couldn't lose my gear too.

"Thanks." I opened the passenger-side door. God, I hoped Earl wasn't a hugger. I might not survive that. "I'll... figure something out."

"You will." Earl settled for a firm pat on my uninjured shoulder as I slid into Holden's car. "See you soon."

"Where were you due next?" Holden asked as the pump attendant washed his already-sparkling windshield. "Got another gig scheduled?"

"Not at present." My voice came out all cagey, and an investigator like Professor Justice wouldn't miss that detail. I kept my eyes trained on my hands, not wanting to give him any other clues as to how rattled I felt.

"Why are you so all fired up to leave town then?"

"Monroe and Knox have new guests arriving, and I don't wanna be a burden on anyone. I'll sort this out. I'm almost out of funds, but if I can get into Portland, I can probably find some day work, get my cash reserves back up. I worked enough manual labor and construction jobs before the military that I can usually count on getting something short-term. I've done it before."

There. I had a plan. Wasn't a half-bad one. I looked up, only to find Holden watching me with a soft smile that made my neck prickle.

"I have a better idea."

I was sure he did and equally sure I would hate it.

# Chapter Seven

*Holden*

"I need a roommate," I blurted, far less gracefully than I'd planned, but Cal looked ready to bolt out of the car at any second.

"Do you now?" He regarded me solemnly, a harsh stare that had me shifting in the driver's seat. Cal wasn't wrong in his skepticism. *Need* was a major stretch. However, the second I'd seen his RV here at the garage, I'd known I couldn't leave Cal to flounder on his own, even if Chief Prickly might prefer that.

"You can ask Monroe. He and Knox have been on me to put up an ad at the Blessed Bean for a house share even before you showed up. I have a spare bedroom with an attached bath, and this last year or so has been my longest stretch without a roommate since buying my house." I'd joked with Monroe, but the truth was that passing by the guestroom door each morning did hit me square in the feels, an unwelcome reminder of how damn quiet my life had become. Perhaps that was why I was drawn to Cal. He might be cranky, but trying to worm my way past his grumpy defenses was an excellent distraction. I remained unconvinced that I was lonely, but having Cal around would be an excellent way to push away that concern. "In fact, I bought the house with an eye to sharing. First, I had my younger brother, then my sister. Maybe the room's a good luck charm to launching to bigger and better things."

"I don't do charity." Cal had his jaw clenched so tightly it was a wonder his teeth were intact. "Family's different."

The distant hint of longing in his voice, not his stiff body language, made my chest clench. If he were simply an irritable jerk, he'd be much easier to dismiss. But those little signs that he'd been wounded, probably more than once, kept adding up, catnip to my investigator brain and tender heart.

"Trust me that I don't do charity either." After getting a receipt for the gas, I put the car in Drive. "I'm going to drive a bit because that always clears my head. Maybe it'll help you consider my idea."

"I'm thinking." Exhaling, Cal fastened his seatbelt. "Not like I'm drowning in options."

"Yep." I wouldn't be offended that Cal wasn't more enthusiastic. There was nothing I personally hated more than needing others, and from the look of things, Cal was well and truly screwed. Out of funds, injured, and without shelter and transportation? I'd be biting off heads too. I took a left out of the gas station, away from Safe Harbor, and kept my tone conversational. "Right now, I have a high schooler who handles my yardwork and trash, but he's about to graduate and has a major case of senioritis, making him unreliable. That was the nice thing about having my siblings as roommates—someone to handle little tasks like carrying in groceries or wheeling the trash to the curb. Wouldn't mind that again."

"Trash duty is hardly worth a free room," Cal scoffed. The day was chilly but sunny, spring slowly but surely making its presence known. I turned right onto one of my favorite country roads that snaked around the town. We'd come out on the other side of Safe Harbor, near where I lived, but in the meantime, Cal could benefit from the sunlight glinting off planters of flowers on farmhouse porches and wide-open fields awaiting their summer yields.

"Room wouldn't be free. I made both my siblings pay rent as they were able. Same for you. Get on your feet, get some sort of temporary job, like you said, and we'll work out a fair amount that will still let you save for a new rig." My eyes narrowed. Cal truly relied on that RV. It wasn't some recreational extra. Best I could see, it was his place of work, living, and solace, all three, not to mention how he traveled between recovery dives. To my mind, someone providing such a service deserved community support. "Couldn't you do a foundation fundraiser of sorts? It's necessary equipment for your work."

"Yeah. I'm...not the best at fundraising." Cal admitting a weakness was surprising enough, but my eyebrows also lifted at his ready agreement that it could be considered a business expense. And that he wasn't insisting he needed to solve his RV crisis on his own made my chest expand with the minor win.

"I could help with fundraising. I'm good at getting people to part with money." I laughed lightly. However, that superpower could be a mixed blessing. People invited me to charity auctions and galas because I could be counted on to bring the jokes and cajole others into donating. Monroe had asked if being the life of the party ever got old, and the real answer was *yes*, but if my skillset could help Cal, I wasn't going to dwell on vague emotions I couldn't even name. "Bet we could dream up some new ways to drum up support for your foundation."

"I'll let you handle the dreaming." Cal gave me a half-smile. "And I'm not opposed to more resources for the foundation. That would mean more dives, more help for those looking for answers. But I've also done okay with taking temp work here and there to get funds for dives. That's a point in favor of Portland—more work opportunities."

"Don't discount small towns." We passed a farmhouse with a fresh coat of apple-green paint and a little yard side for Measure Twice Remodeling. "You got construction experience? Knox is in the middle of a couple of big remodeling jobs. Let him put you to work until his usual summer crew of college kids arrives for the break. After your neck heals a bit, of course."

"My neck is fine." Cal's stoicism was almost comical at this point, given how he winced with even small movements or bumps in the road.

"You look like an extra in a zombie flick." The pain had given his skin a pasty quality I knew only too well. "You're a scene away from demanding brains for lunch."

"Ha." He laughed, and luckily, I managed a glance over at him at precisely the right moment to catch the crinkling of his eyes and the hint of dimples lurking near his unshaven jaw. Even in his ordinary grumpy mode, Cal was easy on the eyes with his rugged looks and wiry build, but laughter transformed him into darn near the hottest person I'd seen in a long time.

"At least come for the night. I'd hate to see you toss what little funds you have at a crappy motel room."

"Suppose that's not the worst idea. And maybe I could

trouble you to collect more of my stuff from the RV later? Gonna need a place to store my gear if nothing else." His tone shifted from pragmatic to mournful with a low groan. "Fuck. I'm gonna miss that RV."

"I know. You'll get another. And in the meantime, I've got plenty of garage space for your gear." We were coming up on the west edge of Safe Harbor, farms giving way to newer housing developments and an elementary school.

"You're more confident than me on getting another RV. My credit's shit. And no idea why I'm telling you my money woes."

"Because despite my chatty rep, I'm a good listener," I said lightly, but my insides buzzed with the thrill of him trusting me with at least some of his troubles. "I'm taking you back to my place now. And later, after we collect your gear, you're going to let me brainstorm some fundraising options for you. Replacing the RV shouldn't be entirely on your personal funds when it's integral to the foundation's work."

"For a guy who was all skeptical that I didn't have a crew, you sure make me sound legit." Cal gave me a smile, another brief flash of those surprisingly deep dimples. "But I guess you have a point. Can't really do the work without a way to haul ass around the country."

"How'd you get the initial RV?" I asked as I stopped for the right turn back into the main part of town.

"Discharge pay. All my accrued sick and vacation leave plus what savings I had in the bank. A buddy on my team had grandparents in failing health who couldn't use that one any longer, and he was happy to take my cash offer. I'm not bad with money." A flush crept up his neck. "It's more that every dive drains my funds a little more than expected, and it all adds up, especially when I'm shit at asking for donations."

"What you're crap at is accepting help, period. And trust me, I get it. I've been there. I fell on my ass a week ago when Tyler, my high school helper, couldn't come do the trash. Foolish thing because a simple call to a friend could have prevented me from being out there at midnight wrestling the damn can."

Cal made a sympathetic noise. "Pride. Fucks all of us."

"Yep." I was damn grateful he didn't try to give me advice about not attempting certain tasks on my own. His commiseration meant more than he could know. I turned onto my street, a wide, sunny side street of seventies and eighties single-level ranches, most updated and in good condition. It was the sort of neighborhood where people put down roots and stayed for a while. After a string of rentals, I'd been drawn to the stability and cozy feel of the street. I pulled into my driveway, flicking the remote to raise one of the double garage doors. "We're here. You going to let me show you to your room?"

I expected him to make a smart remark about how he was only staying the night, but instead, he gave a solemn nod. "Thank you. I'll earn my keep."

Smiling, I reached over to lightly duff his uninjured shoulder. That was probably as close as Cal would come to outright accepting my offer, so I'd take the victory.

"Welcome home, roomie."

# Chapter Eight

*Cal*

"Nice house." I kept my tone polite but bland as Holden pulled into his garage. His house was a well-kept ranch with clear late-seventies roots and a distinct Northwest vibe with the dark-blue paint choice and hardy front-lawn landscaping. Most houses tended to look similar to me. All the base housing I'd grown up in blended together. My grandparents' suburban Atlanta home had been nearly identical to its neighbors and equally lackluster in character. Ev's family's stately historic Abingdon home in Virginia had been a rare exception, seared in my memories with the scent of sweet rolls and lilacs and the sound of boots on wraparound porches.

"Thanks. I like the neighborhood a lot." Holden smiled fondly before opening the car door and transferring to his wheelchair. A narrow ramp replaced what would usually be a step from the garage into the house. "I was specifically looking for a one-level with two bedrooms with ensuite bathrooms because my brother Greg was house hunting with me, and I knew Marley would likely want the room eventually."

"Mm-hmm." I made a noncommittal noise to show I was listening, even if I had trouble imagining having siblings, let alone ones who cared enough to tour houses with me.

"When this three bedroom-three bath came on the market, I knew it was perfect. It didn't require a lot of retrofitting to make it accessible either." Holden rolled up the ramp to the door. "Let me give you the tour."

"Sure." I followed him in. His pride of place was cute. House might look the same as thousands of other ranches, but this one was his, and clearly, that mattered to him. We entered a mudroom area with two rows of hooks, one at chair height. A pair of forearm crutches stood next to a neat shoe bench.

Holden whizzed past a laundry room and bathroom, emerging into an open-plan living and dining area with an adjacent kitchen.

"Sorry about the stacks of grading." Holden paused at the oak dining table to straighten one of several piles of papers. "I have an office, but that's been mainly taken over by podcasting equipment. And I prefer to grade while watching terrible TV."

"I see how it is," I teased, something I'd forgotten I knew how to do. "Like that dating show. Poor Timber with his big decision."

Holden grinned like I'd given him a gift by ribbing him. "Hey, you want to see how that season ends? I have all the streaming options."

"Says the guy who was impressed by hospital cable."

Suppressing the urge to smile, I kept my tone gas station-biscuit dry.

"Well..." A faint blush crept up Holden's cheeks. Yup. I'd known it. He hadn't stuck around for free TV.

"Thanks. You didn't have to stay, but I'm... Thanks." God, even thank you was hard with my painfully rusty social skills. I wanted to say I was glad he'd stayed with me at the clinic, but I bailed on that sentiment at the last second. Instead, I paced to the seating area, crouching to note blue squares by the couch and table legs. "What's with the tape?"

"That was my sister Marley's idea. It's for the cleaning folks, so they know where we have things placed for optimal wheelchair maneuvering. I'm an easygoing guy. My only pet peeve as a roommate is stuff on the floors or things left out where I could trip or run over something."

"Makes sense." I nodded. He wouldn't have to worry about a mess with me. "After living in barracks and then the RV, I'm used to tight quarters and picking up after myself. Clutter makes me itchy."

"Ha." Holden laughed like I'd intended a joke there. "You're a diver. I can always trust scuba folks to share my attention to detail."

*Huh.* My neck ached, an ever-present reminder of the day before, but I'd forgotten Holden was a diver too.

"Maybe we can make a trade."

"Oh?" Eyes wide, Holden sounded legit startled.

Crap. I realized too late how that likely sounded. I leveled my breathing, willing myself not to blush. "I might not be able to pay cash right away for the room, but what if I promised you dive time?"

"I thought you only dive solo?" Damn Holden. He

knew what a big offer this was for me, and he had to go and point it out.

"I do. But I also know folks in the diving community. I bet I could organize something." I tried to sound way more confident about this plan than I actually was. "Or I'll take you myself."

"Cal." Holden gazed up at me with soft hazel eyes that saw much more than I wanted. "You don't have to make yourself do something you hate."

"I don't hate diving with a buddy or in a group. Used to be my favorite thing in the world." I knelt to press a stray piece of masking tape back down.

"I'm sorry." Holden's voice was soft, almost timid, but when I straightened, his eyes were alert, seeming to bore into mine, clamoring to know my story. But to his credit, he didn't voice that demand.

"You seem up on current events." I flopped onto the sofa in front of the picture window. "You hear about the Indonesian incident a few years back?"

"The one where three SEALs died trying to rescue those miners?" Holden wrinkled his forehead like he was thinking hard. "There was a whole inquest after... Oh, wait. That's how you know Monroe?"

"Yep. Good work, Professor." I gave a mock salute to his deduction. "That was our mission. Those were my men. Lost the best dive buddy I ever had, my best friend, my..." I couldn't go on. Let Holden read whatever he wanted into that pause. Gruffly, I added, "Other two we left behind were also damn fine divers, fathers, and husbands."

Leaning forward, Holden dug his fingers into his thighs. "Tragedy."

"Clusterfuck," I corrected him. "Didn't need to happen that way. And I was the team's chief, running point. It's on me. I listened to the higher-ups. Followed every damn order, but I knew better."

"Those moments we ignore our gut are the ones that haunt us." Holden gazed off into the distance like he knew a thing or two about second-guessing and self-recrimination. But whatever emotions he wrestled with over his accident, they weren't the same as my marrow-deep conviction that Ev didn't have to die that day.

"I left him behind." I put it out there, raw but accurate. I hadn't simply swum away. I'd powered through a multistep ascent as ordered, knowing full well what the consequences might be and trusting that someway, somehow, Ev would be okay. But he hadn't been, and that was what I had to live with. "I had some emergency air left. There's a chance I could have saved Evan. The others too."

"And a chance where you both died."

"That's a risk I'd happily take. There's not a world where I wouldn't have given my life for his. Besides, he had so much more to lose. He was the hub of a big family and friend group, the sun at the center of so many orbits. Shattered a whole damn universe."

"Yours too." Holden's voice was soft but firm.

"Not gonna lie. Might as well have died that day," I whispered.

"Don't say that."

"It's true." I shrugged, which pinched like a fucker and made me grimace. "My career ended with that inquest. The medical discharge for PTSD was convenient, but the brass wasn't sorry to see me gone."

"That's so unfair." Holden shook his head, and I closed my eyes, unable to look at his sympathetic expression any longer.

"You wanna talk unfair? For ten years, I spent nearly

every damn leave with Evan and his family. Then I came up, and he didn't. Worse, conditions shifted, and we couldn't get the casualties out, return them to their families. Didn't even get that closure." My voice was rough, and I kept my damn eyes shut.

"You can't spend your whole life blaming yourself."

"Pretty sure others do." I tipped my head back, then regretted the motion and groaned. The invites to Abingdon had dried up after Ev's funeral. Not surprising. But one more loss all the same.

"And that's on them. If they can't see that you're hurt and grieving, that you loved your friend and would have died for him, then their lack of compassion is about them, not you."

"Love. That's a word." Opening my eyes, I gave him a level stare.

"Sorry. I didn't mean to imply..."

"You wouldn't be wrong." I pursed my lips, taking a moment to consider how much to say. Fuck it. I'd already opened a vein for Holden. Might as well tell the rest of it. "Like I said at the clinic, I could write a whole damn script on how to pine for your best friend. But it wasn't like that. He was a newlywed. Sweetest, kindest woman. She's remarried now with a baby. Says I remind her too much of Evan to stay friendly. At least she's honest."

"Her honesty doesn't make your pain less valid or real. Or make those unrequited feelings hurt less. I've been there on that too. I..."

"What?" Not only was I curious, but the potential to shift the focus off myself had me leaning forward.

"I've never said this aloud before, but when Monroe arrived senior year, I was quick to adopt him for our friend group. Friends first. Friends only." Holden huffed a breath, and Lord, I recognized that resigned tone. "But when he came out a few years later, part of me regretted never making a move in high school. Neither of us was out at the time, and I didn't want to risk awkwardness."

"I feel that. And if silence sucked for me, it must have been even harder on your chatty ass." I chuckled.

"Fear of rejection is powerful stuff. I went on to have a crush on this hot detective I shadowed as a rookie and, trust me, she never had a clue. And neither did Monroe."

"And now it's too late?" I phrased it as a question, but I already knew the answer.

"Well, hindsight is twenty-twenty and all that. He's stupid-happy with Knox now, and with the benefit of age, I can see how we would've driven each other up a wall. And the long-term chemistry wasn't really there, but I still had some real emotions about not shooting my shot when I could have back then."

"I don't." My tone came out sharper than intended as words poured out of me, gritty and raw. "I regret plenty, especially not telling my LT where he could shove his by-the-book worries about my reserve air canister. But I don't waste time wondering what if I'd told Ev. Fear of rejection? That's kid stuff. Losing the most important friendship I ever had, the guy who had my six all through SEAL training, the family who welcomed me like an extra brother, the only person I could ever talk to, *really* talk to, was a risk I wasn't willing to take. Standing up as Evan's best man at his wedding, I was proud. No regrets."

"Wow." Holden's eyes were wide, and he swallowed hard.

"Sorry. I...guess I kind of got going there."

"Don't apologize. Not for talking and never for your feelings. And you had a point. My thing wasn't at all the same, and I should have known better than to try to compare."

"Nah. You're okay." Suddenly, I was dog-dead tired. I sank farther into the cushy couch. "It's not like anyone knew. What I said right there? That's more than anyone else has ever heard from me. Must be that investigator gene in you because hell if I even let myself think the word crush around anyone else. For all the world knows, Evan was my best friend, end of story."

"Or the start of one." Holden leveled me with that intense stare of his. And maybe he wasn't wrong. Ev's story had ended while mine, improbably, had marched along.

"Yeah." Like it or not, all those painful, confusing feelings were indeed part of the tale.

"Well, I'm humbled that you shared. Truly." Holden scooted closer in his chair like he was about to touch me. And I might crumble to dust if he did, so I quickly stood, ignoring the protest in my muscles.

"Thanks." Sidestepping him, I headed to the opposite side of the living area, where a hallway led farther into the house. "What's this way?"

"Oh, the tour. Yes. Sorry." Recovering admirably from my abrupt shift, Holden rolled after me to point out various doors. "My office. My bedroom is the door at the far end of the hall. This is the linen closet, and I'm grabbing you a few extra pillows."

"Only need one. If that," I scoffed as he retrieved an unnecessary stack of three and placed them in his lap.

"Yeah, yeah, you SEALs eat gravel for breakfast and use cacti for pillows." He rolled his eyes at me. "But you had a significant neck injury, and every time you move, you wince. Hell, I'm tired simply from looking at you. Unless I can convince you to take those pain meds the doctor prescribed, pillows are your ticket to finding a viable napping position."

"What is it with everyone thinking I need a nap?" I groaned as he continued past the linen closet to open another door.

"Because we're worried you're about to topple over? And long gone are the days when I could haul your ass up. No, you fall, and I'll have to call 911. That army captain Dr. Washington will not be amused if you show up again on her watch with a lump on your head."

"I'm fine," I said, but Holden continued on as if I hadn't lodged a protest.

"And this is the guestroom." He swept an arm around the space, which was cozy in a grownup sort of way. Tan walls with dark-green wainscotting. Desk with a lamp and comfortable-looking chair in the corner. A sturdy double bed with a carved wooden headboard and footboard draped in a plaid quilt. And two pillows already there, both in covers with moose on them. "Feel free to move furniture, bring your stuff in from the RV, etc. Make it yours. Marley had maps of the world all over. Before her, Greg had video game posters and black lights. He works for a big gaming franchise now, so his obsessions paid off. I went for something more neutral, but you won't hurt my feelings if you change it."

"It's nice. I like the green." I ventured into the room, exhaling like I might be staying a minute. "Like old-school camping vibes."

"Was that a compliment? From you?" Holden hung out in the doorway.

"I do have manners. Somewhere. And this is nice. Reminds me of fishing trips with my dad and then later Ev and his family."

"Your family must have been proud when you made the SEALs."

"For an investigator, you're not very subtle." My head felt way heavier than usual as I perched on the edge of the bed. "Dad died on a deployment. Shipboard accident. Mom and I went to stay with her folks, but she drowned her grief in a bottle. Passed a few years later of chronic pancreatitis. Not much family left, but you likely figured that out already."

"I won't say sorry or offer condolences because I know firsthand how hollow those sound. My dad died when I was in my early teens, leaving Mom to raise the three of us." Holden's eyes were soft and distant. "Younger two were little more than toddlers. I helped where I could, but it wasn't easy on any of us. Fuck. And there I go again, sharing my shit like that's any help."

"I get it. You're a born storyteller. Probably why you're such a damn good professor and podcaster."

"You've heard my podcast?" Holden grinned so wide I saw the back of his pearly white teeth.

"Your ego that in need of stroking?"

"Ah." He went from grinning to coughing. Damn it. I'd been unintentionally flirty. Again. So not like me.

"You know what, maybe I am tired. Probably won't sleep, but I guess it wouldn't hurt to put my feet up." After taking off my shoes, I carefully stretched out on top of the quilt.

"Rest." Coming the rest of the way into the room, Holden tucked his stack of pillows around me, effectively making a little nest. He even grabbed a fuzzy cover from the end of the bed and pulled it up over me. "That army captain doctor has nothing on me if you don't take care of yourself."

The last thing I saw as I drifted off was his expression,

fierce but caring. When was the last time I'd been tucked in? By a stranger, no less. And when had I ever, ever seen eyes that intense? I didn't take naps and I didn't catch feelings, but damn if Holden didn't seem determined to break all my rules.

# Chapter Nine

*Holden*

I'd forgotten how good it felt to cook with someone else in the house, knowing I likely wouldn't dine alone. Or maybe repressed was a better word. I'd tried so hard to be happy for Greg when he got married and moved to Seattle and for Marley when she started her traveling nurse adventures. But the truth was I missed Greg's bottomless pit appetite and Marley's insistence that every meal should include something green.

As I chopped and mixed, I had music on low, a soft, happy mix, and my smile was as much for the fact that Cal was on hour six of napping as for my favorite tunes and a tried-and-true recipe.

"My God. How long did I sleep?" Cal wandered into the kitchen, rubbing his face, adorably rumpled and sleep-creased.

"A while." I hid my grin behind a potholder as I removed the cornbread from the wall oven. If ever anyone had needed a long nap, it was Cal.

"Long enough for you to make a whole lunch?" He surveyed the bubbling pot on the stove with a critical eye.

"Dinner. But who's counting?" I shrugged, trying not to chuckle, but I seriously was pleased he'd had such a deep rest. "And it's just chili. Not a particularly involved recipe, but it's my mom's and good. I texted Knox, and he was pretty sure you ate meat."

"I do." Mouth twisting, Cal stepped closer to examine the skillet of cornbread. "Is that a whole cornbread too?"

"Well, a half would be hard to do." Using a potholder, I flipped the cornbread onto a plate. "Seriously, though, my mom gifted Greg and me the cast-iron skillet as a house-warming present, but like hers, my cornbread starts with a box."

"I'm still impressed." Cal hadn't cracked a smile, but I'd take managing to impress his cranky self.

"You're easy," I teased, knowing he was anything but, and that got a half-smile.

"Hardly."

"If you really want to be impressed, look in the garage." I waved him toward the mudroom, and he obediently followed my direction to peek into the garage.

"You got my gear here?" He returned to the kitchen, frowning.

"Are you mad? Earl called, and she was worried about you having pricey scuba gear in the motorhome's pass-through compartments overnight at the garage." I'd had a feeling Cal wouldn't be amused by my and Earl's overstepping. Cal's scuba gear was all in neatly labeled plastic storage tubs, which made for easier fetching and transport but also meant easier for stealing, especially given the flimsy latches on the compartments under his RV. "Earl had your keys, but she was concerned about guaranteeing that much equipment. I sent Tyler, my high school helper, a text because he has a truck. He and a buddy retrieved your stuff before the garage closed. Just the gear though. I figured you wouldn't want them riffling through your personal effects inside the RV."

"You figured." He crossed his arms over his chest, gaze even harsher than normal.

"So that's a yes. You're pissed."

"Earl could have called me."

"She did." I gave the chili a good stir. It wasn't quite ready, but it was getting there. Maybe food would mellow Cal back out. "I heard your phone buzz all the way in my office, but you stayed asleep. It seemed like you needed sleep far more than you needed to cram all that gear into multiple trips in my little car."

"Well, when you put it that way, you and Earl meddling sounds downright practical."

"It was." I grinned at him. My car was amazing, but trunk space was at a premium. "And I can run you back there tomorrow for your clothes and stuff. I found some sweats and a T-shirt here that might fit if you want a shower." I pointed to a stack on the corner of the counter with two fresh towels. The old *Space Villager* gamer T-shirt was likely Greg's, but it would fit Cal's slimmer build. "You'll need to watch your stitches though. Your best bet might be a sponge bath."

"Uh." Cal made a strangled noise, eyes dropping to my hands with barely disguised horror.

"That wasn't me volunteering!" I held up both hands. "Just sharing advice from someone who's had plenty of experience with stitches in inconvenient places."

"I see." A muscle in Cal's jaw twitched like he was trying hard not to think about where I'd had stitches.

"Tell you what. You go get cleaned up while I finish dinner." I gestured back behind us toward the living area and bedrooms beyond.

"That you nicely saying I stink?"

"Not at all." I gentled my tone further. One day, I would win Cal's trust, and when I did, I would feel like a rock star. I wasn't sure which I wanted more: to make him belly laugh or for him to let me indulge him more. "You'll feel better if you wash up."

"I don't need taking care of." His chin took on a stubborn jut, and I disagreed, but no way was I winning that argument. Taking care of him spoke to some deep need inside me. Heck, merely tucking him in earlier had made my chest all warm and tingly.

"I know. That's what makes it fun."

"You have a seriously skewed view of fun."

"Probably." At this point, I was going to keep on grinning until Cal grinned back. "Heck, I was just happy you slept such a big chunk of hours. You said that's not your usual jam, right?"

"Right. I don't sleep." Stubborn. So stubborn. And why I wanted to hug him, I had zero clue.

"Your body has to catch up sometime."

"I...dreamed." Cal sounded equally astonished to be sharing this fact as he was that it had happened.

"What about?" I sliced the cornbread into eighths like I wasn't dying to know.

"I was swimming. In warm water, blue and clear, sun above. The Maldives. You made me dream about the Maldives." Cal's tone shifted from awestruck to accusatory.

"Um. Sorry?"

"No. It was a good dream." He sounded confused, possibly even shaken by this development. And Lord, how I

71

wanted to take him to the Maldives, and not simply because I also dreamed of diving there again. "If I dream, it's never ever good."

"You need a vacation."

"I haven't worked a real job in five years." Cal's scoff only convinced me that much more of my assertion. "I think I'm good. But I will go wash up."

He grabbed the stack of towels and clothes and retreated to his room. By the time he emerged, I had placed bowls of steaming chili, plates with salad and cornbread, and a few toppings like cheese on the table and switched the music to a more dinner-appropriate instrumental.

"You set the table." He used the same tone he'd given me for moving his gear and inspiring his dream, but I didn't let it faze me. He was oddly endearing in the clothes I'd provided: too-big sweats, a slightly tight T-shirt, and the fresh scent of the same soap brand I used.

"Trust that my mom would come smack me if I didn't set the table. A guest and eating in front of the TV? Never."

"Sounds like a great lady." Cal took the seat opposite me, and I wasn't sure if he was being sarcastic, but I decided to give him the benefit of the doubt.

"She is. High school math and physics teacher. Her students both fear and worship her. People come years later just to tell her how they turned out. She's on leave this quarter because Greg and his wife are expecting my first nephew up in Seattle, and she went to help because Kathleen is on bed rest. Our mom is pretty awesome for sure, even after Dad died when it wasn't easy at all."

"I can imagine." Cal's voice sounded far away as he placed his napkin in his lap, and I remembered too late about his own parents' deaths.

"Mom had her moments." I tried to soften my usual

superwoman-level praise. "She ended up seeking medical help for OCD and anxiety. Luckily, she always had good insurance through the school, and my grandparents were pretty great about helping."

"Mine were too. They were strict." Frowning, Cal buttered his cornbread and added cheese to his chili. He'd clearly learned good table manners somewhere, but I already irrationally disliked these grandparents. "But they put a roof over our head, made sure I finished school after Mom passed. Keeping up appearances and all that. Couldn't have a dropout, but I think they were honestly a little relieved the day I reported to basic training."

"You deserved more," I said empathetically.

Cal snorted. "Hugs? Praise? Maybe. But there was always food on the table and clothes on our backs. Can't really ask for more."

"Sure you can." Only my sense of self-preservation kept me from coming around the table to offer him both.

"Chili's good. Thank you for cooking. Those fresh peppers in there?" Cal nodded decisively, not even trying to disguise the change in topics.

"Roasted poblanos. Mom's secret ingredient."

"Nice." Next, he admired his slice of bread. "Cornbread has a great crust."

"That's cast iron for you." The rest of our dinner conversation was dull as dishwater, and I wasn't surprised when Cal leaped up the second he finished his bowl of chili.

"I'll clean up for you." He collected our empty dishes and headed to the kitchen without waiting for an answer. "Dishwasher need emptying first?"

"You don't have to help." In truth, the cooking had tired me out, but I'd managed to clean the kitchen on worse

73

nights, and I had everything arranged so I could do the job largely from my chair.

"Course I do." Cal gave me an incredulous look. "Even after pulling a twelve or more, if Mom cooked, my dad cleaned. Someone makes a meal for you, you help with the mess. Those are the rules."

His expression brokered no objections, but his tone earned a smile from me as I was simply relieved that his determination had more to do with morals than my abilities.

"Well, in that case, have at it. Dishwasher's ready to be loaded." I packed up the leftover chili and then moved to the edge of the kitchen area, staying out of the way but watching him work. And never once in all my forty-odd years had watching someone clean turned me on, but Cal attacked my counters and stove like it was a sacred obligation. And then he scrubbed my fridge, microwave, and dishwasher fronts until they gleamed, and I had to resist the urge to swoon. "If you clean like that every time, I'll cook more often."

"I'm serviceable in the kitchen." Cal shrugged like compliments hurt. Or perhaps that was his stitches. "And I can cook. Fish. Meat. Basics. I can pull my weight as a roommate, but if you make more stuff like that cornbread, I'm in for clean-up duty."

"I'll stock up on mixes," I promised, although Cal sure made me want to pick up some from-scratch skills. "Skillet works great for brownies too."

"Neat trick." Cal sounded all nonchalant, but his hungry eyes gave him away. I was making brownies tomorrow, and that was that.

Kitchen done enough for the moment, I rolled toward the living room before Cal could decide to mop or clean the baseboards.

"Now, who do you think our friend Timber will pick for the final group?"

"You want to watch the next episode of that dating show?" Cal trailed along after me.

"Do you have a better idea of how to spend the evening?" My tone was off-handed, but then my gaze caught Cal's and something unexpected sizzled between us. Call it heat or potential or even unintentional innuendo, but whatever it was, it was potent, thick, and heady. Suddenly, I had a whole list of ways to spend the evening, none involving the TV. Although more than one involved my couch.

"Nope. Guess your idea is as good as any." Cal headed to the living room, shaking his head like he was also trying to break free of the spell between us. He plopped on the couch, a wide number with a chaise on one end that was easily the coziest place in the house. I grabbed the remote before transferring to the couch to sit next to Cal, who made a startled noise. "Oh."

"Sorry. Should have warned you. I usually leave the chair to watch because the viewing angle is better, and also, it's good for me to move around some. This okay?"

"It's fine." Cal's mouth twisted, and I moved toward the chaise to give him more space. Scrubbing a hand over his super short hair, he made a frustrated noise. "You... Not sure how to put this, so I'll just say it, and you tell me if I fuck it up. But if there are things you need help with, some-thing drops and you can't reach it, or like that night with the trash where you fell, you ask, okay? I ain't a mind reader, and I don't know what you might need doing because I don't have the most experience with wheelchair users, but if I can do it, I will."

"Wow. Cal. That's a lot of words."

"Sorry."

"No, you did great." I laughed so he'd know I hadn't taken offense at his offer. "And honestly, I suck at asking for help. I have Tyler, the cleaning service, and I handle my personal care myself these days, although I did have home health in the early days as I learned how to handle stuff like showers. But if I need something specific, I'll try to ask."

Cal responded with a mighty glare, and I held up my hands.

"Fine. I'll ask. But you have to promise to do the same."

"You're already giving me a place to stay. You fed me. What more could I ask for?"

My chest thumped. *Anything.* Cal could ask me for anything, and I'd likely try to give it. But I couldn't scare him off with such a fanciful thought, so I simply said lightly, "Friendship? Or is that on your list of things you don't need?"

"We can be friends." Cal's voice was gruff, but I still felt like I'd won a major victory in the war to break through Cal's defenses.

# Chapter Ten

*Cal*

I was bored. Rest made me itchy, like an allergy attack I couldn't shake. I wanted to get started on my new job with Knox, wanted my replacement dive suit to arrive, wanted my stitches to heal, and wanted something, anything to do on this sleepy, dreary Monday. But no, I had to wait.

Alone.

Knox had called first thing, offering me the chance to work on a remodeling project, which was undoubtedly Holden's doing. However, Knox had ordered me to rest until Wednesday, when he could use me for painting prep. I didn't buy that he had no use for me until then, but I wasn't exactly in a position to argue. Man wanted to give me a job, so I promised to rest even if my skin started crawling before I ended the call.

Holden had left for campus after taking me to the RV to collect my clothes and personal items. As he'd gathered papers and his laptop case, he'd added to Knox's rest orders with an invitation to help myself to the fridge, avail myself of his many streaming options, and make myself at home, like I had the first clue how to do that.

Six years in my grandparents' house, and I'd never once felt at home. Barracks rooms had been just that, rooms. And my RV was secondhand. Supposed it was as close to home as I'd come as an adult, but five years on, it continued to feel borrowed. And now it was done for, so it was probably for the best that I wasn't sentimental.

And making oneself at home seemed to imply an ability to relax or perhaps an assortment of hobbies to fall back on. My weird nap the day before notwithstanding, I wasn't the lay-around-all-day type. I did Holden's breakfast dishes, gave the floor a good once-over because I hadn't gotten to that the night prior, scrubbed the dining table, and finally gave up on cleaning after one too many protests from my neck.

Venturing into the living area, I perched in the center of the couch. I had limited taste in TV, having little regular access to recent shows, and strangely, I wanted to wait for Holden that evening to follow Timber's dating adventures. We had a bet going that Eva from Dallas was a plant to stir up drama. He favored Marie from Tennessee for the final winner, while I thought she was too flashy. I thought the quieter Brandy from Minnesota might be a dark horse contender and, holy hell, how had we managed two episodes last night? Since when did I have opinions on dating shows? And why the hell had I been so...*aware* of Holden's larger body next to mine? It was a tossup as to which had kept me more riveted to the TV for the second episode, Timber's antics or the crackly awareness of Holden's every breath.

Deciding my brain needed a purge from reality TV, I watched some of a World War II documentary, but my restlessness persisted. The living room felt too hollow, too big, too...something. Clearly, I was out of practice with being in an actual home, a place with multiple rooms, throw pillows, and surround-sound speakers. If possible, it was too welcoming, too spacious, and too cozy at the same time.

I headed back to my room. I'd already made the bed, placed my clothes in the dresser, and neatly stowed my duffel bag and backpack in the closet. Duffel. Unbidden, my mind drifted to a few specific items hidden deep in the bottom of the bag. Huh. That was one way to pass the time.

Others might call my twitchy inability to settle down horniness, but that wasn't how I usually operated. An orgasm was a decent pinch-hitter for a sleeping pill and a good tension reliever, but on its own, it wasn't something I often did as a time waster. Average porn clips did nothing for me, ditto dirty stories.

Add rope, though, or handcuffs, or any other type of restraints, and suddenly, I was plenty interested, dick included. Watching others be tied up wasn't nearly as satisfying as doing it myself, although it was good for gathering ideas for solo rigging. I wasn't sure when I'd first discovered that trapping one of my hands did it for me, took jerking off from perfunctory to mind-blowing, but over the years, I'd gone from lying on my right arm to tucking it into a loop of rope or tie to using a few specialty items, especially an electronic key case on a countdown timer.

Yeah, that was what I wanted, a solution to restlessness, inability to nap, and boredom all in one. Resolved, I spread a towel on the bed, stripped down, and used the headboard to stage my rigging. Since I had hours in front of me, I went for securing both hands and lying on my stomach. I found a comfortable position that didn't put undue stress on my neck or stitches, even with my arms outstretched. If my key safe failed, I was a SEAL, and I could be free long before Holden came home from dinner.

Hands restrained, I shifted my hips. The deep peace that only came from this settled over me. I shut my eyes, letting myself drift on an intense wave of relaxation. Eventually, I'd get serious about getting off, but I liked to draw it out, start with enjoying the rare quiet of my brain, then slowly ramp up my movements against the bed.

*Vroom.*

Oh shit. I heard a car in the driveway, then noises coming from within the house. Holden must have come home for lunch. Clearly, I'd miscalculated.

*Okay. Breathe.* My door was closed. He'd likely assume I was resting, like he'd ordered. I flexed my right wrist. Heck. No give at all. The left side was worse because of my injuries. Couldn't wriggle my fingers without searing pain jolting up to my neck. Forget trying to rotate that wrist. Damn it. I was out of practice. I'd have to wait out the key safe because creating a bunch of noise while freeing myself was likely a bigger risk. All I needed to do was breathe, not unlike a dive.

Strangely, my cock pulsed. Apparently, like bondage itself, the threat of discovery did something for me. But I was sure as hell not going to make the bed squeak by giving in to the urge to hump against the towel. So I held still. Waited.

And then the smoke detector went off.

# Chapter Eleven

*Holden*

I didn't come home for lunch to check on Cal. No, that would be silly. I'd forgotten my everything bagel and left-over salad in the flurry of getting out the door after taking Cal to collect his stuff.

*Lies.*

I'd known exactly where that damned bagel was the whole time. And leaving it in the counter bread box was a convenient excuse. I could have stayed on campus. The cafeteria was accessible and well-stocked, and the friendly staff knew exactly how I liked my panini or stir fry noodles. I was a regular there and at Blessed Bean, which also had lunch options.

I'd come here precisely to check on Cal, but he was nowhere to be seen when I entered the house. Kitchen sparkling, table gleaming, living room untouched. Oh wait. A throw pillow had been moved from the chaise to the other side of the couch. Perhaps he had sat still for half a second. The backyard was similarly empty, but his bedroom door was shut. If he were napping again, I certainly didn't want to be the one to wake him.

Deciding to check on Cal before I returned to campus for a late-afternoon class, I started preparing my lunch. I set the bagel going in the toaster, then rolled over to the fridge, wanting to add some red pepper and carrots to my salad. On stiff pain days like this, I usually found it easiest to chop at the table or the lower portion of my island, which meant I was well away from the toaster when it started smoking.

Damn it. I'd been distracted by worries about Cal's whereabouts and well-being and forgot, yet again, that my cheap toaster hated extra-thick bagels and especially despised bagels with lots of little toppings. I could only move so fast in my chair to rescue the smoldering toaster and the desiccated husk of bagel. I scrambled for potholders to free the bagel from its fiery prison and open a window, but I was too late. The smoke alarm started shrieking as if I'd personally offended it.

Well, if Cal had been napping, he likely wasn't now. I made it to the mud room as quickly as possible, grabbed my crutches, returned to the kitchen, and stood long enough to use the tip of the right crutch to reset the blasted smoke detector.

But no Cal.

Not even a peep or a crack of a door or muffled curse. Nothing. And the stupid alarm had blasted for a good twenty seconds at least, plus the whole place now smelled like burned onions and poppy seeds. Even the most chill of roommates would have come to investigate. Further, given Cal's awkward-yet-heartfelt speech about wanting to help me without overstepping, I would have expected Chief Hypervigilant to spring into action.

Something was wrong.

"Cal?" I called out, but there was no response, so I tried louder, rolling toward the hallways that led to the bedrooms. "Cal? You home?"

All my investigator instincts prickled. He was in a bad spot with the lack of funds, probably feeling trapped in Safe Harbor, dealing with PTSD, and injured to boot.

*Please don't let him have done something,* I prayed at his door. I'd never forgive myself if I'd left him alone and feeling desperate. Taking a deep breath, I rapped hard on the door, a knock honed during my years on the police force.

"Cal?" No answer, so I didn't bother knocking a second time. Opening the door, I couldn't hold back my gasp. Cal was nude, lying in the center of the bed on his stomach, very much alive given the rise and fall of his back muscles, but his hands were stretched above his head, tied to the headboard with some kind of elaborate restraint system that involved black rope. "Cal? What the hell?"

"Leave." He didn't turn his head toward me, either because he couldn't or wouldn't, neither of which were great developments.

"Were you attacked?" I demanded. There was no one else in the room, but I still kicked to raise the bed skirt and rolled over to check the bathroom. Empty. No signs of a struggle. "Was there a break-in?"

"No. Leave, please." He ground out each muffled word, face buried in a pillow. "I did it to myself."

"You did it to yourself?" Now I was seriously alarmed, my worries about self-harm flooding back in. I glanced at the empty desk and bedside table. No evidence, but that didn't mean anything. "Did you take something? Too many pain pills?"

"Chill, officer." Cal let out a mighty groan but still

didn't look at me. "It's a...kink thing. I'm sober. Not self-harming."

"Oh. Um. Okay." My gaze continued to flit around like a hook-up partner might materialize at any moment. Anxiety retreating, I took note again of his nude state, more leisurely this time, registering one hell of an ass and a toned back with an impressive backpiece featuring a ship on a churning ocean between his shoulder blades. "Kink? Like bondage? By yourself?" Not waiting for him to answer, I added, "How do you get free?"

"You want a demo?" Even tied up, Cal managed to be cranky and commanding. And hot, although I had no business registering that. If my pulse pounded, it had to be from residual fear and adrenaline, not desire. I forced my eyes away from his ass as Cal continued, "There's a key safe by my right hand. It'll open in a bit and drop the key into my palm so I can loosen the rigging."

"And what if it doesn't open?" I was picturing all the ways in which Cal could die from this little hobby.

"Christ. Come closer, push 9292, and put me out of my misery so I can sit up and show you I'm fine."

I didn't need a second invitation to approach the bed and get him loose from the rope. Putting the brakes on my chair, I steadied myself enough to stand and punch in the code on the little box with a countdown timer. Thankfully, the key code worked, which loosened the central attachment point and allowed Cal to slip free even before I finished untangling him.

"There." I lowered myself back into my chair.

"You can go now." Scooting around, Cal wrapped himself in the camp-themed quilt from the bottom of the bed, sitting up in the middle of his messy sheets.

"We're not going to talk about this?" I made no move to head for the door.

"No." Cal pulled the quilt more snuggly around him, ending my cataloging of his various injuries and tattoos and one hell of a nice chest with sparse hair and dark-pink nipples. When I stayed put, Cal huffed a breath. "Sorry. Thank you for the help. It won't happen again while I'm here, I assure you. I don't often do this."

"I'm not worried about what you do when you're alone. Jerk off all you want. Watch porn. Enjoy the good Wi-Fi and privacy. And I'm sorry that I and the smoke alarm interrupted your solo time." I tried to counter his stiff, formal tone with relaxed concern and humor. "But I'm worried about *you*. Are you okay? Safe?"

I wasn't sure precisely how to inquire about Cal's mental state, and from the looks of his tight-lipped frown, I'd missed the target.

"I'm fine. I know what I'm doing."

"It's natural to be a little embarrassed and awkward, but we need to talk about this. I can't pretend I didn't see."

"I'm not embarrassed." Cal gave a long-suffering groan. "And you could pretend you saw nothing. That would be appreciated. I like what I like as far as getting off. Have you never known anyone kinky before? You're awfully close to pearl-clutching and calling for the manager at the horror of someone liking a little rope."

"I'm not a prude." I held up my hands, trying to relax my body language more. I didn't want to kink shame. I only wanted Cal safe. "And sure, I know kinky people. I have a few turn-ons some might find kinky myself. I'm only trying to understand why you'd do something potentially risky solo?"

"Okay. Apparently, we're having this conversation.

One, I don't play the hook-up game, even for kink. I tried once and..." Trailing off, Cal wound a fistful of the quilt around his fingers, and my heart twisted. I wasn't a violent dude, but the idea of someone hurting Cal had all my protective instincts awake and growling.

"It's all right. You don't have to tell me details." I kept my voice soothing even though that protective part of me wanted names, dates, and addresses.

"No, nothing happened. I chickened out. Deleted the app. That's the thing. Can't trust strangers for the sorts of things I like. And like I said the other day, I do pining much better than random lust anyway."

"Understandable." I nodded, trying to will away the last of my own random fit of lust over his toned body. "But plenty of people of all genders play kinky inside a committed relationship."

"Ha." Cal snorted, dropping the cover to tap his bent knee. "Finding a permanent partner who might not run if I confess to liking rope isn't happening either."

"I bet you could find someone." I was nothing if not encouraging, and while a certain part of me was all too willing to volunteer to read up on bondage, I tried to focus on being Cal's friend, not making an unwanted pass.

"Your faith in me is staggering." Cal finally met my gaze, only to roll his eyes at me. "Anyway, sure, solo play has risks, but it beats the alternatives."

"Similar to your preference for solo diving."

"Yep." Cal nodded like I was finally getting the idea, but in actuality, my brain was racing. I wasn't sure where this need to keep Cal safe in and out of the water was coming from, but I couldn't seem to turn it off. There had to be a way. If the stubborn man had let us send divers down with him Saturday, he might not have been injured.

*Oh.* That was it. I smiled wide. "You need a spotter."

"Uh?"

"Like a lifeguard. A kink lifeguard. A dive buddy? Maybe that's the better metaphor." Warming to my idea, I gestured with my hand. "Someone where you can say, 'Hey, I'm thinking of doing my thing tonight. If you don't hear from me by midnight, check on me.' And then you tell them when you're...done."

"It's rope. Not internet dating, but I get what you're saying about having a backup plan." Cal sounded like he was trying hard to humor me even though he found me stuffy and insufferable. "I could have gotten free on my own. It would have taken some time and likely some noise, but I could have. And which friend am I supposed to saddle with getting a call whenever I want to rub one out?"

"Me." I grinned at him, doing my best to look as nonthreatening and nonjudgmental as possible. "I could be your kink dive buddy. Safety check-in. And I know you hate talking. You could just shoot me a text: *Do not disturb for an hour.* Or use the college door code even—just text me a tie emoji."

"Ha." Cal gave a short, sharp laugh.

I leaned forward. "I want to be your friend, Cal, and I want you safe. I don't care that you're kinky. I care that you don't hurt yourself."

"Wow. That's some words." Cal echoed me from the night before, and then the most wondrous thing happened. He smiled. Like really smiled, big and wide, dimples and parted lips like he might even laugh, a real one, not the sarcastic barks. Cal belly laughing would be a sight indeed. "You wanna be my kinky lifeguard."

"Yes. I can't pretend to not know or be concerned, but I think there's a balance where you can have your privacy." I tried to press my advantage while he still thought I was humorous. "Like I'm here until my afternoon class at three. I could help you resurrect your rigging in a way that won't cut off circulation, then go and listen to some pod recordings. Loudly. With headphones on. As long as I see proof of life before I leave, I won't bug you again."

Cal's smile morphed into something thoughtful, eyes widening like he was seeing me for the first time. I had to resist the urge to make sure I wasn't wearing bagel crumbs or break the suddenly thick tension with a wisecrack.

But my patience was rewarded when Cal finally spoke. "Or you could not leave."

# Chapter Twelve

*Cal*

I was either making a monumental mistake or having the best idea I'd had in a long time, and it was a tossup as to which. Possibly both. Once upon a time, I'd been more spontaneous. Some might even say fun. But the last few years had hardened me, sharpened my edges. Holden gaped at me, clearly shocked at my invitation. The very idea that I might propose something fun was out of character, and honestly, I was more than a little shocked myself.

"I could stay?" For the first time, perhaps ever, Holden sounded unsure of himself, and I had to laugh. Like really laugh, the kind that involved my abs along with my facial muscles, and Holden looked as startled by my chuckling as my offer.

"Lifeguards usually stay by the pool. Dive buddies go down with you." I was joking, but my voice came out dry. Holden's eyes went wide as he made a strangled noise. "Don't go all seventh-grade humor on me. You wanna keep me safe. Shouldn't you be close by? Watching out for... danger?"

"Are you putting me on?" Holden asked softly, as uncertain and quiet as I'd seen the guy. "Like, as soon as I say yes, you're going to rescind the offer and laugh about how I went from pearl-clutching to an eager participant?"

"Why would I prank you?" I might have a rep as a cranky bastard, but I'd never been cruel or a bully, and I sure as hell wasn't a jokester. But something in Holden's eyes said he didn't trust me. I gentled my voice as much as possible. "What happened?"

"Middle school was brutal. I was already teased because my mom was a teacher and known for being strict. Then came my dad dying. Construction accident involving an overturned portable john. You can imagine how much fun the kids had with that." His mouth twisted as he glanced away, eyes distant. "Then came first crushes. Girls. Guys. My hormones ran amok, and I fell for the whole fake note or pretend attention type thing a time or ten before I finally realized that if I laughed first, the jokes didn't sting so bad. And thus, I went from class nerd to class clown."

"I'm sorry." I knew exactly how inadequate those words were, but I didn't have much practice in offering comfort. "What was that you told me last night? You deserved better."

"Thanks. I guess those early experiences left a mark. I usually make the first move when it comes to sex. Don't always trust come-ons from others. Not that you were making a pass, but..."

"Old habits die hard. I get it." I flexed my fingers. His hand wasn't so far away. I could reach out, but my chest tightened. He wasn't the only one with old fears and scars. "I don't joke about sex."

"I know. You don't joke about much." Holden's tone was kinder than I deserved, fond even, like my grumpiness was a cute quirk. "But you were mad I discovered you. Seems like a pretty big leap to ask me to stay and watch."

"Trust me, I'm shocked too." I laughed again, and damn, it felt good, like clearing out rusty pipes.

"You don't have to make the offer. I don't want you obligated—"

"I'm hard." I cut him off before he could nice-guy his way out of my invitation.

"What?" Forehead creasing, Holden leaned forward like I'd confessed to a fever, not an erection.

"My dick. It's hard." I couldn't believe I was sharing this, but the truth was I'd been hard since I'd heard him come into the house. Flagged a little when he'd come in ready to battle whatever had tied me up, but fresh blood had surged south when he'd tenderly untied me. And when he'd said he also had kinks, my dick had legit pulsed. Then he'd offered to leave, and the part of my brain I didn't usually give free rein to had an even better idea, one that made me harder, unexpected as that was. "Hard-ons don't usually happen to me in random conversations. Not that I have conversations about kink often, but I'm hard. Apparently, my dick likes the idea of you checking my circulation and, uh...watching."

"Okay." Holden measured out the word carefully, expression impassive.

Oh. Maybe I'd misjudged his interest and offer. Damn it. I was no good at reading signals when it came to shit like this.

"Never mind if you're not into the idea." Releasing my grip on the covers, I waved away my offer. The quilt pooled in my lap, revealing more of my bare chest. "I mean, I know you don't share the kink. I just thought..."

"Oh, I'm into it." Holden's gaze raked over my torso, hot and hungry. Well, if nothing else, he wasn't immune to my body. "I'm trying like hell not to take advantage of the fact I discovered you in a compromising position. I'm a good guy."

"I know. And you're not taking advantage. The opposite really. The way you offered to be my kink lifeguard was cute."

"For once, I wasn't trying to be funny." Holden's mouth quirked. "And trust me, my reluctance isn't me being judgmental about your kink or not liking it. I admit I haven't had experience with bondage, but like I said, I've got my own kinks."

"Such as?" I drawled, as close to flirty as I was capable of.

"I can be bossy. And...talkative."

"Shocker." I smiled and laughed again, which felt more natural with each chuckle. "You with a mouth on you. Never would have guessed."

"Hey, I'm not that predictable."

"Yeah, you are, and it's adorable." I shifted on the bed, which revealed a little more skin. Unintentional, but if it got me more of Holden's hot glances, I wasn't complaining.

"Well, if it makes me adorable, I suppose I'll take it." Holden gave me a dopey grin before sobering. "Does orgasm control count as kinky? I've never tied someone up, true, but I've sure as hell played around with edging and making someone wait."

Below the covers, my dick went from intrigued to *hell yeah* in point six seconds. Edging was exactly what I did on my own, and the idea of someone making me... Oh, I liked that. A lot.

"Huh. What do you know? My dick seems to dig the idea of the word no."

"So you'd be okay with me talking?" Holden cocked his head to the side, studying me. "I'm good with staying silent, observing, whatever would make this feel the best for you. What do you want, Cal?"

"Wow. No one's ever asked me like that."

Holden frowned, continuing to look at me like I was some new species of wildlife. "No one's ever asked you what you wanted and needed in a sexual experience?"

"I'm a SEAL. Everyone wants to get banged by a SEAL, and they usually come complete with their own fantasy." I sighed, the heaviness of every night out with the guys, every ill-fated setup, and every awkward double date weighing me down. "Not that I've got a ton of experience, but everyone I've met expects me to do the leading."

I had a feeling if I said the word *virgin* to Holden, he might balk further, but if we got technical and used any sort of penetrative sex as the benchmark, the label might be accurate. But I was dancing toward my mid-thirties, and using the word felt more than a little ridiculous.

"I don't expect you to lead." Holden's expression softened as his mouth quirked. "And I have the opposite problem. I'm a top. I've always been a top, regardless of my partner and my injuries. But after the accident, potential dates stopped seeing me in the top role as much."

I did a double-take at that. "People stopped noticing you're bossy as all get out?"

"You'd be surprised how invisible the chair makes someone. And don't even get me started on the caretaker or wheelchair fetishists." Holden's sigh sounded exactly as weighty as mine had. "I get that you SEALs have it rough, but I've struggled with being a different type of notch on the bedpost for partners, and it sucks. And not in the good way."

"I imagine not."

"I suppose if I have a kink for anything, it's control. Leading, like you said. Being in control of when someone gets to climax." His tone was thoughtful, not particularly sexy, but my dick still took plenty of notice. "But also delivering precisely what it is my partner most wants. I like to please, and if I get to control the pleasing, so much the better."

"Huh." I pursed my lips. He sure managed to make edging sound like an entire damn entrée. "Never ordered off the menu before..."

"Start. What do you want, Cal?" Ah, there was the bossiness, and damn if I didn't love it. "You asked me to stay. Tell me what image flashed through your head."

"You. In that chair over there. Feet up, all casual-like." I pointed at the chair in the corner. Inhaling deeply, I let myself drift, trying to channel my rogue impulse into a series of coherent thoughts. "Your body language is relaxed, but your eyes are so intent. Watching me. I can't see you the best because I'm on my front, but I know you're there, eyes on me the whole time."

"Trust me that watching you isn't going to be a problem." He chuckled roughly.

"Yeah. Watching. And you're telling me what you see and what you'd like to do to me. Like narration?" The more I mused, the more I warmed to the idea. I loved his voice, deep and rich and melodic, so nuanced and emotive, and listening to those back podcast episodes had made the miles pass quickly. I hadn't considered the sexual potential before, but now my cock was almost painfully hard at the thought of Holden talking me through the experience. "And control-ling. The...orgasm denial thing you were talking about? That sounds good."

"I can do all that. My pleasure." He gave me a down-right wicked grin, and if Holden was attractive normally, he was irresistible when in a sexy mood. Surprising, how much I liked that mood on him. He rolled away from the bed, heading toward the chair.

"Wait." I held up my unbound hands before flipping over to my front. "Check my rigging first."

I could have done it myself, of course, but I was getting into Holden being in charge. He moved far more carefully and gently than I would have as he looped the rope around my wrists and followed my instructions for attaching it to the headboard with the special carabiners and bolts. With him standing next to his chair, I was acutely aware of his bigger size and how he probably had a couple of inches on me in height as well as a much wider frame. He kept stop-ping to check the rope tension and my circulation, making me feel delicate. Fragile even. I shuddered, the unexpected pleasure almost too much.

"Doing okay?"

"Great." I wasn't lying. I was already drifting on a wonderful haze of good feelings. So good I almost missed Holden threading the rig through the timer. "You don't have to use the key safe timer if you're staying in the room."

"Yeah, I do." He nodded solemnly. "I want you to feel totally safe. Trust me, if I have my way, you'll come long before the timer dings, but it's your...flotation device. In case of lifeguard failure."

That he thought there was any chance of me kicking him out of the room was cute. But it was the level of thoughtfulness and caretaking that was most appealing. "You're a pretty damn good guy, Professor Justice."

"Thanks." An uncharacteristic blush spread across his cheeks. And being Holden, he fussed over my position, adjusting the pillows for my head, neck, and upper arms. "There. All set."

# Chapter Thirteen

*Holden*

Cal was set, all trussed up and ready for...*me?*

Whatever we were about to do, I was woefully unprepared for. Not only was I in the middle of the longest dry spell of my adult life, making my libido into crackling kindling ready for a Cal-sized spark, but I liked Cal. A lot. I didn't want to let him down. And sure, I liked to playfully take care of and boss around partners in bed, but I didn't have much experience with someone willing to give up as much control as Cal.

I wasn't even entirely clear why he'd asked me to stay, but I wanted it. I wanted to be what he needed, to fulfill his every kinky fantasy, and while I might not have had a prior thing for rope, I was rapidly developing a Cal kink. Whatever he was into, so was I.

And accordingly, I was nervous as I settled into the padded armchair in the corner of the room. Marley had dragged it in here from a thrift sale as part of helping me redo the space after she'd moved out, and it was a comfortable chair with a small matching ottoman. Comfortable as it was, I still had to resist the urge to shift around or clear my throat. So I did what I did best and cracked a joke.

"Damn. I have to admit bondage hasn't been in my personal spank bank before, but I think that was a grave oversight on my part." My voice came out a little too hearty. For once in my life, joking didn't feel natural. "Sorry. You look...hot."

*Really, Holden? No better adjective than that?* I exhaled hard, looking at Cal, really looking at him. Not the collection of muscles, triceps, lats, delts, each more defined than the last, or the acres of sun-kissed skin, more freckled than mine, or the intriguing tats, but *him.*

"Hot's not the right word."

Cal snorted. His head rested on a pillow, and he turned slightly toward me. "You don't have to—"

"No takebacks." I talked over him before Cal could send me packing. "What I was starting to say was that you're... stunning. Like an erotic art installation. The afternoon sun filtering in, perfectly lighting your...supplication. And you're bound, but you also radiate so much power, so much potential. You're a vision."

"You can go back to the cheesy one-liners. I'm not all that."

"Now, now, I've got you restrained, so you're going to have to take a compliment." Relaxing more into the chair and my role, I smiled. "You're hot. Beautiful even. Like a sculpture."

"Well, I'm sure hard as one." Cal subtly hunched his hips, rubbing against the towel underneath him. The pressure on his cock must have felt good because he groaned, and I nearly did too. The flex of his ass muscles was undeniably erotic, but the greater turn-on for me was the evidence that Cal truly was into bondage. Not as punishment for some unspoken transgression, but the restraints turned his crank, made him hard and needy, and apparently, so did my presence.

"Did I say you could move?" More confident now, I adopted a far sterner tone than normal and earned myself a sexy-ass whine from Cal.

"But it feels good."

"Yeah, but I'm in charge. Move all you want, but I say when you come." I gave him a hard stare until he stopped wiggling.

"You said I'd come before the timer went off."

"And I plan to keep that promise." I smiled wickedly. "You didn't ask how long I gave the timer."

Cal glanced upward before making a frustrated noise when he couldn't see how many minutes were on the timer. "What if I get chilly?"

"I'll just have to warm you up with my words."

"Prove it." His tone was demanding, but it also held a brattiness that was new and surprisingly provocative. Did something for me, made my own cock pulse even as he complained, "So far, you're a lot of talk."

"You're sorely tempting me to add spanking to my list of kinks."

"Hmm. Yeah. I could dig that." He sounded thoughtful, a sexy hitch to his breathing. "I've played around with too-tight ropes and things like binder clips. A little bite to the restraint."

"All the more reason you need a kink lifeguard." I frowned at the idea of him causing serious unwanted pain to himself, yet I couldn't deny I was also intrigued. I'd been joking, but now I envisioned that ass of his with pink handprints, and I liked it. Way more than I would have expected. I'd always prided myself on being a cool, calm guy. Gentle even, careful not to use my greater strength in bed. With Cal, though, the idea that someone might want that strength was intoxicating. "And apparently, you need one who's not afraid to put a hurt on you."

"Think you could?" God. The note of hope in Cal's voice made me hard enough I needed to shift in the chair. Cal also moved around, pushing against the mattress.

"Since the mere suggestion has you wiggling again, yeah, I'm in favor of anything that makes you come gangbusters for me."

"Want it." Cal's voice was all breath.

"But I wouldn't start with pain. No, I'd start with the thing you hate as much as you need it. Niceness."

Cal gave a barky laugh.

"No laughing during my narration. I want to sit next to you. Kiss the back of your neck. Your arms. I want to feel the tension from the restraints, lick your flexed biceps. Stroke you all over with the tips of my fingers."

"Ticklish." His voice was needy and definitely not a rebuttal to my plan.

"That's exactly what I want to discover. What makes you gasp and sigh, and what earns me another laugh. You have an amazing laugh, by the way. You should do it more often."

"Give me a reason." And like that, he was back to bratty, but I only gave him a fond smile. I'd put up with the brat for more of those needy sounds and hot sparks in his blue, blue eyes.

"I will. Later. I've got jokes for days. But right now, I want to trace that tattoo on your back with my tongue. Outline each ocean wave."

Cal sucked in a sharp breath. "That's a lot of tongue action."

"Yep. Trust me, I'm up for it. I'll lick your spine. Maybe, if you seem sufficiently docile, I'll give you a hint of teeth," I said experimentally, testing for the edges of Cal's desire for pain.

"I can be good." Yep. He dug the idea of light bites, and so did I. *So did I.* Wow.

"I know you can." My voice came out warm and liquid, arousal making it deeper. "And I want to rub you all over."

"Like a massage?" He sounded skeptical, but I wasn't. I could make him love all kinds of touch, from caring to rough.

"Exactly like a massage. Make you all boneless and relaxed, still restrained, still mine to do with as I want."

"Yeah."

"I'll rub you from your neck all the way to your thighs and calves. And don't think I'm going to neglect that ass of yours." Thoughts of more licking and biting flitted through my brain, and I considered narrating rimming, but Cal moaned shakily at the word *ass*. Unsure whether that was a *yes, please* or a *not now*, I switched directions. "Imagine I've researched a tie that would let me flip you over without dislocating a shoulder. And I flip you onto your back—"

Cal interrupted me with a frustrated noise. "But I want to come."

"Baby, you've got to be patient and let me tell my story." I chuckled. The air in the room felt thick and potent. "You think I don't have hands or a mouth?"

"Oh." Cal hissed like he'd been burned. "You wanna put your mouth..."

"Everywhere. There's nowhere on you I don't want my lips, tongue, and teeth."

"Fuck."

"Yup." I grinned, truly getting into this scenario. And strangely, I didn't feel like pushing to make it a reality. Maybe someday, but at this moment, there was a pleasure in simply painting a picture for Cal, making him groan and writhe. "And you're thinking I'm going to go right for your cock. But you're wrong. I'll kiss your chest, your nipples. Those I might bite. If you like binder clips, I bet I could do better."

"I was right." Cal laughed, and it was the best sound in the world, as much a turn-on as a kiss would be. "You do like to talk."

"Yup, definitely biting until you stop trying to goad me into that spanking you deserve."

"You could spank me." Cal was back to that thoughtful tone like he, too, was trying out new ideas.

"I could. And I likely would. But right now, I want to lick your belly, the smooth parts and the fuzzy parts, and those abs. God bless the navy's PT requirements."

He snorted. "I'll tell my old master chief you appreciate my commitment to put in maximum effort."

"You do that." I watched him move for several long seconds, the way he hunched his hips and the tension in his powerful ass and thighs. In the quiet, he sped up, but I made a warning noise. "And if you come before I'm ready for you to, you'll be sorry."

"Yeah?"

"You come too soon, and I'm going to keep right on teasing you, work you back up, make you give it up a second time."

"That...might not be a punishment." Cal's voice was uncertain as if the news he could potentially go doubles wasn't a most welcome treat for me.

"Don't make me threaten a third."

"My record is around four in a number of hours," he countered. I loved how need made him provoke me, challenge me to push him further and harder. "Last one hurt when I went for number four."

"Shouldn't have told me that. I'm competitive. Now I want to break your record."

"Do it." He moaned.

"Anyway..." I made my voice casual, indifferent to his increasing desperation. In truth, I was painfully aroused myself. Forget doubles or triples. Coming even once right then might do me in, but I wanted all my focus on Cal. "Back to licking your abs, hoping I don't crack a tooth on those hipbones of yours, and making my way south. Licking—"

"I need to come."

"I know, baby, but you've got to wait for it," I encouraged, loving how he slowed his motions in response to my command. "Let me play with you a bit."

"Sadist."

"Nah, but I can play one for you." The brattier he acted, the more certain I was that I could dole out what he needed. "You all needy and mouthy is turning me all kinds of on."

"You hard?" His tone was mainly curious, but there was a note of arousal there too.

"You think there's a chance I'm not? Gorgeous, naked guy all tied up and mine to do with as I please? Yeah, I'm hard."

"Good." He adjusted his head position slightly, eyes fluttering shut. "You can...stroke."

"Oh, I think you'd like that too much." Actually, I was the one who'd like that, and my cock throbbed, protesting my restraint. "Tempting me to go faster. Right now, I want to lick just your tip. Very, very lightly."

Cal moaned, his most erotic noise yet.

"And if you make noises like that, I might give you my hand, jack you while I tease you all over with my tongue."

"I'd come."

"You would not," I said sternly. "Not unless I wanted it. And I say you can wait, let me get you close, then back it off. You'll feel your balls start to buzz, legs tense, and then—"

"Yeah." He gave another breathy moan.

"And then I stop."

"No." His objection was closer to pain than anger.

"And I start all over again. Lightly, softly, slowly. Maybe a little more pressure now. If you're good."

"I'm good."

"Yeah, you are." Breathing deeply, I surveyed him again, the flush that had come over his skin, the slight sheen of sweat, the flex of his muscles as he moved in jerky thrusts against the bed. "So good. Letting me play. Letting me do whatever I want. Bet you can really feel those ropes now. You'd like to touch, to reach for your dick, push my shoulder to make me go faster."

"Yes."

"But you can't. You're mine now." Growling, I was at my most commanding, and judging by his increased movements, Cal liked the tone shift. "At my disposal, and you don't get to touch unless I say. Don't make me tie your legs next time."

"Yes. Please. That." Cal's voice was broken, interrupted by breathy moans.

"Well, since you said please." My abs were so tight with arousal that my chuckle hurt. "Imagine that. Legs spread. A cuff on each ankle. The bed has a pretty sturdy footboard, don't you think?"

"Yes. Yes." Cal's voice and motions were frantic, so I kept my tone measured, speculative.

"Yeah, your legs could take a bit of rope. I dig the idea of you thrashing against the bonds because I won't go at your speed. I go at mine. And my kink is enjoying every damn inch of you."

"Need it." A shudder racked Cal's body from his outstretched arms to his back and all the way down to his thighs and feet.

"I know, baby. And I'll give it to you. I'll suck on your cockhead, work it over with my tongue—"

"Oh my fucking God." The intensity of his shuddering increased, a knife's edge of arousal where I wanted to string him out more but didn't want to push him over until I said so.

"And I'm going to suck you close, then release, work you with my hand, then do it all over again."

"Dying." Cal really sounded like it too, voice stripped of all pretense and attitude, whittled down to pure need.

"Good. That's when you know you're alive."

"Yes." Cal said it like a prayer, moving faster and faster, then slowing down of his own accord. Damn. He was trying so hard to please me. Sexy as fuck.

"You are the hottest fucking thing, humping that bed. Want you grinding on me like that."

"I'm tied." He said it like a protest, but I chose to take it as a request.

"Fuck yes, hands tied behind you so all you can do is grind."

"Holden." He said my name, and it was the sound I'd

been waiting my whole damn life to hear, so much urgent need, like I alone could end his pleasurable misery.

"Yes, baby. And right when you think you really are dying, that you can't possibly last another second—"

"I can't." He moaned, barely moving now, trembling all over.

"Just. One. More. Second."

"Please."

"And then I let you come. Go on now, sweetheart." I gentled my voice to sexy encouragement. Cal hesitated slightly, then started thrusting again, hard and fast, making the bed shake and squeak. "You did so good for me. Come."

"Fuck. Fuck. Coming." Cal cursed and pressed his body hard against the mattress. It was bar none the hottest thing I'd ever seen, and I had no choice but to reach down, grip my fly, and—

"Oh damn." The words tore out of my throat along with a climax so intense I saw entire nebulas flash before my eyes. I groaned along with Cal, both of us breathing hard.

"Did you just come?" he asked, opening an eye to look me over.

"Not intentionally." I had to laugh. I seriously had intended to make the entire thing about Cal, take care of myself later. But my cock didn't care for all my good intentions. "God damn. Barely touched the thing, and I went off like a rocket."

"You edged yourself too well."

"Apparently." Leaving the chair, I transferred to my wheelchair, then quickly made my way to untie Cal's hands. I rubbed his wrists, dropping light, grateful kisses on his forearms.

"You don't have to..."

"It's called aftercare, Cal." Smiling, I shook my head at him. "Even a vanilla dud like me knows about aftercare."

"You're not vanilla." His face wrinkled like he was sorting something out. And since I was too, I had to laugh again.

"Nope. Go figure."

"Thank you." He didn't smile, but his eyes were so intense they made my breath hitch nonetheless.

"Feels like I should be the one thanking you." I meant that on multiple levels—for letting me watch, letting me participate, letting me see him so vulnerable, letting me discover some important truths about myself. All of that.

"Where... What now?" He licked his lower lip as I continued to rub his arms, and damn, if I didn't have a whole list of ideas for that tongue.

"I go take the world's fastest shower, get back to campus, then tonight, I'm turning the leftover chili into Mom's famous chili dog casserole." I knew perfectly well what Cal was asking, but I continued on in a blandly clue-less tone. "It has a can of crescent roll dough. You'll love it."

"Uh-huh." Cal sounded anything other than certain.

"Then we watch the next episode of Timber's dating adventures."

"You're giving me a schedule." His mouth twisted. "Not what I meant."

"You'd think after coming so hard, you'd be less cranky. I know what you were asking, and that's my answer. We'll have dinner. We'll watch TV. Wednesday, you'll go to work for Knox. The world keeps turning even though we got a little kinky together."

"So we pretend it didn't happen?" He huffed a short breath. Was that disappointment in his tone? I chose to believe it was.

107

"Oh, it happened. And if you want to play again with me or simply want to text me that tie emoji to let me know you're playing solo, you know where I live. You've got my number. Just ask."

"I might," Cal whispered. "Especially the first thing. Playing...with you. Damn. That was...unreal. So...maybe."

"I'll be honest. I hope you do ask." In the face of his uncertainty, I kept my voice soft, undemanding. "But I'm also going to leave that ball in your court. Has to be your call."

Cal nodded slowly, and my pulse sped up. I'd take dinner and TV and whatever else Cal wanted to offer, but Lord, how I hoped he'd find his way to wanting to play more because I sure as hell wasn't done with him.

# Chapter Fourteen

## Cal

"You packed me a lunch?" I eyed the two insulated lunch bags on Holden's kitchen counter as if they might be full of C-4 explosives. The exterior of one bag featured a talking sushi roll and the other was faded blue with a character from *Space Villager*, the company Holden's brother worked for. Funny, the little details I'd already picked up.

"You don't have to sound shocked, Cal." Holden handed me the bag with the game character. "It's only a tuna sandwich, some chips, and an apple."

"That I didn't need." As soon as I snapped, I regretted my rudeness. It had been a long, strange two days waiting for my first day working construction with Knox. Trying to rest up. Trying to cope with downtime. Trying not to think about kink with Holden. All that made me punchy, but Holden didn't deserve my crappy attitude. "Sorry. It was kind of you to think of me. I meant to say I would have come up with something."

"I'm sure you would have." Holden was so much more

patient than anyone else would be. And his tone was all reasonable, not condescending, even though we both knew how short I was on funds. "But one can of tuna makes two decent sandwiches, and since I was packing a lunch for me, it was no trouble to make yours as well."

"Well, I suppose if you needed a lunch to take to campus anyway."

"Yup." Holden glanced away, but not before I saw guilt creep into his eyes. Damn it. He likely knew the name of every cafeteria worker at the college. If he kept this up the rest of the week, they'd probably send out a search party to find out why Professor Justice was suddenly bringing his lunch. But I could hardly refuse the food again at this point.

"Well, since you got lunch, I can cook tonight." I tried to sound as chipper as him and failed miserably.

"Excellent. There's a package of chicken in the fridge. Do whatever you want to it. I'm not picky." He smiled, no trace of wickedness, but all I could think was how easy he was to please in all the ways. Food. TV. Me tied up and begging to come. All those things seemed to make him happy. And this would be a long damn week if I kept having *those* thoughts. In fact, I was trying so hard not to think about Holden and sex that I almost missed him motioning me to follow him to the garage. "Come on. I'll drop you off on my way to campus."

I opened my mouth to protest, but Holden cut me off with a raised hand.

"It truly is on the way. And if you say no, Knox will insist on picking you up himself."

"When you put it that way..."

Holden gave a wide easy grin as he unlocked the car and got his wheelchair situated. "Sometimes accepting help truly is the most reasonable course of action."

"I don't have to like it," I grumbled as I settled into the passenger seat, lunch in my lap. "But thank you. For the lunch and the ride."

"No problem, sunshine." He chuckled. "Besides, I want to see Knox's progress on the Stapleton house."

I was due to meet Knox at the Stapleton house, a run-down older home with a wide porch near the bed and breakfast. It had a low fence around an overgrown front yard and a large, stately tree that undoubtedly predated the whole neighborhood. The peeling paint in various shades of green, saggy roof, and dusty windows gave the place an undeniably creepy vibe, even without the connection to the case of the missing woman. Apparently, Sam, a friend of Knox, Monroe, and Holden who ran a coffee house in town, had bought the place with an eye toward making it a halfway house for troubled teens. Sam was working with a tight budget, so Knox's remodeling business was working the job between other projects, making Knox only too happy to put me to work here.

"Man, this poor house. Makes me sad. You should have seen it when our friend, Worth, lived here with his folks. Riots of flowers every spring. Of course that was before his mom—before everything." Holden shook his head as we parked in the driveway, which was overgrown with weeds poking out of the cracks. "I'm glad Sam bought the place, but damn, does it ever need work. It's hard to believe it'll ever be inhabitable again."

He shuddered, and it was my turn to laugh. "Why, Professor Justice, are you one of the locals who thinks this place is haunted?"

"Nah." He shook his head, but his shifty eyes called him a liar. "And I don't want to see it razed. But it's going to take more than a little elbow grease."

"Luckily, I'm not afraid of hard work."

"No, you're not." His expression turned more serious, and his gaze held mine long past the moment I should have exited the car. The air quickened, the memory of Monday afternoon heavy and potent between us. All it would take was a word from me, maybe even simply a look, and we could be counting down to kink later. He'd told me he'd let me do the asking, but I didn't want the responsibility. Which wasn't fair to him, yet I'd be happier if he'd take all these long pauses, meaningful looks, and nice gestures and tell me to go find the rope. But he didn't. Only nodded. "Have a good day."

"Will do." I said it blandly like my day wouldn't be filled with hundreds of tiny memories of his voice, the feel of crisp sheets, and the pull of ropes. As I exited the car, Knox pulled up next to us in a truck adorned with a Measure Twice Remodeling logo. Before I could shut the car door, Holden's phone buzzed, and he held up a hand.

"Hang on a second. It's Rob. The police chief and also Knox's dad. Let's see if we've got news from the state crime lab," he said before turning his attention to the phone, greeting Rob.

Meanwhile, I waved at Knox, who made his way over to us. And while Holden was still on the phone, a reddish-haired dude around my age in a Blessed Bean hoodie came loping up the sidewalk. He had to be Sam, the property owner, and he, too, paused for Holden to finish his call.

"Yep. Not surprised." Holden nodded up and down like Rob could see. His broad shoulders radiated energy and high color rose to his cheeks. There was news, all right. "Okay, talk soon."

"Well?" I barely waited for him to hit End on the call.

"That was your dad," Holden said to Knox before his

gaze settled back on me. Despite the seriousness of the subject, there was still a certain warmth in his eyes that hadn't been there when he'd looked at Knox. "And he had some news."

"I know." Knox gave an offhand shrug. "He called Monroe first."

Holden frowned at that, but he wasn't the type to pout over being called second. "So he did. Anyway, he and the task force will be holding a press conference soon because the remains have been identified as Mrs. Melanie Stapleton. The presumptive cause of death is strangulation, same as the suspect's other three victims."

"What happens next?" Sam was the first to speak. He had a surprisingly intense voice that belied his choirboy looks, each syllable holding gravity that ensured we all turned in his direction.

"Like I said, there will be a press conference. Not sure if they'll ask Monroe and me to attend." Holden's mouth twisted. "Then the prosecutor's office will likely pursue the indictment as well as continue to find evidence linking the suspect and the victim."

"No, I mean, what happens to Mrs. Stapleton?" Forehead creasing, Sam took on a vaguely censuring tone. He was the kind of dude no one wanted to let down, what with his air of infinite patience. "And Worth. Who's calling Worth?"

"Rob said he notified Worth first, but he didn't mention his reaction. As for the remains, I'm not sure. Guess that'll be up to the family."

"There's not really anyone. Just Worth." Sam's lament made my gut clench. *Remains.* I'd participated in countless recovery operations, and even so, the reminder hit like a buoy to the face. And I wasn't surprised that the son hadn't been on the scene. That many years of not knowing had to scar a person, and Sam seemed as concerned about Worth as the victim. "She deserves a proper burial. Worth needs closure, but so does the whole town. So many people searched over the years."

"Yeah, some sort of memorial would be a good idea." Holden's tone was thoughtful. "Doubt Worth wants to plan it though."

"Maybe he shouldn't have to," Knox mused, the same tone he'd used for proposing I rest up at the B&B. My back prickled, on edge for whatever plan he was about to suggest. "Safe Harbor needs to do right by all of them and hold a memorial."

"It's not the town's fault," I snapped without thinking. Or rather, thinking of the perp. The criminal who'd done this to the victim, the family, to this town. The loss that couldn't be measured also couldn't be healed by some pretty words and somber music. Closure was important, but what was closure without justice? Without someone held accountable? Nothing.

"Fault doesn't have anything to do with us doing the right thing," Sam said reasonably.

"There will likely still be a trial," Holden added as if he knew the Ev-shaped direction of my thoughts. "But Sam has a point. You brought Mrs. Stapleton home. Returned her to all those who wanted answers. She deserves a dignified burial."

"I didn't do anything," I mumbled, perilously close to telling them to keep me out of whatever performative grief they thought the town needed. My reaction had far less to do with Mrs. Stapleton and what she deserved and more to do with Ev and what he'd never received and with how fucking awful that funeral had felt, knowing his family could never get the closure they deserved. Or the justice.

And Holden seemed to sense that distinction. "You did what you could," he said firmly, catching my gaze. "Sometimes you have to accept the minor win. Closure is a process, not a single event."

"True." Sam had a voice that deserved a pulpit, but hell if it did anything to soothe my churning thoughts. "However, certain types of events, a time to honor and reflect, can help."

"Hey, Knox? Why don't you show Cal the interior of the house? I know he's itching to get his hands dirty." Holden had a voice that went right to every achy part of my soul, and he also knew exactly what I needed. Distraction. "I'll brainstorm with Sam about what the town could do for the Stapletons, but you guys go ahead and get to work."

"Thanks." I nodded at him as I turned to follow Knox into the house. The cement pavers leading to the porch were wobbly. Maybe this place had also been waiting for closure. Fanciful thought, but I was a man of action, not pretty words. I'd leave those to Sam and Holden. And I couldn't serve up justice, much as I'd like to. But I could hammer and sand and paint and put my back into doing right here. More than a job, more than a paycheck and a way to pay off my diving debts and get out of this town, doing the work this house needed felt like a mission.

And I didn't fail at missions or bail early. I glanced back at Holden. Guess it was a good thing I had an understanding roommate lined up. He paused his conversation with Sam, the corners of his mouth turning up. Not the wide, easy grin he gave the whole damn world, but a little private smile, all for me.

The same certainty that said I needed to see to this

house also said it was damn inevitable that I'd eventually find my way to asking Holden for another round of kink. Soon. And while the uncomfortable conversation had given rise to a deep need to escape my head, my certainty had more to do with the man himself. We had unfinished business, and that was a fact.

# Chapter Fifteen

*Holden*

I arrived home in a foul temper, but the meaty smell of chicken and something spicy greeted me. My mood immediately brightened several degrees. I wasn't coming home to an empty house, and the sounds of someone cooking were soothing enough, but that the someone was Cal? Well, that was even better. Things might be ever so slightly weird between us after the Monday afternoon kink-fest, but nothing during the following couple of days had dampened my ever-growing attraction to the man.

Consequently, I had to squash the urge to call out something absurd like *Honey, I'm home*. Instead, I wheeled into the kitchen, taking a moment to admire Cal in a clean white T-shirt, loose sweats, and damp hair with a fresh-looking bandage over his neck.

"Hey." He swiveled away from the stove to greet me. "Knox sent me home with time to spare, and I knew you had a later class, so I started some dinner."

"Thank you." I smiled broadly, a feat I hadn't thought

possible two minutes prior. "Whatever you did to that chicken smells amazing."

"Don't thank me." Cal quirked his lips, as finicky about taking a compliment as ever. "Thank that bottle of organic, local barbecue sauce in your pantry. Made my job easy. Sear, simmer, shred. Easy."

"What can I do to help?" I asked because no way was I passing up the chance to watch Cal cook and enjoy his company, prickly though it was.

"I was debating on a vegetable." Striding over to my fridge, he opened the freezer as easily as if he'd lived here for years. "Do you eat corn?"

"Sure. Let's do that and broccoli." I gestured toward the produce drawer as he opened the refrigerated section. "Marley got me in the habit of always adding something green at dinner."

"You got it." He handed me the package of seasoned corn to heat in the microwave while he quickly hacked up the broccoli and set it to steaming on the stovetop. "Your sister sounds smart."

"She's a traveling nurse. And brilliant about more than just nutrition, but I'm a biased big brother." I grabbed a spice blend to add when the broccoli finished.

"Was it fun having siblings growing up?" His tone was offhand but with the same wistful note I'd heard from other only kids over the years.

"Hard to say. Both of mine are quite a bit younger. There was a gap after me where Mom was working on her master's in teaching, then came Greg, then Marley was the surprise bonus baby." I tried not to oversell the sibling experience, but my fondness for Greg and Marley shined through nevertheless. "They were both fun kids, though, and their energy really kept Mom and me going after Dad died. Later, after my accident, having them around as they did college helped me transition back to independence, and now that we're all adults, we're actually closer than we were as kids."

"Nice." He sighed like a cranky teakettle before removing a tray of potato wedges from the oven. "Being an only... It's isolating, I guess is the best word. Been thinking all day about your friend, Worth, and how he's all that's left. No one to share the burden of the mess of the investigation and stuff."

"That's true." I hadn't realized the similarities between Worth and Cal until this conversation, and it spoke to Cal's subtle empathy that he'd been dwelling on a man he'd never met. "And that aloneness is why Sam wants to plan this memorial. Worth hasn't been back to Safe Harbor in nearly twenty years. And he's been on his own in the bay. No partner or spouse. The news about finding his mother's remains has to be hard on him, but he's not one for talking."

"Understandable." Cal's eyes were distant.

"Yeah, you and he are similar in that way. You do broody well." I'd pressed Rob and Monroe both, but neither had gotten a response from Worth. Meanwhile, Sam could occasionally rouse the guy via text, but he'd also reported crickets. I was at a loss as to how to ensure his well-being short of a flight to California. But maybe someone cut from similar cloth would have answers. "I bet you'd know how we can help Worth. Is there anything we could say that would encourage him to open up?"

"Keep trying." Cal fetched two plates from the cabinet near the sink and then turned back to me. "Sorry. That's mainly what I have. After...*after*. A lot of people reached out. But that dried up fast, especially when I didn't reach back. Don't wait on Worth. And don't expect talk to help, but give it a go regardless."

"I'm sorry." I had to take a deep breath to push past the temptation to make this conversation about Cal. He flinched at my words, a clear sign he wouldn't welcome sympathy about how much it sucked that he'd been hurting, unable to accept to help, and that those around him either hadn't seen or hadn't known how to help. "What about distraction?"

I was asking for Worth because maybe Sam, with his endless stream of G-rated funny memes, was onto something, but I was also asking for Cal. Had Monday been a needed distraction? He was a bottomless well of despair and grief, and if fooling around with me was a distraction he desperately needed, I was more than willing to help. To learn. I might not be what either Worth or Cal needed, but I wanted to be.

"Maybe." The hint of color along Cal's cheekbones said he too was thinking about Monday afternoon. "And don't be surprised if Worth nopes out on this memorial idea."

"You don't think Sam has a point about closure?"

"It's a point." Cal shrugged, then winced, putting a hand to his neck. "But guys like me...we don't really do closure."

He dumped the now al dente broccoli into a dish and added the seasoning I'd set out. I waited him out, catching his gaze as he straightened. The pain in his eyes was unmistakable, and I'd give an awful lot to help him find a way to move past. Not forget, but Cal deserved something resembling peace.

"No closure leaves an open wound," I said softly.

"Yup." He gave a curt nod.

"Cal—" I started, but he cut me off, bustling around

plating the barbecued chicken sandwiches, potatoes, and vegetables.

"Chicken's ready. I found these neat-looking rolls in your freezer. Toasted them while the potatoes finished."

"Thank you." Helpless to lessen his burdens, I trailed behind him to the table. However, my own pain, physical not mental, got in the way of enjoying the hearty portions he'd dished up. I was still poking at my dinner as he cleaned his plate.

"Food okay?" he asked, glancing over at the stove like he'd have a reckoning with the chicken if it wasn't to my liking.

"It's wonderful. It's my stomach that's off. I'm just not as hungry as sometimes. Had to take some pain medication before class, and it's always a complicated calculus of when I need the meds, which med will work best, and finding the smallest dose that won't bring side effects."

"That sucks. What hurts?" He cleared the plates, returning to frown at me.

"Everything. Which I know is a vague answer, but that's the nature of chronic pain. Today, it's mainly been my lower back, hips, and legs, like always, but also my neck because I slept wonky. Or maybe it's sympathy pains for your injury? Who knows." I gestured with my hands, yelping as he touched the back of my neck. "What are you doing?"

"Have you never had a neck rub?" Cal asked like this was the most reasonable question in the world, continuing with his firm massage. "If you get banged up enough on active duty, they send you to physical therapy, and lordy, do those folks love ordering therapeutic massages. Picked up a few tricks."

He did something with his broad thumb, digging into

121

the worst of my knots and effectively loosening my tense muscles with a few targeted maneuvers.

"I'll say." I barely managed to stifle a moan. He was clinical. Precise. Not sexy in the slightest, and I was still so turned on by his casual touch that it was hard to breathe. And then, just as abruptly as he'd started, he was done, floating back to the kitchen.

"Let me handle the dishes, then we can watch the next episode."

"Hey, you cooked." I wheeled after him. "There are rules!"

"Which are made to be broken." He waved me away like he hadn't been the one to explain to me how nonnegotiable post-dinner chores were. "Go get the show ready."

Grumbling under my breath, I made my way to the living room and cued up Timber's hunt for a spouse. I'd just settled on the couch when Cal came in with two small bowls of ice cream.

"Think your stomach can handle some dairy?" he asked as he handed me a bowl. "It's from that local place y'all rave about."

"Dessert?" I blinked. Dinner. A neck rub. Dessert. TV. Were we dating, or were we roommates? The lines were getting awfully damn blurry. Tasty. But blurry.

"Hey, it's your ice cream." Cal stretched as he sat down next to me, slightly closer than he had the first few episodes. And, of course, I noted the minor shift, my left side seeming to heat from little more than simply his nearness. "I just served it up. Felt like I burned a million calories today doing painting prep."

"How'd your stitches hold up?" I cast a critical eye on his wound dressing. I didn't rush to start the show, the dual pleasure of watching Cal eat ice cream and the conversation taking priority over trashy TV.

"Fine. I only swapped the bandage because I showered before I cooked."

"I noticed." I meant it conversationally, but my tone came out a bit too appreciative, and Cal blushed.

"Anyway." He studied the caramel stripe in his ice cream intently. "Guess I'll be sticking around a bit. Between my dive suit and the replacement RV, I need all the hours Knox wants to give me. But also, that house needs seeing to."

"And you're the man for the job?" I couldn't keep the skepticism out of my tone. Cal was the last person I thought would have feelings about an old, run-down house.

"All that talk about closure." He made a clucking noise. "Not one of you thinking about the house, other than maybe Sam. And Knox said the place has been through a long list of bad news owners in the last twenty years. Not the house's fault it got caught up in rumors and neglect."

I had the same thought about Cal, but I knew better than to say that outright. "No, not its fault at all. About time someone treated it right."

Cal paused exactly long enough for me to know he'd heard the unspoken message. Good. I wanted to be the one to treat him the way he deserved.

"When Knox gets around to my paperwork, I'll work out something fair on rent, especially since it's likely to be more than a couple of days."

"I'm in no hurry." That was an understatement. I wanted him to stay as long as he wanted, as long as it took for him to start healing on multiple levels. "And if you're going to be here awhile, that's more time for us to work on your fundraising plans. Your pay will go further if you have donations to help with the RV costs."

"I'm in no hurry," he echoed me with a rare chuckle, scraping up more ice cream from his bowl. "We've both had long days. It'll keep."

"Yeah, you're not kidding on a long day." Even with the pleasant distraction of Cal's company, the exhaustion I'd battled all afternoon continued to loom large.

"Still battling pain?" Turning more toward me, Cal narrowed his eyes. "Or something else?"

"For someone averse to conversation, you're remarkably perceptive."

"It's called listening, Professor." He gave me a pointed look, one which made me chuckle.

"Touché." I glanced away, reluctant to fess up. "And it's stupid, but the task force didn't invite Monroe or me to the press conference to announce the finding of the remains. And the official press release didn't mention your charity or my podcast. Like I said, it's silly. Of course the task force isn't going to want to credit the pressure from a podcast for the recovery of remains, but..."

"You kinda wanted the credit. I feel you." Cal duffed my shoulder lightly.

"Yeah. Guess my overinflated ego is a little bruised." My tone was wry. I hated that I cared so much about credit. "The important thing is that answers are finally emerging for the Stapleton case, not who gets kudos."

"As you'd tell me, you're allowed to feel your feelings, but if you're mad about being hurt, maybe you should put a hurt on me instead." Cal gave a very uncharacteristic smile.

"Pardon?"

"Never mind." His smile rapidly diminished. "That was the cheesiest come-on in the history of come-ons."

"Wait a sec." All my nerve endings went on red alert, the possibility of more than casual banter tantalizing. Goodbye exhaustion, hello arousal. "That was a request to play around again?"

"Uh-huh." A flush spread up his neck. "Was thinking your ego could get some...stroking, and if you wear me the fuck out, I might have a prayer of sleeping tonight. God knows I'm tired enough."

Oh, thank God. My patience in waiting for Cal to ask had finally paid off. "You're on."

# Chapter Sixteen

*Cal*

The trek from the couch to my room had never seemed longer than when Holden shut off the TV with a decisive click and headed for the back hall.

"I better shut down my computer too." Wheeling ahead of me, he quickly darted into his office, pocketing something as he returned to the hallway.

"Tell me what you'd like for this time." He paused at the door to my room so I could enter first. "Whatever you want is fine by me."

"I'm not used to ordering kink off the menu." I busied myself in retrieving my gear from the bag in the closet, tossing the rope and connectors onto the bed. My neck muscles tugged, and my back itched. The only thing worse than never getting what I wanted was being offered exactly what I needed. "Feels...indulgent."

"Well, get used to it." Holden smiled, waiting patiently in his chair by the side of the bed. "I want to indulge you."

"I want touching." The words barked out of me, cannon fire in the quiet room.

"Touching?" He tilted his head, clearly in a mood to make me get specific.

"Like you narrated last time. You touching me with me tied up...likely on my back, but don't leave me hanging." I gave a rusty laugh. "Sorry. Poor word choice."

I'd meant to imply that I wanted the relief of an orgasm, not that I wanted to be strung up, and Holden chuckled right along with me.

"Yeah, no suspension bondage tonight. And you don't have to worry, baby." Holden was all kinds of loose and relaxed, breaking out the *baby* even before I was trussed up. "I'll get you off even if I make you suffer a little orgasm control to earn it."

"Suspension bondage. Orgasm control." I narrowed my eyes. "Where did you pick up the kinky vocabulary?"

"I've maybe been doing some research." He glanced down at his big hands. And damn, why hadn't I noticed before how sexy his hands were? They were big, strong, and capable, leading to even sexier forearms poking out of his rolled-up shirtsleeves.

"Maybe?"

"Okay, definitely a little poking around on the internet." His tone was sheepish. "Some articles, a few how-to videos, a couple of class descriptions, and a visit to an online adult store to see what various gear looks like."

I blinked. "You did that much research for me?"

Holden might be a little embarrassed, but I was awed. Had I ever inspired that kind of concern from anyone?

"For both of us. I wasn't kidding about liking what we did the other day. I want to know more." His curiosity was damn adorable, the way he went from sheepish to enthusiastic. "But also, I was hoping you'd ask, and I wanted to be prepared. I want this good for you."

"Hell, you caring about getting it right, that pretty much guarantees it will be." I kept my tone practical, but in truth, my muscles buzzed with anticipation, eager to see what tricks Holden had learned.

"Someone caring about the details is the bare minimum you deserve." His stern tone made me laugh again. Apparently, being cared for was the key to loosening my vocal cords because I'd laughed more tonight than any time in recent memory.

"Such a conscientious kink lifeguard. I'd call you a bodyguard, but not sure you can protect me from myself." I gestured to indicate that the vast majority of my kink experience had been on my own.

Holden gave a legit growl. "I can damn sure try."

"Not sure whether you're hot or infuriating when you go all fierce." I pulled off my T-shirt, careful of my neck and shoulder bandaging.

"Let's go with hot." Tone flippant, Holden pointed at the bed. "Where do you want me?"

*Everywhere.* I wanted him everywhere, all at once, the need so all-consuming as to be overwhelming. "Sitting next to me on the bed? Then you can...touch."

"And play. I'm digging it." Grinning, he transferred himself to the right side of the bed and started sorting through my ropes and gear. He glanced up as my sweats hit the floor. "And is ogling allowed? Because damn."

"Oh." My skin heated as I gathered my clothes to set them on the chair. "Was I not supposed to strip?"

"You most definitely were supposed to strip." His stern voice was back, but there was a smile there too, a playfulness. "What about me?"

"Hmmm." I considered the vibe I wanted since, apparently, this was all about me and what I liked. And damn, Holden looked good in his white dress shirt, sleeves rolled up, collar loose, and gray slacks that hugged his frame well. "Clothes on. Not because I don't wanna see..." My cheeks reached supernova-level warm. "Sorry. No idea why I'm blushing. It's...appealing. Sexy, kind of? You clothed. Me not."

"I can see the draw in that. On the bed now, arms overhead." He went from thoughtful to commanding in a single sentence. "How do you feel about having your legs cuffed like we talked about?"

"Yes." I groaned at the mere idea as I stretched out next to him. The position was strangely intimate, cozy even, and I had to resist the urge to curl around his warm bulk like a cat. "I want my legs restrained."

"Good." Holden set to rigging my wrists first, working with sure fingers and some sort of internal agenda as he maneuvered me this way and that, stopping to inquire about my stitches and making sure I wasn't stressing my healing wound. "According to my research, you should have a word in case you need me to untie you in a hurry or don't like something I do."

Holden with a little kink knowledge was a dangerous thing. "You think I have a problem using the word no?"

"I think part of you is dying to be even brattier and tell me where to stuff it, but you want to know I'll keep going." He gave me a look so pointed it pierced my bluster effortlessly. And yeah, I wanted that. Badly.

"Okay, okay. Red. That can be the safe word," I grumbled, but as he sat up and hunched forward to work on my ankles, every brush of his fingers against my skin felt like fireflies, electric and wondrous, and I'd give him a dozen safe words if it got me more of his touch.

"Well, damn." Holden whistled low as he glanced up, looking right at my bobbing cock, which was as hard as I could remember. "At least part of you likes the leg restraints."

"Apparently." As soon as he had me set with the rigging, I tested the bonds, flexing my arms and ankles, loving how the pull of the ropes made my cock throb and abs tremble.

Holden made a clucking noise. "That you think wiggling around will get me to touch you sooner is cute."

"More like I can't hold still. Feels too good."

"Try." He dropped a kiss on my forehead, tender, chaste, and absolutely soul-searing. And damn if it didn't make me give a happy sigh and silence my restless limbs. Anything to earn his praise. "Good. Now, what to do first?" Shifting around, he pulled two binder clips from his pocket. Devious man. I should have guessed shutting down the computer had been a ruse. "Have you been nice or naughty?"

*Both.* I wanted more of his tenderness, but I also needed the bite of pain, and I had no idea how to ask for either, especially the caring. Trying to come up with words made my back itchy and my tone cranky. "Stop making me choose. You decide. Just wanna not think."

"No thinking. Got it." He tweaked one of my nipples, an all-too-brief electric sensation. "I am but your humble servant, yet if you give me the power to choose..."

Grinning, Holden brushed featherlight kisses across my shoulders, avoiding my injuries, down my collarbones, gliding between my pecs, and ending with a teasing lick on my sternum.

"Should have known you'd pick nice." I pretended to be put out.

"You're lucky I don't mind your bratty complaints." He gave me a loud, smacking kiss right below my nipple. "Otherwise, I might develop a kink for gags."

"No. I'll be good," I promised quickly because the thought of a gag wasn't sexy to me, and Holden, ever perceptive, picked up on my hesitance, nodding.

"I know you can. You're already doing so good." He gave me another of the exaggerated kisses on my pec, then started teasing my chest earnestly with little licks, openmouthed kisses, and scrapes of his teeth.

Hissing, I stretched against the limits of the rope, chasing more of the delicious contact.

"Look at you, so desperate for my teeth." His tone was chiding, but his eyes were unmistakably pleased.

"Do it. Bite me," I ordered as if I were remotely in charge. But blessedly, Holden actually listened, nipping at my chest with light bites. Then he reached my nipple and sucked hard, the press of his teeth absolutely perfect. "Oh my fucking God."

And then, as he abandoned that nipple in favor of the other, he deftly applied one of the binder clips. And I fucking levitated.

"There." He sounded all satisfied. "Nice and naughty."

For once, my endlessly sarcastic inner monologue gave way to blissful static, a state where all I could do was float on the sensory overload and moan. Holden, for his part, was a damn scientist, precise and methodical in alternating mouth and clips until I was trembling, abs trampoline tense, teeth gritting. Each sharp bite of pain from the clips or his mouth was met with an even greater amount of pleasure, the interplay between hurt and ecstasy overwhelming me until I no longer cared which was which, only that I got more of it.

"Fuck." I strained toward him.

"Wow." Straightening, he peered down at me, clearly impressed with his own efforts. "Can you come this way?"

"Keep it up and we'll both find out," I ground out, as close as I could get to demanding more.

He gave a playful shake of his head. "Tied. Suitably distracted. And still, you find your way to bratty comments. Your stubbornness is the stuff of legends."

Grinning diabolically, he resumed his torturous assault on my chest, inching me ever closer to erupting. I'd never been so close yet so far away from climaxing. I whimpered, a needy sound I'd never heard from my own throat.

"Damn." Holden ran a hand down my torso, stopping short of my cock, running a finger through the trail of precome painting my abs. "You made a river."

"Sor—"

"Sexy as hell." He licked his finger, and I moaned, which made him wink at me. "Love that you make a ton of pre. Makes you that much more fun to edge."

He moved to kissing my arms and stroking my legs, undoubtedly checking my circulation, but the sweetness of the gesture was enough to back off my imminent need to come. I exhaled, only to immediately jolt as he gripped my cock without warning.

"Aaah." I moaned, right back on the edge, the pleasure of his touch mingling with painful urgency.

"Doing okay?" Holden kept right on stroking, coaxing more beads of precome from my cock and more moans from my throat.

"Dying."

"That's a yes then." He grinned at me.

"You're surprisingly evil." Somehow, I managed to grin back, which made him laugh.

"I know. Isn't it great?"

He resumed stroking me with one hand while the other roamed all over my body, from my bound wrists to my trembling thighs. Every pass of his sure grip nudged me closer to the edge without tipping me over. Seeking that last elusive push, I tested my bonds, letting the bite of the ropes ratchet me higher.

"Fuck. More. So. Close."

"I have a theory…" Holden said conversationally.

"Is now really the time for science?" I snapped.

Ignoring my whiny tone, he continued, "If I get you super close and then switch to your nipples, at what point do you think you'd spontaneously blow?"

"Fifteen point three seconds." That insubordination earned me a gust of warm breath across my aching nipples, which was far from the contact I craved. "Please. Holden. I really need to come. Now."

"And I really need you to wait. You sure have a lot of orders for someone all tied up with nowhere to go." Amazingly, his reasonable tone turned me on that much more. He made it so damn easy to give up control to him, making my only job pleasing him with my patience. He tugged lightly on my arm, making the restraints dig into my skin. The reminder he was in charge helped me to drift back to the pleasurable haze where the strokes of his hand mingled with the kisses from his mouth on my nipples. He sucked hard, finding a particularly sensitive spot, and it was all I could do not to shout.

"Please," I begged, voice broken into jagged syllables of pure need.

"Come." Apparently, he'd been waiting for that *please*

because he immediately gave my nipple a firm flick and sped up his jacking of my cock. "Come for me, Cal."

"I..." I opened my mouth to protest that I couldn't possibly come on command, and then he used even tighter suction on the same nipple, grazing it with his teeth. Bang. Done deal. I came so hard my body bowed, pulling hard on the ropes, each spurt more intense than the last. "Oh fuck. Oh fuck."

Holden petted me through the last of my shudders, gentle touches that should have soothed me but instead inflamed one last glowing desire. I lunged toward him, then cursed the ropes. And my stitches, but I was careful not to wince where he could see.

"Fuck. Untie me so I can blow you," I demanded, voice rough.

"That's quite..." Holden gulped, making no move to loosen the ropes. "You don't have to."

"What? You're seriously going to turn down the opportunity to shut my mouth for ten minutes?" I was joking, but I also needed to make him come with a ferocity I couldn't begin to understand. Never before had I been this obsessed with another's pleasure, especially after coming myself. Not that I was selfish, but this craving, the tingling in my mouth, the need churning in my gut, was new.

"Minutes is a wildly optimistic estimate given how turned on I am." Holden gave a wry smile as he loosened my bonds, maddeningly starting with my feet, then cleaning up the come on my belly before undoing my hands and finally sitting back against the headboard.

"Fuck yes." I was on him the second he got into position, and I wrenched open his fly. He wore a pair of black briefs, and I quickly bypassed that fly to draw out his dick. His cock was thick and ruddy, jutting out of a nest of hair, and I'd never wanted something in my mouth so badly. I'd had a few dark-and-dirty fumbling experiences with oral, enough to know I liked it, but nothing in the past had prepared me for Holden, for what desire was truly like when I craved his taste and his pleasure like a shot of a narcotic.

I knew exactly how I wanted this to go, and my confidence that Holden would indulge me was another hit of intoxication. Stretching my hands, I grabbed his wrists. "Hold my hands. Go as hard as you want. I can take it."

"Don't want to hurt..." Holden trailed off on a broken moan as I took him deep without absolutely no warm-up, just sank my mouth down on his delicious girth. Heck, I even surprised myself with my grace and ease. Holden clutched hard at my hands. Apparently, my enthusiasm made up for my lack of practice. Emboldened, I went all the way to his base, letting my face nuzzle the slick fabric of his gray dress pants. Felt so damn good that I stayed down there a long while. "Oh my God, Cal. Do you even need an air tank for diving?"

"Now who's sarcastic instead of sexy?" I pulled all the way up to ask but kept my mouth right against his cock, making him shudder.

"Oh, I'm sexy, all right." Using his grip on my hands, he urged me back down. Gentler than he needed to be but firm enough to be sexy as hell. "Keep going. Please."

I resumed my work, going deep, holding, retreating with intense suction, then repeating until he babbled a sexy stream of filth, muffled curses, and pleas. However, I could feel him holding back, body trembling with restraint, hands tight on mine. The time for his careful control was over, and I needed everything he had to give me. I sucked harder and faster, but apparently, I'd met my stubborn match.

"Come on, Holden. Please. Let go."

"You want that?" he asked, eyes hooded, mouth slack. "Want me to fuck your face? That's what you want?"

I moaned my enthusiastic agreement around his cock, working the underside of his shaft with my tongue, hands tensing in his grip, my whole body rejoicing as he loosened the reins on his control. Careful thrusts, rocking gently up to meet my mouth, then more and more. He shifted my hands to one of his, freeing his other to stroke my short hair and guide my motions. Yes. I loved that, and I groaned my approval until he completely took over ownership of my mouth.

"Okay, baby, okay. It's...close." He was breathless, mile twenty-six of a marathon, and I was determined to get him over the finish line, going even deeper and working him with my throat. "There. Oh fuck."

He came with a series of low moans and delicious sounds that had me swallowing every drop. The taste was overtly sexual, earthy and salty, and if I hadn't come minutes prior, I totally would have blown when he did. I finally released him with a satisfied groan, laying my head on his stomach and letting my eyes drift shut.

"Oh my sweet Lord." He petted my head with tender drags of his long fingers, a hypnotic sensation. "How did we go from me supposed to wear you out to me boneless and not wanting to move?"

"Me too." I didn't bother opening my eyes.

"And how was that the best orgasm of my life, and we still haven't kissed on the mouth?"

"The best, huh?" I gave him a sleepy smirk, stretching to invite more touching.

"That's what you focus on?" He chuckled affectionately. At some point, he'd likely leave for his own bed and more comfortable sleeping attire, but I fully intended to enjoy every touch and sleepy cuddle before then.

"We'll get there on kissing." I yawned. My string of sleepless nights was quickly catching up with me. I probably wouldn't even last until he escaped, but I also wasn't going to deny wanting to kiss Holden. It seemed inevitable that we would be right back here again, preferably more awake.

"We better." He gave another of those possessive growls of his, cuddling me closer and arranging the covers more on me than him. This was too good to be a one-off. But I wanted to be awake for the kissing, fully present. And why it mattered to me that I gave him my best stuff, I refused to think about. Sex. This was sex. Anything else was unbearably complicated.

# Chapter Seventeen

*Holden*

The wait to kiss Cal was going to kill me. He'd said we'd "get there" like it was an item on an awfully long to-do list of middling priorities. Whereas for me, after round two of the kink-fest, I'd assumed we might be headed toward a nightly thing. Preferably with kissing and plenty of it, but I'd made the fatal mistake of waiting for Cal to ask again.

And waiting.

And waiting.

And now here we were, the start of a new week, and I was in line for an afternoon pick-me-up at Blessed Bean, unkissed and in dire need of more than caffeine. When I'd accidentally fallen asleep in Cal's bed after the most epic orgasm of my life, my last conscious thought was a wish to wake up together, sneak in that first kiss before coffee. The possibility was enough to make it worth sleeping in my clothes and away from my ultra-supportive mattress. But Cal had already been in the shower when sunlight hit my eyes, and I'd snuck off to my own room to peel off my hope-lessly rumpled dress clothes and regret lost chances.

I'd packed him lunch while he'd finished up in the shower, and that had been that, back to whatever normal was between us. I'd wanted to leave repeats up to Cal because I didn't want him to feel obligated since he was staying with me. Quid pro quo for a place to stay was gross. Thus, I stayed exactly the same level of approachable and friendly, mildly flirty, but not crossing the line. We ate dinner together every night, watched reality dating shows like it was our job, roared through various local flavors of ice cream, and thoroughly enjoyed each other's company. At least, I thought so.

But no kissing, no asking, only a long awkward pause after we clicked off the TV each night. And me, ready to climb the blinds at Blessed Bean at the mere mention of Cal.

"Your new roommate is pretty awesome," Sam observed as he made me a mocha. The coffee house specials board advertised a seasonal lavender white chocolate mocha, which sounded tempting, but I wasn't sure I trusted Sam or his ever-revolving crew of teen employees to not end up with something approximating soap.

"Careful. We're not allowed to compliment Cal." Leon cackled from a table near the door. The retired owner of Measure Twice and his husband, Frank, were town fixtures and even more up on gossip than me.

"Says who?" Frank scoffed, big shoulders rolling as he stood to carry their empty cups to a nearby bus tub.

"Cal. He's opposed to niceness." Leon wasn't wrong, but I didn't so much as nod. Cal might be cranky, but he was my kind of cranky, and only I got to tease him about his prickly nature. Instead, I let Leon continue to prattle on. "Also, Holden glares every time the man's name comes up."

"I don't glare." I held up my hands and schooled my expression. Had I been that damn obvious of late? Apparently so, because Sam laughed right along with Leon.

"Glower protectively?" Leon suggested with a knowing smile. "How are things going over there anyway?"

"Leon, quit fishing." Frank mercifully returned to fetch his husband, steering him toward the door. "Let's get to the grocery store before it gets busy."

"I love Leon, but he's wrong here," I said to Sam as they left. "I want to hear about what Cal did well."

"Oh, I think Leon's got it exactly right." Sam's eyes sparkled. "And Knox has the vision for what the Stapleton house could become, but Cal is an absolute workhorse. A beast."

Despite my protests, I felt some kind of way about the compliment for Cal. "He's injured."

"Is he?" Sam frowned as he slid me my drink. "He said he's doing great other than itchy stitches."

"He still shouldn't overdo it." I ignored my drink in favor of fiddling with the wrapped straw Sam handed me.

"Yup. There's that protective glower." Chuckling, he gave me a knowing look. "I'd say you're cute, but you might sock me."

"I care about his health." I ground out the words, dry as one of Sam's biscotti. Undoubtedly, part of my crankiness had to do with the spike in my pain levels after my totally worth it night in Cal's bed. One stiff wakeup was enough to create days of issues until my body cooperated again.

"Mm-hmm. Anyway, I hope Cal sticks around." Sam said it offhand like Cal was as mercurial and welcome as the sun in the Northwest. And like the sentiment wasn't the first and last thing I thought every day. Smiling, Sam grabbed a rag to wipe down the counter. "He's done wonders on the ground floor. Hand-washed all the baseboards. About to turn him loose on the upstairs, and Knox talked me into finally scheduling the exterior painting. The house might actually be inhabitable soon."

"That's good." As far as I knew, Sam had yet to spend a night in the house, but maybe all the remodeling progress would prod him into actually moving in. And the longer the house took, the better. If Cal felt saving the house was a personal mission, then loyalty to Sam notwithstanding, I was fine with the work dragging out months. Hell, get crazy and make it years.

"What's up with you? Other than the obvious?" Sam asked as I finally took a sip of my drink. "I figured you'd be crowing to anyone who would listen about solving the Stapleton case."

"I didn't solve it." I sounded petulant as a tween. What I meant was that the indictment hadn't been handed down and that we had a body but no justice and more questions than answers. But I could have modulated my tone, made it less easy for Sam to nod smugly.

"Oh. That's it then. Not enough credit for your liking?"

"It's not only me. Neither the press release nor the press conference mentioned Cal and his contributions." I knew perfectly well I was adding more fuel to the gossip fire, but I couldn't let Sam think this was all ego. "That sort of publicity could really help him."

"And you," Sam added mildly.

"I don't need funding in the same way."

"Yeah, but you love being out front." Sam scrubbed at the counter, tone almost loving, which was possibly more infuriating than if he'd been pointed.

"I'm not that bad."

"Of course not. You're more comic relief than a braggart. But you can't deny enjoying being the center of attention."

"You'd be surprised." I pursed my lips. That was me. The guy with the jokes. Why did it feel like only Cal saw me as something more? And perhaps that was why I'd enjoyed the kink with him so much. I wasn't a clown with him. Wasn't the comedian or the life of the party. I was the one in control, the one he respected and begged. The one he *needed*.

"Don't be cranky. We love you exactly as you are." Setting aside his towel, Sam reached down to pat my shoulder. "And I need your town crier rep to help me with this memorial and ensure people turn out. I'm considering holding it at the community center rather than a church to make it more about the community than a formal funeral."

"What does Worth think?" I asked, thinking of my conversation with Cal about what Worth needed. His insights and compassion inspired me to try harder with Worth and consider what might truly help versus what I thought Worth could benefit from.

"No clue." Dropping his hand, Sam huffed, unusually frustrated. "He texted a thumbs-up emoji to the initial idea, but nothing other than random likes on silly memes since then."

"Are you going to be okay if he doesn't come?" I had to agree with Cal that the chances of Worth no-showing were high. If he wasn't talking, the idea of coming back to Safe Harbor was hardly going to be more palatable.

"Of course." Sam nodded too crisply. "I'm doing this for Mrs. Stapleton, not Worth specifically."

"Not a thing to do with your old crush—"

"I'm well over thirty, a business person, community leader, and homeowner. I don't do crushes." Sam bristled like an old broom, blowing his dusty mood in my direction.

"Well then." I gave him the same pointed look he'd given me earlier. "I'll keep texting Worth too. Got to keep reaching, even if he can't reach back."

"Exactly." Shoulders slumping, Sam leaned against the counter. "And that's all I'm trying to do. Sorry for getting cranky on you."

"It's going around. You're all right." I offered him a quick fist bump. "I better get to class."

"And we better see you at trivia night this week. Bring Cal."

"So you all can interrogate him?" That sounded like utter misery for Cal and me both. I didn't need Cal catching wind of me having a...something. Not a crush. But more than friendly interest. And heck, even friendly interest might be enough to make Cal run.

"I was thinking so he could contribute," Sam said patiently. "We've got a top-three streak to defend. But if questioning him is likely to yield tasty gossip..."

"It's not." I groaned. "Lord, why do I love this town so much?"

"Because we've always got your back? And usually, you're first with the gossip. You're only having an issue because you're the subject."

"Possibly." Sighing, I headed for the door as Sam waved me away.

"Go on. Go forth and educate."

I tried to focus on my afternoon class and meeting, and as I exited my last meeting of the day, my phone buzzed with a text from Cal. My pulse galloped.

You out of class? I need a favor.

I quickly typed a reply.

Just finished for the day. Happy to help.

I need a ride to the clinic to get my stitches out. I was planning to ask Knox, but he's waiting on a plumber at another job site. I could walk, but I figured I'd ask.

I responded before the stubborn man could start walking.

I'll be there in ten. We can pick up a pizza for dinner after.

Cal's reply made me smile.

Sounds good.

What truly sounded good was Cal proactively asking me for help. With a little luck, maybe he'd ask for kissing next. Or perhaps I'd get out of my own way, do the kissing my own damn self.

# Chapter Eighteen

*Cal*

"Do you have everything you need?" Holden asked as we pulled up to the Stapleton house on a sunny, warm morning the day after I got my stitches removed.

"Yep," I lied. Or rather, I ignored the *everything* in Holden's question. I had my food in the borrowed lunch box from Holden, a large water bottle from my stack of gear now residing in Holden's garage, my phone, and other essentials, and I'd already suffered a handful of reminders from Holden about not overdoing it simply because my stitches were out. What I didn't have was...heck. If I knew how to describe it, I'd be in a better position to ask for it. A kink repeat? A make-out session? A goodbye kiss or hug, as silly as that sounded? An excuse to touch Holden?

I had no idea how it was possible to be so comfortable and so restless simultaneously. In a little over a week, we'd developed routines for everything from the morning drop-off to dinner to pre-bed TV watching. And somewhere in there was room for...*more*. But more was a damn frightening thought because if I got any more settled into the present situation, I might drift off on a warm cloud, forget my mission, forget that I didn't do coziness, relationships, and routines dependent on other people. Instead, I clung to my restlessness, my inability to come right out and ask Holden for what I wanted, even knowing full well he'd grant any request.

"Sure is a pretty day." I made no move to exit the car, drinking in these final few seconds with Holden. Sweeter and a better day starter than fresh-squeezed orange juice, and something I had no business getting used to, yet, here we were.

"Hmm. A weather compliment from you." Holden chuckled, hazel eyes crinkling. "Either you actually slept last night, or you want to make the point that you could have walked."

I could have easily walked, and we both knew that, but no way was I admitting aloud that I preferred the ride and the time with Holden.

"Not much sleep." I yawned. Outside the car, Oregon spring was in full swing, riots of flowers and color up and down the tree-lined street of older homes. My insomnia was slightly better, but what little I did sleep remained broken and too shallow. I chuckled. "Real sleep seems to only happen when you tuck me in."

The *tuck me in* line was supposed to be a joke, but Holden gave me a particularly intense, pointed look. "You do understand that can be arranged, right?"

"I suck at asking for things that will benefit me." I kept my tone as light and airy as the flimsy cherry blossoms drifting along the sidewalk. But it was also true. No matter how good our evening TV time felt, I was hardly going to invite Holden to lie next to me simply so I could sleep better. The idea alone felt selfish. And if I had trouble asking for kink, which Holden did seem to enjoy, no way was I requesting something that would be for me alone. "Witness my reaction to most of your fundraising ideas."

"I'm not talking about fundraising." Holden used an unusually stern tone, one he'd reserved for kinky fun times prior to now. The back of my neck went slick and hot. Was he losing patience with me? If he was tired of waiting on me, why couldn't he make a move himself?

But, of course, I knew the answer. He was a good guy. He was my landlord of sorts, and he was the type to worry about things like pressure. He thought he was doing the right thing, leaving it up to me.

"Actually, I was thinking more about the idea you had last night to sell bumper stickers." My words tumbled out quickly because I was only too eager to avoid talking more about beds and sleep and us. Over pizza the night before, we'd taken a break from dating shows and watched a documentary about the making of a war memorial. Holden had been inspired by all the bricks and plaques donors had purchased. He was into the idea of covering my future RV with sponsor stickers, but I'd needed time for the idea to grow on me. "It's a decent idea. Make it about the donors and the RV, not me."

"And what if someone wants to make things about you?" For once, Holden didn't allow me the grace of a subject change, and frustration laced his words.

"Then that person might need to remember I suck at reading signals, and I get all caught up in finding the mythical right moment. I'm the king of patient pining." If he could be frustrated, so could I. Maybe if I simply asked him to stop waiting around, we would be free from this limbo land we were stuck in.

"Pining, huh?" Holden gentled his tone. "We can't have you wasting away. And apparently, I need to take out a damn billboard advertising my tuck-in services."

"Neon lights," I countered, wanting to hear his chuckle, but he didn't laugh. His expression stayed too somber, too serious, and I had to resist the urge to squirm in the passenger seat.

"Cal, I want to put you to sleep." He put a hand over mine.

"Huh?" My few remaining brain cells fled in the face of Holden's electric touch.

"Poor word choice." Holden groaned and ran a hand through his dark hair. "Can I—"

He was cut off by a rap on the passenger-side window. In a case of the worst timing ever, Sam stood by my door, holding a coffee cup and offering a broad smile.

"I came to see the progress on the house," Sam said cheerily. "And I brought you coffee."

"Many thanks." I nodded curtly before turning back to Holden, who was staring straight ahead, expression wooden. "Holden—"

"Go on." He pointed at my door. "I'll keep."

I couldn't help but wonder for how long. How many chances would he grant me to sort myself out and just ask already? Or do? How hard would it be to simply plant one on the guy? Heck, Sam had already headed up to the porch. I could lean in, kiss Holden goodbye, and that would be that, and maybe tonight he'd...

*Nope.* I'd survived SEAL training, multiple deployments, and cheated death on numerous dives, yet the idea of closing the gap between us made another round of cold sweat snake down my back. I beat a hasty retreat from the car, joining Sam on the front porch. He handed me my coffee before he finished unlocking the door. Turning back to the driveway, Sam frowned as Holden zoomed away.

"That was a fast exit. I was about to ask him in to see... *oh.*" He slapped his head and gestured at the steep porch steps. "Crap."

"Need a ramp, boss?" I asked, forcing a cheerful tone. Sam didn't need the dregs of my confusion over Holden, and Sam's realization that his house wasn't accessible for Holden and others was far more important than petty worries over kissing. "I'm no woodworker, but I could talk to Knox. If he's got plans from other ramp projects, I bet I could bang something basic out."

"Something that would let Holden see the first floor?" Sam smiled as we entered the house, greeted by the scents of paint and industrial cleaners, the air still dusty with age. But the house's vibe was slowly transforming from neglected relic to work zone to the possibility of being a home again someday.

"Yep. Gonna need permission to remove some of the higher thresholds between rooms as well." Striding into the living room, I pointed out the thick wooden divider between the living and dining rooms. Not only a hindrance for wheelchair users, the old-fashioned thresholds were a hazard for anyone with unsure footing or high distractibility.

"Good call. Start on that whenever you get a chance." Sam nodded as he walked around the large, open living room. "Your work so far is looking amazing. And I absolutely want the house as accessible as possible. Might also add a chair lift to the second floor at some point."

I whistled low even as I nodded my agreement. "Those are a pretty penny."

"That's what fundraising is for." He grinned at me, but I only groaned in response.

"Now, you sound like Holden."

"If this is about your RV dilemma, you should listen to him." Sam gestured broadly, completely oblivious to my rising tension. Undoubtedly, the whole damn town knew my business. Broken RV. Injury. Rooming with Holden. Sam was hardly the only one picking up on all the good gossip. "Holden has a knack for encouraging people to donate. Guess all benevolent comedians have that skill, but he's among the best at it."

I made a warning noise. "He's more than a comedian."

"Is he now?" Leaning against the fireplace, Sam cocked his head at me, but I chose to ignore that I'd inadvertently tossed more fuel on the gossip fire.

"Holden's ideas are sound. I'm just allergic to asking for help."

"So don't." Sam shrugged like this was the obvious answer. "Why do you think so many charities have celebrity spokespeople? You're not the only do-gooder who hates to ask for money."

"I'm not a do-gooder." I scowled, summoning all my badass SEAL vibes, but Sam chuckled.

"See? That kind of humility is exactly why you need to let others do the asking."

"You got a spare celebrity?" Unable to keep still, I took a piece of sandpaper to a rough edge on one of the shelves I'd painted the day before, smoothing out a dried drip that was a testament to how distracted I was by everything with Holden. I didn't make silly mistakes, nor did I make friends, and yet, Sam kept right on with his advice like we were pals and he cared about my fundraising woes.

"As it turns out, yes. That iconic eighties coming-of-age movie, *Treehouse,* was filmed in Safe Harbor. My dad was an extra, and he became friends with one of the stars. Monte Ringer?"

"I've heard of him. Won an Oscar, right?"

"Yup. And he went on to be a big-name director after getting bored of acting awards. It's not a favor I ask Dad to call in often, but Monte lost a sister to a drowning accident. I think this charity might speak to him."

"I'm not profiting on some family's tragedy."

"It's not profiting." Sam shook his head like I was missing the point. "Everyone has a tragic backstory in some way. What sets people apart is what they do with the tragedies that define them. Some stuff them down. Some try to make amends or find other personal motivations. And a few will try to use the bad stuff as inspiration to advocate for changes that might prevent future tragedies."

"Suppose that's a point." My jaw was so tense it was a wonder it didn't pop loose like an over-tightened spring. I'd tried all that—stuffing the feelings down, trying to make things right, directing my life course—and Sam was wrong. When the tragedy was senseless, it didn't matter what a person did.

"It's all about what helps someone process." He sounded like Holden, firm in the belief that grief could be transformed into something manageable, maybe even useful. I knew better, but I let Sam continue. "In fact, in addition to my dad's friend, we should look into testimonials from those who have benefited from your recovery work."

"I ain't a restaurant begging for reviews."

"No, your work is way more important than that." Sam

bounced on the balls of his feet, cheeks flushed and eyes lighting up. He and Holden were peas in a pod, energized by thoughts of donations. Publicity. *People.* I wasn't ever going to understand extroverts.

"My work is necessary, sure. But it's also a reminder of dark times for folks. Don't wanna make them dredge that up."

"Cal, the dark times are there whether you call asking for a favor or not. Your call might be the very thing someone needs to not feel so helpless and powerless." Sam's tone was earnest and passionate, a combo that made it easy to see why he had so much respect from Holden, Knox, and others in the town. "Most people will be only too happy to give you the testimonial. It's an honor to be asked to help, especially if it's something specific, personal, and cost-free."

"That's not bad advice." Sanding done, I wiped the shelves down with a nearby rag. I'd do another coat of paint later, even out the final finish. "Similar to what I told Holden about your friend, Worth. Sometimes you have to make the call, even if the other person never picks up. Kinda weird to think he once lived here."

"I think he'd prefer to forget it." Eyes narrowing, Sam took on an uncharacteristically pessimistic tone. "He's not even giving likes to my messages right now."

"What did you just tell me? Your message might be what he needs." I swallowed hard. There were so many messages I'd never replied to myself. How many people had stopped reaching out simply because I couldn't reach back? Guilt and grief had created a toxic inertia, and I wished I had better words to explain to Sam. "Him not replying is about him, not you. Be...easy on him."

"I'm trying." Sam's expression softened, and his mouth

opened like he might have more to say, but Knox bustled in through the front door carrying a foil-wrapped plate.

"Hey, Sam! And, Cal. I meant to be here earlier to discuss your work for the day, but...running behind." Knox's faint blush said Monroe was undoubtedly involved in his late start. Lucky duo. I lacked Holden's gift for teasing, so I simply nodded as he held out the plate. "But I have breakfast sandwiches! Leon's latest culinary invention."

Sam and I each grabbed a sandwich, but Sam didn't stay much longer than some small talk with Knox and a discussion of adding a ramp to the front porch.

"I'll leave you guys to work. Hopefully, we can figure out a ramp." Sam patted my shoulder on his way to the front door, expression thoughtful. He certainly had a way of making people feel heard. "Thanks again, Cal. Oh, tell Holden the new monthly flavors just dropped at Dairy Mart."

"Will do." Funny how I hadn't been in this town long at all, yet I was all invested in ice cream flavors and pizza toppings and the fate of people I'd never met, like Worth. For the first time since leaving the SEALs, I felt part of something bigger than my own cause. I wasn't sure I liked it, this feeling of connection. Like with Holden, the coziness was both reassuring and panic-inducing.

I ruminated on that all morning as I removed thresholds and prepped for hardwood refinishing. While working on the doorway between the kitchen and the dining room, my eyes kept drifting to a built-in display hutch with glass doors on top and drawers on the bottom. Giving into the impulse, I abandoned my work to examine it closer. It smelled musty, like old paint and disuse. The glass needed a thorough scrubbing, and the drawers all stuck, especially the last one.

I pulled harder.

Nothing.

Determined, I tugged with all my might.

Papers. A whole stack of papers rained out of a hidden compartment behind the drawer. A single glance told me I'd found something that might change everything.

I dug my phone out of my pocket, knowing exactly who I needed to call first.

# Chapter Nineteen

*Holden*

As soon as my phone rang and I saw the call was from Cal, my pulse sped up.

"Are you alone?" he demanded. No greeting, and with certain others, I might have assumed the question was a prelude to sexy phone fun, but with Cal, my heartbeat went from gallop to full-out sprint. Something was wrong.

"What's wrong? Are you okay?" I wheeled out from behind my desk to firmly shut my office door. "I'm alone in my office. Just finished a meeting and have a rare free afternoon for grading. Or whatever you need. What's going on?"

I slowed my rapid-fire questions so Cal had a chance to answer, and in typical Cal fashion, he took a long pause first.

"I found something. At the Stapleton house. I called you before anyone else." He sounded breathless and on edge, so I let him continue rather than thanking him for making me the first call. This wasn't about my ego. It was about whatever had Cal spooked. "I need to show you this. I know the chain of custody rules for underwater dives, but I'm murkier on land-based items. I probably should have called the police station, but the chain of custody is only the tip of the ethics iceberg here."

He stopped for a few deep breaths, and I breathed along with him, trying to radiate calming vibes. "First things first. Are you okay? Safe?"

"Yeah. Not injured. Just...antsy." Antsy was probably as close as Cal would come to admitting he was shaken up. "Can you...? I know it's a big ask, but could you come over? I can help you come in the house through the back way. The door by the kitchen only has a step or two. I'll help you in. But I need to show someone what I found."

"I'm on my way." I'd hit Send on an out-of-office email before Cal finished making his request. I usually avoided inaccessible situations where I'd need help with my chair, but if Cal called, I'd deal with any amount of inconvenience. "Don't touch anything else until I'm there."

"I'll be here. Thank you." Cal sounded decidedly calmer. I liked being able to provide that for him. I wanted to be someone he could count on and not simply for kink or conversation.

When I arrived at the Stapleton house, Cal met me by the rear door. I had my crutches with me, so with Cal's assistance, I tackled the steps and let him carry my chair in.

"Thanks," I said gruffly as I settled back in my chair in the kitchen. Several cabinets were missing fronts, the sink was chipped, and loose tiles marred the floor and back-splash. The space was a far cry from back in high school when it had been a sparkling kitchen filled with baking smells and peaceful vibes.

"No, thank you for coming." Cal laid a hand on my

shoulder. "I didn't know what else to do, but I wanted your take first."

"I'm always happy to help." I didn't want to sound too grateful for being his first call, but I loved how he seemed to think of us as a team and valued my input. I'd grabbed some latex gloves from the first aid kit in my car, and I handed Cal a pair. "Here, put on gloves, and show me what you found. Take me through the discovery."

I followed him into the dining room, where he stopped in front of the large, built-in hutch. It had likely been natural wood colored at one point but was now painted a grimy, faded white under several layers of dust.

"This cabinet kept bugging me. Something about it..." He pursed his lips. "Anyway, I went and tested the drawers. When I freed the bottom drawer, this happened."

Crouching, he yanked at the bottom drawer, which revealed a space behind the drawer that opened to reveal a stack of papers.

"A hidden compartment." I whistled low as I pulled on a pair of gloves myself. "Worth's parents always were particular about having cash on hand and stashed in odd places. His dad called it mattress money, but he had hiding spots other than under the mattress."

"This stuff is more likely the mom's. And it's more letters than cash, but there is some of that." Carefully, Cal removed the stack, revealing an envelope of cash, pamphlets and papers with the cheerful Kitchen Kingdom logo, and many notes in scrawled handwriting on lined notecards.

"This is good potential evidence." I nodded slowly, trying to force the investigative part of my brain to stay in control, not give in to the rising emotions at these tangible reminders of Mrs. Stapleton. Although the house remained heavy with signs of neglect and the scents of paint and cleaner hung in the air, I swore I could smell oatmeal-raisin cookies and hear the strains of the oldies Mrs. Stapleton always had going. "The Kitchen Kingdom pamphlets, order forms, and cash envelope are significant for showing a link beyond secondhand hearsay reports she was involved in the cooking equipment parties."

"But it's these notes..." Cal showed me the first card, which was on heavy stock with a line drawing of a bird on the front. I was immediately drawn to the first line. A quote from a classic Katharine Hepburn movie.

"Movie quotes." I sucked in a breath. The main suspect in this case was known for speaking in riddles and using quotes from movies to answer questions. And sure enough, a brief riffle through the notes revealed countless quotes, all of which seemed picked to flatter Mrs. Stapleton and conveyed a significant depth of romantic emotion. "He had a crush. Obsession maybe. But she saved the notes."

"Exactly. She saved them. Hid them even. If she hadn't wanted the attention, wouldn't she have trashed them?" Eyes narrowed, Cal worried the edge of his lips with his tongue. "And there's more."

He revealed several handwritten notebook pages in a different, more feminine writing with lists of pros and cons and drafts of letters with words scribbled out and sentences in the margins.

"Oh." All the air left the room. "It wasn't one-sided. She was thinking of leaving or at least trying to work out how she felt in return. It's like she was..."

"Pining." Cal finished my thought for me. "I know pining. And that's someone who was pining for...an escape, maybe? Or perhaps the other person specifically."

"Sociopaths can be very charming, and it sure looks like she was tempted to go with him." I studied the documents closer. "If it wasn't a physical affair, there were, at the very least, strong emotions involved on both sides."

"Exactly. And this information changes everything." Cal, who was always serious, had reached a new level of grimness.

"Yeah, can't argue with that. She didn't deserve to die, but this will influence public opinion. Cracks in her perfect housewife image." My chest felt strangely hot and tight, instant heartburn. "Worth already told Monroe his folks argued that summer, but he didn't report it to investigators at the time, so it's not public knowledge. But now it will be much clearer that their marriage was on the rocks."

"And everyone's gonna have an opinion. It sucks. You and Sam are planning that memorial. And Worth isn't gonna like this news at all. Maybe we don't have to share?" Cal's tone was mournful but resigned like he already knew the answer, so I allowed him space to work things out aloud. "The task force has enough to get the suspect now. The indictment should come down any day now. But what if they do end up needing this evidence? Fuck. I don't know what the right thing to do here is."

"Cal. We can't play God." I gave him a hard look, but he likely didn't need the reminder. He knew what we had to do here, but he was right. It was going to suck. "If it damages her reputation, that is a shame, but the truth needs to come out. And if she was the first victim of this killer, establishing a pattern and motive may help locate others beyond the known Florida victims. It could end up helping more than this one case."

"Yeah..." Cal sighed, sagging back against my chair, and I rested a hand on his tense shoulder.

"She was human and made some mistakes, but she still

deserves justice, and the killer needs to be held accountable."

"Agreed." Cal's voice sounded far away. "Guess that's the problem with pedestals. People are humans. Not sure why this has me all in knots."

"Come here." I pulled on his shoulder until his head was against my thigh, arms around my torso. Cal took big gulps of air.

"I feel stupid."

"You're not stupid. You're caring. That's a good quality."

"It's a liability because most folks see the world in black and white." Anger laced his tone, but he still sounded closer to tears than rage. "With my mom, all anyone remembers is the last few years. The grief-induced depression. The drinking. The chronic pancreatitis. And with Ev, everyone only remembers the good, not the complicated reality. Wild teen who made good in the navy, reckless daredevil but also a highly decorated SEAL, hook-up king turned loving husband. Last impressions matter. Apparently."

"Others might see it that way, but you can honor those shades of gray." I stroked his short hair and muscular neck. "It's okay to admit the people you loved were human."

He shuddered, burying his face against me. My shirt grew damp as I held him as tightly as I could.

"Damn it. Why am I crying?"

"Because you're human too." I clung to him as much as he clung to me, my own emotions close to the surface. "You're human, and you hurt. It's good to let it out."

"You shouldn't have to deal with me all sloppy."

"You're emotional, Cal." I leaned down to kiss the top of his head. "This isn't you falling-down drunk. I want to be here for you. And hell, I'd be here even if you were shit-faced."

"Thank you." Tilting his head, he gazed up at me with glassy eyes. And then he stretched, mouth right below mine. I held perfectly still, letting him be the one to close the gap. He brushed his mouth over mine, the softest, sweetest kiss on record.

"I'm glad you trust me," I whispered.

"You make me feel...safe." He kissed me again, another kitten-whisker soft kiss that made me gasp. Safe was a start. I wanted to make him feel all the things, but if I could make this wounded man feel safe, perhaps I stood a chance of protecting him from his demons. When he released me, I kissed his forehead, keeping him close as he rested his head against my torso. "Will you stay while I call Sam and then the station? It's Sam's house, so he should know, but we need to turn in the evidence, even if it complicates things."

"Yes. Of course. I'm not going anywhere." And I wasn't. The case wasn't the only thing complicated. Each interaction with Cal tangled me up further, increased the risk of hurt for us both, but hell if I could be anywhere other than right here.

# Chapter Twenty

*Cal*

"Sleepy?" Holden's voice gently awakened me from a pleasant couch snooze. We were, for all intents and purposes, cuddling. Holden's arm was along the back of the couch, my head was perilously close to his shoulder, and our feet were cozied on the same ottoman. And warm, fuzzy energy had enveloped us since the sweet kisses at the Stapleton house. It blanketed us, made us sit that much closer, made our voices more tender, made our looks longer, and our casual touches more lingering. "We can watch the episode again tomorrow. You missed some epic backstabbing drama."

"You're too good to me." I yawned and gave into the impulse to let my head drop the rest of the way onto Holden's shoulder.

"Nah." Chuckling, he gently pushed me off. "To bed with you."

*Boom. Boom.* My heartbeat sounded like cannon fire in my ears and my palms sweat. I could head to bed, same as always, nothing changed even though everything had, or I could take a deep breath and leap into the icy unknown.

"And to bed with you."

"Yeah, yeah, I'm going." Holden yawned even wider than I had. Clearly, my leap had landed far off target because he didn't even look in my direction as he transferred back to his chair. "I have to lock up first and—"

"I meant *with* you." Making a frustrated noise, I itched behind my ear. This wasn't supposed to be difficult. "You said earlier? About a neon billboard advertising your sleep aid services?"

"*Oh.*" Holden's eyes went wide and pleased. "Absolutely. You wanting the tuck-in service or..."

Studying me carefully, he trailed off, leaving me plenty of room to ask for what I truly wanted.

"It was nice that night you accidentally fell asleep in my bed. I slept all night. Most of it using you as a pillow, which..." Now it was my turn to trail off because I needed a better word than *nice*.

"Was wonderful." Holden had enough enthusiasm for both of us. "Yes, we can do that. My mattress is bigger and more supportive, so could we sleep in my room?"

"Yeah." That was an easy request, so I waited by the hallway for him to lock up and show me to his room. He quickly flipped off the lights and checked the deadbolt.

As he approached me, he waved toward my room's door. "You can get whatever you were planning to sleep in."

"I don't own pajamas." I gave him a very pointed look as I grabbed my pillow and a toothbrush, enjoying his flushed face.

"Or nothing. Nothing works too." His voice was a little on the bright side, but surprisingly, things weren't that awkward as we made our way into his room. Felt...natural almost. I'd never been inside the space, which had pale blue-green walls, warm wood accents, and soft lighting, but the peaceful, ocean-like vibe served to relax any lingering nerves over my request. The split king bed was heaped with white linens, which made it look like something out of a hotel photo shoot despite the adjustable functionality.

"Are the underwater photos yours?" I stepped closer to look at the row of pictures over the bed and the dresser, which featured schools of fish, coral reefs, sunny spots, and hidden caves. Familiar pleasure-diving sites, and it added to how comfortable I felt in the space.

"Some. Few are ones Marley took in Hawaii, and I purchased the big one of the Maldives because none of mine were as frame-worthy." Still in his chair, he twisted the hem of his dress shirt. "Are you wanting me to stay clothed again?"

I outright chortled at that. Apparently, I wasn't the only one battling nerves. "No, Holden. If I'm sleeping naked, you are too."

"Oh. Okay." Holden sounded tipsy like he'd had a few beers with dinner, but the dude was as sober as me. After the long day at the Stapleton house and talking to the police, neither of us had been in the mood for much dinner beyond a few leftovers.

However, like me, he settled down as we got ready for bed, brushing our teeth at the double sinks in the attached bathroom and stripping our clothes off on either side of the big bed. The mood was cozy and familiar, pressure-free, but even without expectations, there was a certain sexiness in sharing a pre-bed routine.

Not to mention, my body thrilled at the chance to see more of Holden, his wide, fuzzy chest with dark nipples and a surprising crop of freckles over his sturdy shoulders. After

I pulled my own underwear off, Holden shucked his boxer briefs quickly, but not before I caught a glimpse of that thick cock my mouth had enjoyed so much. His legs were thinner than his build might suggest, with various surgical scars, but he slipped under the puffy comforter before I could appreciate him further.

Bedside lamp casting warm shadows across the bed, he lifted the edge of the blanket for me to climb in next to him. His eyes were heated, but somehow he managed relaxed body language and a casual tone.

"Requests?" he asked as he pulled me close under the covers, onto more of his side of the bed. The gesture was more sweet than sexual but romantic nonetheless. "Big spoon? Little spoon?"

"How the hell are you so nice?" Making a sound partway between frustration and chuckling, I arranged myself exactly how I wanted, on my side, head on his shoulder, an arm and a leg across his big body, chest pressed to his, warm and perfect.

"I train hard." Holden stroked a hand down my bare back. "Maybe you make it easy to be nice?"

I snorted. "Try again."

"Maybe I like being nice to you." Pressing a gentle kiss to the top of my head, he held me close, and wonder of wonders, I relaxed into the embrace.

"Huh. I guess I like it."

Holden laughed and kissed my head again, this time on the temple. "You don't have to sound so startled."

"Hey, my surprise is real. I used to hate being fussed over. Still do, honestly. Only seem to tolerate it from you." My admission made him squeeze me tighter against him, hand firm on my back.

"Good. I don't want to share you." He gazed intently

into my eyes, a message there about far more than nice gestures. "I'll do all the fussing you need."

"That you asking if we can go steady?" I joked to relieve the sudden tightness in my chest, but Holden cocked his head, more serious than silly.

"Are we dating?" The tiny note of hope in his voice darn near killed me.

"Um." He deserved far better than a flip answer, especially after the day we'd had. He'd been there for me, no questions asked, yet again. Lacking clarity, I went for the truth. "I was hoping you'd know the answer to that."

"Living together certainly makes things confusing." He sighed. "I mean, I'm your landlord—"

"Never had dinner and TV with a landlord. That ain't how I think of you, and you know it." I gave him a hard stare. "You telling me roommates never date?"

I had absolutely no clue what I was doing, advocating for us to be anything other than casual friends. But the answer mattered to Holden. That much was clear in his every look and gesture, and what he wanted mattered to me, even if it was unfamiliar territory.

"All right then." He gave a crisp nod. "Come with me to trivia night at the pub. Wear a nice shirt. I'll buy you fried pickles, and we can hold hands under the table."

"It's a date." Swallowing hard, I tried to calm my pulse rate out of cardiac-event territory.

"Your heart is pounding." Holden's voice was kind as he stroked my back some more.

"Yeah." There was no sense in lying. I sagged against him. "Not like I have a lot of dating experience. I'll probably screw it up."

"It's trivia night with the guys." He offered me a crooked smile. "Pretty hard to mess up. I know you can't make me any promises." His smile dipped a tiny bit before recovering. "But I want this. I want to see where things go."

"Me too." My heart continued to hammer like an out-of-control nail gun. Humor was usually Holden's weapon of choice, but right then, it was the only thing standing between me and emotional Armageddon. "So we lived together first, then did kink, slept next to each other, finally kissed, and now we're gonna have a first date? At this backward pace, I'm gonna be sending you love notes on looseleaf next week."

"I'm counting on it." He tipped my head back, eyes telegraphing his intent, but I didn't pull away. In fact, I leaned toward him as he lowered his mouth. Earlier, the kisses had been more about connection and comfort. And this started in a similar fashion, a light brush like I had done to him, but then the kiss turned far more seductive. His tongue coaxed mine out to play, and his lips, while still soft, were active, encouraging more responses from me. If earlier had been a kiss, a singular noun, this was *kissing*, a verb, a very *active* verb.

"Oh." I gasped as he pulled back. We were in exactly the same position, lying next to each other in his bed, under the covers, but every cell in my body felt as though I'd traveled through space and time, a cosmic event. I released a shaky laugh. "All those songs and lines about butterflies and fireworks. I always figured everyone else was either liars or damn good poets or both. But that..."

"Butterflies?" Hopeful crinkles appeared around Holden's hazel eyes.

"More like the butterfly effect. Time travel." I laughed, not entirely comfortable with this level of poetry from myself, but I lacked the appropriate vocabulary for kissing Holden. Anything I'd experienced prior was fast

167

and fleeting, ultimately disappointing. "You...took me places."

"Even better." Clearly loving the praise, he kissed me again, intensity ramping up as he delved deeper and lingered more. I let myself match his urgency, mimicking his actions because everything he tried felt equally amazing when I did it to him. This, too, was new, the playfulness, the time to explore and discover. He lightly sucked on my lower lip, and I shuddered before returning the favor, loving his low groan.

He roved his hands all over my shoulders and back, encouraging me ever closer. My hips moved restlessly, my thigh dragging against his erection as I pressed mine into his side. I groaned because it felt so good, both too much and not enough.

"What do you need?" he whispered.

"I don't know." I made a frustrated noise, and he went completely still, hands dropping away from me. I pulled them right back. "I didn't mean stop. You choose something, and I'll probably like it."

"Have you fucked before?" His voice was carefully neutral.

I shook my head against his shoulder. "No, but I would with you. I trust you."

"Not sure I trust me this turned on." His wobbly laugh said he wasn't as collected as he tried to appear.

"Maybe I like you this turned on." I nudged him with my midsection, loving how he groaned. I liked him nice and sweet, but I loved him human best of all. Like I'd said earlier in the day, people didn't belong on pedestals.

"Good. And we'll get there on...other stuff, but how about for now we keep making out?" He stroked my face with gentle fingertips, a reverence there that made my breath catch.

"Yeah." If more kissing was what he wanted, I was only too happy to go along with that plan. Holden kissed me again, hands even more active now, kneading my neck, rubbing my shoulders, stroking my sides. And I touched too, memorizing his crinkly chest hair and muscular shoulders and biceps. There was a sweetness to our explorations that made them stretch on and on. That, too, was new—my few prior experiences had all been zero to sixty fast dashes. What Holden and I shared truly was in a different universe. Hours could have passed, and I would have been right there, totally happy. Well, most of me would have been happy. The more we touched and kissed, the more my cock throbbed. It was trapped against Holden's side, and my subtle grinding wasn't nearly enough relief. A needy noise escaped my throat. "Want..."

"I got you, baby." He gave me a fast, firm kiss before rolling toward the nightstand and returning with a sample-size bottle of hand lotion. "Can we try something?"

"Sure." I didn't have to think about it. If it was something Holden liked, I wanted to give it a whirl, much as he had with my kinks. "Show me."

"I like you all prickly and stubborn, but I sure do enjoy it when you let me be in charge." He chuckled as he rearranged us so he was spooning me from behind. I went even more pliant at the praise. A dick pressing against my ass was a bit new, and I trembled, though more from arousal than anything else. I liked how big and thick and strong Holden was everywhere, and I loved how safe I felt as he held me super tight. I might be the SEAL, but he made me feel absolutely secure under his protection.

"I like this idea already." I relaxed against him, letting

him adjust us further so his lotion-slick cock rode between my thighs, but even more intriguing than his cock's new home was the way his arm snaked under me, hand resting right above my sternum, fingertips grazing my throat. "Your hand feels good there."

"Still good?" He moved his hand slightly, more deliberately splaying his fingers across my collarbones and Adam's apple. "I'm not about to try for breath play or anything like that, but holding you this way is hot as hell."

"Yeah it is." I stretched against him, testing to see if he'd increase the pressure. He did, but as promised, he kept his grip possessive, not constricting. His other hand started a slow, slippery jack of my cock.

"Mmm. You smell nice." Holden kissed the back of my neck as he slowly started thrusting between my thighs. For the first time, I could see the appeal of fucking, being this close to another person, closer than close, taking him inside me. Yeah, I wanted that. But despite how amazing his moving against me felt, how connected and special, I couldn't stop the restlessness in my arms and legs, my body searching for something. He kissed me again, lips against my ear. "Do you need the kink? Restraint?"

"No." I huffed. "I don't think, at least. Not sure why I can't settle."

"It's okay. Whatever you need." Holden stroked me, touch firm and reassuring. "Try this. Tuck your hands by your sides and cross your legs. Let me hold you extra close, baby."

"Oh wow." I exhaled hard at the difference the adjustment made. His strong arms completely enveloped me now, and he used his top foot to pin my legs. His thrusts and the strokes of his hand were more limited but also far more erotic this way. And it wasn't about force or feeling like he was taking something from me. Rather, he was *giving* me this, making me feel surrounded by safety and the freedom I only seemed to find in restriction.

"Fuck. You're so sexy." His breath was warm on my neck, his voice urgent.

"Wanna make you come." Like the last time we'd fooled around, my need to hear and see and feel him get off rose, even more so than any need of my own.

"Oh, you will. But not before you."

"Not sure I can," I admitted. The want to make him come was so great, and while my dick pulsed in his slick grip, climax seemed maddeningly just out of reach, even on Holden's command. But then he sped up his thrusts and tensed his entire body, torso rigid, arms and legs clasping me tightly. I inhaled, meeting sharp resistance, and that did it. "Oh fuck."

I strained against him, the elusive orgasm suddenly right there, no stopping it. The first spurt fucking hurt, like an exorcism followed by intense, unending pleasure that pulsed and pulsed even after I'd finished shooting.

"That's it. That's right. Let go, baby." Holden's voice was rough, and right as I made a broken noise that might have been an attempt at his name, he groaned deep, hips stuttering against my ass, warmth blooming along my thighs. "Fuck. Cal."

He kissed my neck over and over, and it was a moment to get lost in, a moment I didn't want to end, and I only reluctantly sagged against him as bone-weary tiredness started to replace some of the orgasmic high.

"Holy crap. I may sleep for a week after that." Continuing to tremble, I managed a yawn as Holden fumbled for some sort of cloth on the nightstand, cleaning us both off. Or at least attempting to do so. I wasn't much help, what with trying to get back into the perfect snuggling position.

"I hope so." He kissed my forehead before groaning softly as he shifted. Heck. I hadn't really stopped to think about his physical needs the whole time, and now guilt crawled up my spine.

"You okay?" I kept my voice as carefully neutral as he always did when broaching a hard topic.

"More than." He pulled me close against him, tucking me in against his side. "My hips will undoubtedly feel it tomorrow, but that's hardly news, and any extra achiness will be more than worth it."

"Good." I yawned even bigger as cuddling nirvana was achieved. "Gotta...sleep now."

"Yeah, you do." Holden's warm chuckle rumbled through his chest, vibrating through my sleepy body as well. "You need all your rest for dating me."

Oh crap. I had agreed to try that, hadn't I? God, I hoped I didn't screw things up for the nicest, sweetest, sexiest person I'd ever known. At the very least, I better study up on some trivia.

# Chapter Twenty-One

*Holden*

The universe had a crappy sense of humor, timing yet another spring rainstorm complete with wind and the sort of barometric pressure shifts my body hated on the same day as my trivia-night date with Cal and a full afternoon of never-ending meetings on campus. Unsurprisingly, I was late arriving home with every bone aching. In fact, I took an extra minute in the car in the garage, trying to summon strength. Canceling wasn't an option for me. Of course my friends would understand, but I held myself to a different standard. Ordinarily, I'd take some medication to help tough out the evening, but the one most effective against damp weather pain flares was also a bit of a boner killer. And as this was supposed to be *date* night, I didn't want to risk that.

I had slept the past few blissful nights with Cal, and I was greedy enough to want more. It wasn't like either of us was exactly orgasm-deprived, but a first date deserved... well, more effort than I was currently capable of giving it, that much was certain. My hips creaked as I hefted myself into my chair, and my biceps strained on the short distance into the house. I was halfway to deciding to take the pain medicine anyway when I almost ran into Cal in the kitchen.

"Oh." I legit did a double-take, like some hero in a music video catching sight of the love interest coming down the stairs. Cal wore a crisp white dress shirt, nothing particularly fancy, but it fit his lean build perfectly and the open button at his collar and rolled sleeves revealing his muscular forearms and tattoo were the perfect tease. "Remind me to order you to wear a nice shirt more often."

"You can order me around anytime you'd like." Cal had a sexual glint in his eyes that I didn't see often. He was definitely in date mode, and no way was I going to waste a playful, sexy Cal. I could live without the pain meds, especially when Cal gave me an appreciative once-over. "You look good too."

"This?" I looked down at my aqua dress shirt. The color was flashy, but it was otherwise yet another oxford to pair with slacks for professor wear. "I wore this to campus. Got delayed by a student coming into my office, so I didn't make it home to shower and change like I'd planned."

"You don't need to change on my account." Cal's tone was serious as he held my gaze. There was a message there, one I wasn't sure I was ready for. Accepting Cal prickles and all was ridiculously easy. Accepting myself? So much harder, especially on days like this. And Cal seemed to intuit that, adding, "After all, you're the one who said this is just trivia night with your guys."

"Only one guy I'm interested in tonight." I managed a flirty tone as I held out a hand to Cal, intending to pull him into my lap, but he merely laughed and sidestepped my grasp.

"Don't tempt me into asking for kink instead of a date."

"You can always ask for a kink date, baby. No rule that says we have to leave the house to date." Winking at him, I chuckled. And perhaps that would be the better choice tonight. Bail on trivia night, tie Cal up, make him come undone, and maybe he wouldn't notice that I wasn't anywhere near my best.

"You? Miss a social obligation?" Cal shook his head. Amazing how well he knew me after a few short weeks. "Your friends are waiting."

"True." I groaned and turned back toward the garage. "Guess we should head out."

The rain continued on the short drive to the tavern, but luckily there was an accessible spot open close to the door, so we weren't too drenched as we made our way to the table where Sam, Knox, and Monroe were already waiting.

"Cal! You came!" Sam smiled broadly and pointed to the seat next to him as Monroe moved a chair away from the table for me. "Have a seat."

"Thanks." Cal nodded at Sam before deftly ducking behind me to take the chair on my other side. "Think I'll sit next to Holden though."

"That's fine." Sam drew out the word *fine,* giving me a pointed look. The other two looked plenty curious as well. The gossip mill would be churning big time by the end of the evening, but seeing as how this outing had been my idea, I couldn't exactly complain. And Cal said he wanted to date, so perhaps he was less likely to be spooked by gossip than a few weeks ago.

"We already put in a food order, but you probably want to flag a server for your drinks." Knox passed Cal a drink menu.

After we both had beers and the first batch of appetizers had arrived, Sam resumed his attempt to chat up Cal.

"I stopped by the house before here. The downstairs is looking so good, but the upstairs was the real surprise."

"Yeah? You thinking about finally spending a night in your own house?" Cal's dry tease made the rest of the table laugh. That Sam had yet to move a single item of clothing or a mattress into the house was becoming comical.

"I'll get there." Sam's pale cheeks turned pink.

"If it feels too strange, you can always finish the work, then flip it for a handy profit." Monroe was always sensible and pragmatic, but I wasn't surprised when Sam made a horrified noise.

"I couldn't do that!"

"Then take baby steps toward moving in. Bet your parents will be happy to have their garage apartment back." Knox was far gentler in his approach, leaning toward Sam. "What would make it easier for you to move into the house?"

"I'm not sure. Probably just need to make up my mind and do it." Something in the way Sam shifted said he might be lying about not knowing what the problem was. Maybe I shouldn't have encouraged him to buy the place. Too many feelings for all of us wrapped up there. "I guess I start by picking a room."

"It's your house. You get the primary suite." Knox shrugged like Sam was way overthinking things. "But let's make the room feel more like you. Cal, do you have any ideas?"

"You want me to give decorating advice?" Cal shook his head and nabbed another fried pickle. "If it were my house, I'd say screw the whole owner-of-the-house rule. Take over the third floor. Full-on bath remodel up there with a walk-in shower or—"

"A soaking tub." Sam's expression turned damn near poetic. "Right under that dormer window."

"If you can envision it, we can figure out how to get the tub up there." Knox was nothing if not encouraging. "And Cal's brilliant. Make a brand-new suite. One with fresh energy."

"Yeah. I like this idea," Sam said slowly, eyes distant, deep in thought. "A soaking tub. Small, black one. Japanese style. Dove gray walls. Cream linens. Plants on the balcony and in the windows..."

"You're the boss." Cal chuckled. "It's on you to keep the plants alive, but I think we can deliver a suite you'll be happy with."

"We?" Sam raised his thin, arched eyebrows. "You gonna stick around to help?"

Cal shrugged, but his face twisted with discomfort. "Guess so. Yeah. Still working on the RV fund."

That was hardly a ringing endorsement. More like he had nothing better to do. If the house project, which he seemed to have made a personal mission, wasn't enough to keep him here, how could I expect to be a good enough reason for him to put down stakes?

"How's that RV fund coming?" Monroe was in a good mood, arm slung over Knox's shoulders, impervious to my mental request to stop talking about Cal leaving. "With summer getting closer, I guess there will be more dive requests and opportunities for you."

"I have an updated website now." Cal sounded vaguely ill. We'd spent an evening installing a new template and fundraising widget on his existing site. Cal had grumbled the whole time then too, but I'd felt compelled to come through with at least some sort of fundraising plans. I might want to keep him here forever, but I was also a man of my word. "With a landing page for Holden's big fundraising plans for selling bumper sticker space. And I guess I need to add Sam's testimonial idea."

"You do." Sam whipped out his phone. "I'm sending you a reminder message to email me a list of contact information for prior dives, so I can gather the praise quotes for you."

Sam's ready offer had me wishing I'd thought of adding testimonials and collecting them myself to save Cal the work of asking.

"You'd do that?" Sure enough, Cal's wide-eyed gratitude had vinegar rising up the back of my throat.

"I can help too." I wasn't sure anyone heard me because none of them glanced in my direction.

"I wonder if the...news will help or hinder Cal's fundraising efforts." Knox twirled the straw for his drink. The five of us knew what Cal had found, but the official investigatory team was still reviewing the documents and had yet to announce another press conference. The indictment process was also still grinding on. Intrastate politics were undoubtedly slowing things further.

"Is it wrong to hope Cal's find doesn't come out till after the memorial?" Sam grimaced, staring down at his share of the fried pickles. "Mrs. Stapleton deserves her dignity a little longer."

I made a frustrated noise, then lowered my voice to a harsh whisper. "Someone trusting the wrong person doesn't make them bad or unworthy of respect."

"Of course." Sam visibly recoiled, sitting back in his chair. "I didn't mean to sound judgmental. The discovery doesn't change all the good she did for the community."

"Gossip won't care how good of a person she was." Cal pursed his mouth. "Last thing I want is a boost in fundraising from the public airing of dirty laundry."

"I know." I patted his leg under the table. "And I think we're all worried about Worth. Whatever the public reaction, his is the one that matters most."

"Yeah." Sam pulled his phone back out, and I didn't need to ask to know he was checking his messages again. The turn in the conversation made my pain flare again, made me that much more aware of how damn tired I was, how long this week had been, and by the time we made it through two rounds of the trivia game, I was more than ready to head back out into the rain.

"Thanks for coming, Cal." Knox offered him a fist bump as we all settled up and prepared to leave. "How'd you learn so much history trivia?"

"A hell of a lot of sleepless nights and documentaries. And last few years, long drives and certain informative podcasts." Cal gave me a knowing almost-fond look. That I wasn't leaving alone was nice. Comforting. Indeed, Cal's presence all evening had been most welcome. Having someone to share long gazes and little jokes with had been a major bright spot in a rough evening, and I returned his look with one of my own, which made him smile wider. "Lot of good...*hypnotic* voices out there."

I heard praise for the podcast all the time, but coming from Cal, the compliment landed in a softer, more vulnerable place and lingered, warm and fuzzy, like an unexpected neck rub.

However, his praise turned to concern as soon as we were alone in my car.

"You okay? And don't say fine. I can tell you're not doing well."

"You can?" I couldn't keep the guilty startle from my tone.

"Doubt the others noticed, but the lines around your eyes and mouth get deeper when it's a bad pain day, your shoulders get tenser, your voice a little more strident, and your humor more forced." Cal rattled off a whole damn list of observations I couldn't argue with as I turned toward my neighborhood.

"Hell." I groaned in defeat. "I was trying hard to not be obvious."

"Like I said, the others likely didn't pick up on anything. Think I'm just tuned into you." Cal gave me a much more tender look than my cranky ass probably deserved.

"I'd rather you be *turned on* to me."

"That too." He stretched as I pulled into the driveway. "But not tonight."

"What? Why?"

"Holden." Cal put on a not-an-idiot voice that made me feel like I was in a remedial how-to-human class. "You're in pain, and the only reason I didn't insist on driving is because I knew you wouldn't trust me with your pricey baby."

"I trust you." Holding up my hands, I gave him what I hoped was a sincere look. Because I did trust him. Maybe not with *everything,* but my car? My house? Sure. My bad days? My heart? I was working on it.

"Then trust me. Take the meds you've been putting off." Cal said this declaratively, and damn it, he really did know me too well.

"But I wanted to sleep with you." I tried one last protest as I transferred to my chair. "The meds make me sleepy. Like *all* of me sleepy, sleepy."

"Then you'll sleep. My insomnia willing, we'll both

sleep." Cal was only too patient as he waited for me to enter the house. "After you take your meds, I'll give you a neck rub if you think it will help, and I can still sleep next to you."

"You touching me is always a good thing. It's our first date, though, and I wanted...*more*."

"More? It's date one, Professor." He grinned at me, right there in the dim light of the mudroom, a full-wattage rare-as-fuck Cal grin. And just like that, I was all his. "Give us time to run all the plays in the playbook. How about you take your painkillers, I rub you down, and you give me a goodnight kiss to remember?"

"Deal." I grinned back, already contemplating how to repay Cal's kindness as soon as my body allowed.

# Chapter Twenty-Two

*Cal*

"Take the afternoon off." Knox, who had already established himself as a nice guy several times over, seemed determined to earn his spot in the Good Boss Hall of Fame. It was a sleepy Saturday, with more of the cold, drizzly rain Safe Harbor had been battling all week. But I'd been scheduled to work on the accessible ramp at the Stapleton house, and I was nothing if not a man of my word.

"I don't mind a little rain."

"A little? It's practically a monsoon." Knox shook his head. "The ramp will get done, but not today. Not in this weather. And before you ask for more work, we're waiting on plumbing and electric for the third floor. The paint for the remaining second-floor rooms is back-ordered. I won't get the floor sander rental until next week. It's Saturday, and you've been working pretty much nonstop on this project since I hired you. Go find something to do with Holden."

*Oh.* Now there was an idea. I'd never been one to make

much of holidays or days off as an adult, preferring to pull extra shifts wherever I could, but the prospect of a few daylight hours with Holden was a rare treat. "Maybe I could do that."

"Need a list of suggestions?" Knox winked at me.

"Nah. I'm sure we'll think of something." I tried to play it cool because being public about dating someone was new and uncomfortable, like a too-tight shoe, but Knox merely laughed.

"I bet you will." He waved me away with more merry laughter. Despite a vague sense of embarrassment, I was amped when I reached Holden's house, choosing a quick walk in the damp weather over calling for a ride.

However, when I arrived home, Holden was recording a podcast, office door shut. The low, soothing tones of his voice made me even looser than the walk. I used his work time to sneak in a shower to warm up after the rainy walk. A bolder guy than me probably wouldn't have bothered with anything more than a towel after the shower, but I pulled on a clean pair of jeans before making a fast brunch of eggs, sausages, and potatoes and venturing to Holden's now-open office door.

"You're home way early." He smiled broadly as he gestured for me to come in with the two lunch plates. "And bearing food while shirtless. I like this turn of events already."

"Knox sent me home. Told me to have weekend fun with you."

"Even better." He held out a hand for a plate, but before I could step away, he patted a clear patch of desk. "Sit. Let the fun begin."

"Okay." Somewhat awkwardly, I perched on the desk in front of him, legs dangling. "Did the podcast go well?"

"I suppose. I want to have Monroe back on the program to discuss the Stapleton case developments, but I'm waiting for the next official press release from the task force to record that one." Holden sounded tired but like he was trying to be his usual optimistic self for my benefit. "So today's pod was the author of a book about the impact of the true crime genre from the POV of a crime victim."

"That sounds interesting." I brushed my leg against his torso as I took a bite of eggs.

"It was. Great thought-provoking discussion." Holden speared some potatoes and chewed before continuing, "On the one hand, there are cases like the Stapleton one where podcast and amateur sleuths are key in cracking unsolved mysteries. But the publicity takes a toll too."

"You're thinking about Worth again?" I rubbed his side with my bare foot. I didn't know Worth personally, but I was also worried.

"After we were done recording the pod, I tried calling him. Nothing. Left a voicemail and text asking him to come to the memorial, offering to pay his way or help in whatever way he needs." Holden's mouth twisted.

"You offered. That matters."

"Not enough." He huffed a breath, sounding suspiciously like my usual dour self before brightening. "But I don't want to dwell on the case right now. It's the weekend. And like you said, I tried."

"You're a good friend." Reaching down, I laid a hand on his shoulder, rubbing the tense muscle. "Maybe I can distract you?" I raised a meaningful eyebrow. "How are you feeling?"

"Right now? With you looking like a sexy-ass dessert on my desk? I feel amazing." He grinned at me.

"I'm serious." Tilting my head, I gave him a hard stare.

His bad pain day had taken a few days to resolve as the weather had stayed rainy and wet.

"So am I." Holden set his half-eaten plate aside. "In fact, I'm starving."

"You want...?" I trailed off on a gasp as he danced his fingers down my bare chest. "Here?"

"Right here." He grinned wolfishly. "My recording equipment is off, promise. And you look like a SEAL going undercover as a pool boy. I love it. Let me blow you? Please?"

"Thought please was my line," I joked to cover my unease over the request. We hadn't done this act yet despite Holden offering a few times. I wasn't sure what my trepidation was. I didn't mind being the focus when I was restrained, but take away the bondage, and I didn't know how to deal with all the attention and affection.

"Oh, you're going to be saying please plenty." Holden waggled his eyebrows at me before turning stern. "Hands back behind you. Hold the edge of the desk. Legs on either side of me, touching the chair. Don't move, and don't you dare let go of that desk."

"Fuck." I exhaled hard. This was exactly what I needed, restraint and command. *Orders.* Orders I could do.

"God, baby." Holden whistled low as he undid my fly and withdrew my cock. "You are so fucking hot."

"I'm not—"

"Only words I want from you are *please, more, yes,* and *close.*" Growling, he gave me a fierce look that set my abs to trembling.

"Yes." Being limited in speech was yet another layer of restraint, and apparently, my dick loved it because it pulsed in Holden's hand. I hooked my feet around the arms of his office chair to increase the bound feeling even further.

Holden made an approving noise. "Good. Remember, don't move."

"I will...er...*yes*." Trying to stick to the rules of this game, I suppressed a smile.

Even knowing what was coming, I had to work to remain motionless as Holden positioned himself so he could lower his head, teasing my cockhead with the very tip of his tongue. As usual, I was leaking big pearly drops of fluid, and Holden lapped up the precome eagerly.

"Mmm." He made a noise more appropriate for hot fudge and brownies. "I love how turned on you get. Can't wait to taste more."

"I...uh...*please*." I started to protest that I wasn't entirely sure I could climax from oral attention, but if he wanted to try, I wasn't exactly in a position to object.

"Good. You're doing so good holding still. I think you need a reward." And that was all the warning he gave before he swallowed me down, continuing until his nose rubbed against my jeans.

"*Yes*. Oh God." I had to tense all my muscles, but I stayed in one place. A shudder raced through me, but I tried to tamp it down. I wasn't truly worried that Holden might withhold pleasure if I didn't stick to the rules he'd laid out, but there was also a certain satisfaction in pleasing him, in trying to prove my worth and obedience. And he rewarded my restraint with a steady rhythm, up and back, going a little deeper each pass before retreating to do more light teasing with his tongue. A frustrated noise escaped my throat. "More."

Holden chuckled warmly. "I think I love you all demanding."

*Think I love you more.* The thought entered my head, uninvited and also unmistakably true. I didn't do poetry.

Wasn't prone to exaggeration. And I was damn glad Holden had limited my words, so all I could do was nod. "Yes."

"Cal..." Holden's face softened, voice going more tender, hand on my thigh turning into a soft caress.

I wouldn't be able to withstand it if he finished the thought, so I made my voice deliberately bratty. "*More.*"

Holden exhaled, and if he was disappointed, he did a fair job covering his emotions as he took my cock deep again. I groaned, gratitude and pleasure mingling. Closing my eyes, I gave into the hypnotic rhythm, ceasing to worry about pesky feelings, whether or not I could climax, or how one-sided this was. All that fell away, replaced by whole-body relaxation, muscles turning warm and liquid.

And then, right when the pleasure turned sharper, more insistent, Holden released my cock only to start licking it with broad swipes, long delicious strokes of his tongue along my most sensitive spot.

"Holden," I whined in a voice I hadn't known I possessed, all needy and demanding. My hips ached with the urge to rock, arms and thighs burning from holding the position. "Want to move."

"Nuh-uh. You have a safe word if you need it." He blew a warm breath against my cock. "You stay in one place and let me drive."

Drive he did, resuming a slow but deadly deep rhythm of sucking until I was right on the edge before pulling back to lick until I was damn near incoherent. Climax went from elusive to all I could fucking think about.

"Want to come."

"You're awfully talky," he said conversationally. "What did I say about that?"

"Sor—*fuck.*" I started to apologize but ended up cursing as he sank all the way down to my root, hands spreading my jeans so his lips brushed my patch of hair, fingers pressing against my heated flesh.

"That's it. Let go, Cal." He pulled back to urge me on, moving his hands to his hips, pinning me further in place. "Let me make you fly."

"Yes." The pressure of his hands was going to do it, the reminder that I was at his mercy and all I could do was accept the pleasure he was pushing on me. No worries about anything, simply existing in this moment where tension kept spiraling higher and higher. "Yes. Close."

"Mmmm." Holden hummed his approval, and that did it for real, the warm vibrations against my shaft pulling my climax loose. My entire body convulsed with shudders, but I managed to keep the position, earning me more murmured praise from Holden. He swallowed and swallowed, drinking me down. Staying still intensified the orgasm, made me more aware of every sensation, the sweet agony.

God, I loved it, and as the waves receded, all I wanted was to give him a fraction of everything he brought to my life. I couldn't give him the stability or structure, his quiet reassurance, all the things I'd never wanted but needed so damn much, but I sure as hell could make him come.

"Now can I move?" I begged. "Wanna get you off."

"That was a treat for you." Releasing my hips, he held up his hands. "Not a quid pro quo obligation."

"Stop talking sexy legal terms and tell me how you wanna get off because if you want to treat me, you'll gift wrap your come for me in all that toppy dirty talk you love so much."

"Well, when you put it that way..." Chuckling, he tugged me into his lap in the oversized office chair. "Come here."

"We're gonna break your chair." Intending to kneel in

front of him, I wiggled around, but Holden held me tighter until I gave up and slumped against his shoulder.

"We are not." He undid his fly, then took my right hand in his, licking my palm in a tease so sexy my spent cock twitched. "Give me your hand."

"Boss man." I laughed as I let him direct me to grip his thick cock, keeping his hand on top of mine, guiding my motions. "You would have made a good officer."

"Uh-huh." Rolling his eyes at me, he leaned slightly back in the chair, looking that much more like an entitled sultan, a vibe I was totally digging. "Only orders I want to give are for your benefit though."

"I know." I made the mistake of meeting his gaze, which had gone soft and warm again, with so much affection there my breath caught.

"Cal—" he started again, but this time I shut him up with a blistering kiss. I tasted myself on his lips, earthy and sexy as hell, and almost enough to get me ready to go again. How did I ever think I could live without kissing? How had I gone so long without this connection? And how was I supposed to live without it? I kissed him harder, more urgently, putting every bit of my uncertain and cresting emotions into my mouth until we were both gasping.

"Fuck. Cal. Keep going." Removing his hand, Holden stretched, cock pushing through my grip. Without his restriction, I started jacking him fast and firm. By now, I knew exactly what he liked when he was close, and there was an unexpected pleasure in that knowledge, in repeated encounters. I reveled in my power as he moaned. "Need it."

"Come on," I urged as he wrapped an arm around me, pinning me against his torso. Funny how I loved him taking charge right up until he gave all the control to me. "Come for me."

"It's there. Fuck. Damn. *Cal.*" He arched his back, groaning as he came in creamy ribbons that ran down my fist. His expression ricocheted between pain and ecstasy, a religious experience simply watching him.

"Mmm. See?" Releasing his cock, I licked each of my fingers slowly. "Definitely for my benefit."

"You're so fucking hot." Groaning as if the fact was a personal insult, Holden grinned and stretched. "I think I want to spend the rest of the day in bed."

"As long as I get to come too." I wasn't sure when I'd ever been this playful with another person. Maybe never?

"Oh, you're coming all right. Again and again." Laughing hard, he squeezed me in a tight hug. "What am I going to do with you?"

*Keep me.* But I couldn't say that, so instead, I lied. "I don't know."

"Cal." Holden's eyes said everything neither of us could voice aloud. *Don't break either of our hearts.* The hope and fear in his gaze packed a punch right to my gut. Because we both knew if anyone was going to screw this up, it would be me.

*I won't hurt you,* I wanted to promise but couldn't.

"Let's go hide away." Standing, I offered him a hand. It was the best I could offer and not nearly enough.

# Chapter Twenty-Three

*Holden*

"What if no one comes?" Sam paced back and forth at the front of the community center, near the double doors. We were awaiting the start of Mrs. Stapleton's memorial service. News of Cal's discovery had broken a few days prior, terrible timing but not entirely unexpected as the task force undoubtedly wanted to get ahead of the news cycle about the memorial and related pieces about the case.

"They'll come." I tried to reassure my friend even as the pacing made me dizzy. I held a cup of cheap coffee from the station set up in the rear of the room. Sam didn't drink coffee, or I would have brought him a cup as well.

"People do love to rubberneck, if nothing else." Returning with his own cup of coffee, Cal joined us right as Monroe and Knox arrived. I glared at Cal, a rare moment of frustration with his bluntness. "What? Not helpful?"

Knox made a sympathetic noise. Like Monroe and the rest of us, he was wearing a dress shirt and dark pants. "Cal's right. People will come for the gossip factor, if nothing else, but I hate that her reputation is being smeared."

"And for what?" Sam's frown deepened. "The convicted serial killer is already spending life behind bars."

"The killer needs to pay for this crime too." Adjusting his tie, Monroe had no more luck soothing Sam's ruffled feathers than I had. "And this is a chance to clear Worth's dad of any suspicion. The full story matters."

"*Pfft.*" Sam pursed his lips. "In your book, maybe. Or for Holden's podcast. But to the people who knew and loved her? Should marital dirty laundry define her legacy? Maybe some things are better kept private."

With that, Sam stalked off.

"He's upset because Worth didn't come," I said helplessly, watching his retreating back as he found a seat near the lectern.

"I don't think it's just that." Cal shook his head. "He's got a point. Maybe I should have burned the papers."

"Don't talk like that."

"The guest author on your pod had a point too." Predictably, Cal ignored my rebuke. "Who does airing all the gory details really serve? And sure, finding out the truth is nice, but what does that pursuit cost?"

Monroe opened his mouth. Shut it again, a thin, hard line. "I'm going to find a seat."

He strode away, Knox following after him.

"Hell." Cal made a pained noise. "I seem to be pissing off your friend group right and left."

"You're not wrong." I set aside my frustration to place a hand on his shoulder. "Glorifying violent criminals serves no one. The truth always comes at a price, and how the information is framed to the public makes a difference. Maybe the press release could have worded things better."

Cal shrugged, eyes distant and full of hurt. "I tried for years to get the navy to acknowledge the truth about what happened on that dive. To publicly admit they fucked up. The evidence is there. But all that righteous anger got me was a wicked case of insomnia and a lot of lost years."

"Cal..." I felt adrift, helpless in the face of his pain, no longer sure what the correct course of action was with anything in my life.

"Maybe being right isn't worth it." Taking a long swig of his black coffee, he slumped against a nearby pillar. "I probably shouldn't have come. I don't belong here."

"Of course you do." I'd been dreading this moment for weeks, the point when Cal felt constricted by Safe Harbor and wanted to run from harsh realizations and big feelings. And me. "The town should be so lucky to have someone like you."

I meant myself too, of course, but I couldn't bring myself to voice that wish, especially not when Cal was already shaking his head.

"Nah." He straightened back up, gazing past me at the rows of empty seats. "But I'll do my part. Pay my respects. At least the house looks halfway respectable if anyone drives by after."

"You've done good work." I dug my teeth into my lower lip, unfamiliar nerves making me desperate. "There's still more to go, right? Sam's new suite?"

"Sure. A lot of that is the subcontractors." His voice sounded a million miles away, made worse when he dug out his buzzing phone and glanced down at it. "Huh. I need this dive shop to stop bugging me."

"What's the problem?" I wasn't sure I wanted to know.

"My new suit is in at the shop in Portland. They need

me to come in, check the fit and seals. It's more involved than checking the inseam on a pair of jeans."

"I can give you a ride. I'm always game for a trip to Portland." I felt honor bound to offer, even if it meant literally driving him away from me, away from here, this way-stop in his otherwise solitary life.

"Don't want to be a burden." His expression was unreadable, fathoms-deep eyes having some sort of conversation with mine, but hell if I could decipher the message.

"You're not. Ever. All you need to do is ask. My answer's always going to be yes." I put extra emphasis on *ask* and *yes*. There was no request of his I would ever turn down, but I needed at least a hint of what to offer.

"I'll take you up on the ride. Perhaps tomorrow? Knox paid me, so I can get you lunch for the trouble."

"It's no trouble." The real trouble was my growing feelings for Cal, the way he'd crawled under my skin, made a home in my heart.

Continuing to stare at his phone, Cal grimaced. "What the heck now? Guess I need to put my phone on silent, but I keep getting website alerts."

"Oh, I set that up when we updated your site, remember? Does it say you've been hacked?" My abs tensed, and I reached for his phone, but he shook his head.

"Not hacked. The messages keep saying I have new donations, but it has to be a hoax."

"If it's from the electronic payment service, it's probably legit. Check the return email address and don't click any links, but the whole point was donations, remember?"

"Huh. Guess your plan is working." He didn't smile, and neither did I. No, no, my plan was definitely not working. I didn't want to give him yet another reason to hit the road, didn't want to watch him RV shop, wasn't ready for him to head on down the road.

Maybe he needed to hear me say that I wanted him to stay. I was loath to put myself out there like that, but I opened my mouth anyway, only to have Earl saunter in with the first crowd of memorial guests.

"Cal! I was hoping you'd be here." Earl clapped a meaty hand on Cal's shoulder. In deference to the occasion, she wore a clean work shirt and shiny black boots. "Find me after the service. Got a proposition for you."

"Huh?" Cal's eyes went wide.

"Not that kind." Earl cackled. "You'll wanna hear this, trust me."

A prickle raced up my spine, and my hand tightened on my wheelchair rim. One more worry, one more thing that might pull Cal even further from me.

# Chapter Twenty-Four

*Cal*

Eulogies were weird. I'd sat through far more of them than I'd ever wanted to. That much was for sure. Each time, it struck me how a person could be reduced to a few sound-bites. With my dad, it was all about his military service. My mom's memorial managed to get by with no mention of her addiction and mental health battles, painting a picture even teen me had known was an illusion. Ev's military-heavy funeral was largely a blur, but the occasion had been tightly focused on family, underscoring my outsider status.

And Melanie Stapleton's memorial was an ode to a town citizen, dedicated churchgoer, loving wife and mother, with no hint of the complexity I'd discovered in her papers, the woman desperate for an escape, the cautious flattery and flirtation. The various speakers all did a fine job. Poems were read. Sam's dad gave a rousing speech, and meaningful music peppered the short service.

But certainly, I wasn't alone in being relieved when

everyone stood to sing the final hymn, an old classic I knew by heart. Too many funerals and all that.

"I didn't know you could sing," Holden murmured next to me. "You're good."

My cheeks heated at the praise. "Grandparents dragged me to enough Sunday services. I guess I learned to sing along. My mom, though, she was the one with the voice."

"She'd be proud of you." Holden's voice was gruff before reverting to his usual teasing. "Better be careful. Sam will recruit you for the choir."

The joke landed flat because we both knew I wasn't sticking around long enough to become a regular anywhere in Safe Harbor.

"I'd scare away the parishioners." I waved my tattooed forearm in Holden's direction before catching his eyes for a meaningful look. "Besides, I'd rather sleep in."

"Me too." Holden's mouth twisted as his voice turned wistful. "Honestly, I would have rather slept in today. But it was a good service."

"Lots of pretty words." I moved so more of the sparse crowd could filter past us.

Holden gave a harsh exhale as a trio of older ladies passed. "I wish Worth could have heard the words. Doesn't matter how nice the words were if they don't reach the right people."

"Clearly, he's not ready to hear them yet." It was the truth, but my voice came out sharper than I'd intended.

"Suppose not." Expression cloudy, Holden pointed his wheelchair toward the coffee and snacks table. "You want more coffee?"

"Nah." Chest aching, I watched him wheel away. This seemed to be my day for pissing people off, not that I usually had to work too hard to do that. Being bluntly honest with a side of cranky tended to do the trick. But with Holden, I wanted to be better. I wished I knew the right words to say or the right gesture to offer him comfort. Instead, I kept saying the exact wrong thing.

Probably just a matter of time before he too was sick of me. A memory of the wall calendar in my grandmother's pristine kitchen flashed in my head, big red marker numbers counting down until I left for basic. And the morning after Ev's funeral, his mom had had my coffee in a to-go mug, muttering about the long drive ahead.

Overstaying my welcome. I was good at that. Knee deep in the muck of my feelings, I almost missed Earl loping up next to me.

"Cal. Guess who I had in the shop earlier?"

"Not good at guessing." I tried to return her smile, but I doubted my lips even moved, not that Earl was deterred.

"An RV enthusiast with an eye on your rig." Earl pursed her garish pink lips, a reminder that my RV had been taking up valuable lot space at the garage for weeks now. "I told him it might need to be dragged off, but he went on and on about how rare the damn thing is and how much fun to restore that make is." She fished a piece of lined notebook paper out of her shirt pocket. "Long story short, he'd like to make you an offer."

She handed the paper over. It had a man's name, phone number, email, and a number I never would have associated with my broken-down RV.

"Wow." I whistled.

"Yep. That's a figure, all right. And you can add it to whatever piggy bank you've got going for a new RV."

"Uh-huh." Dazed, I bobbed my head like an unsteady doll. "I've been getting donations too. Holden made me a new site."

"I saw. It's a right pretty website. Holden, he does good work. Man of many talents." Something in her tone made me blush.

"Yeah."

"I'd bet between this offer and whatever funds you've raised, Bud, my RV dealer friend, could get you in a new rig, maybe even soon as next week. Get you on the road in no time."

Next week? Was that what I wanted? To hit the road again? Leave Safe Harbor in the rearview? Head...where? I wasn't sure. Anywhere but here. My chest pinched tight and hot, making it hard to get a full breath. "I suppose."

"Free up Holden's guestroom." Earl cackled like she knew perfectly well I hadn't been sleeping in that room.

The pain in my chest intensified, blooming behind my ribs, that feeling of having overstayed my welcome almost overwhelming. All I could manage was a nod.

"Not saying he's ready to be rid of you." Earl's tone was apologetic, but I shook my head. From one blunt person to another, I appreciated the honesty, even if it hurt.

"No, you have a point."

"Didn't—" Earl held up a meaty hand, but I cut her off by talking faster.

"I'll call this number. And your RV dealer friend."

She sighed like I'd personally disappointed her. "Make sure you get the veteran special."

"Will do."

Earl drifted away shortly before Holden rolled back to where I stood. My feet felt heavy, stuck in wet silt. The place was nearly empty now, but I wasn't in a hurry to head out. I was intensely aware of the paper in my pocket, crisp and crinkly. Yeah, I could stand here a while longer. Holden didn't have a coffee cup, but a mostly eaten store-bought sugar cookie on a napkin rode on his thigh.

"What was Earl's proposition?" He did us both the favor of not pretending he hadn't seen me talking to Earl, undoubtedly hanging back until she'd moved on.

"Buyer for my old RV." I quickly summarized what Earl had said, and Holden's eyes narrowed more and more as I talked.

"Oh," he said at last, tone as dry as the cookie crumbs.

"Guess I better take it." I shrugged like I wasn't desperate for a reason to turn the buyer dude down. "Probably not getting more cash for that heap of screws."

"Better call the guy before he changes his mind. Get that cash." Holden flashed a smile that didn't reach even half-wattage before fading again. "Suppose that means you can buy a new RV now."

"Yep." My heart pounded an anxious rhythm made worse by Holden's too-calm demeanor. "Next step is figuring out that donation business. Gotta see how much is there."

"I can help. I still have the website login." Holden whipped out his phone and clicked around. "Damn."

Making an impressive noise, he held up the phone to show a very robust number.

"Wow. Must be those testimonials." I shook my head. "And Sam's celebrity friend."

"You do good work, Cal." His voice was soft and tender. We were the last two in the meeting room at the community center, and in that moment, we might as well have been the last two on earth.

*Ask me to stay.* I wanted to demand that even as I knew I'd have to turn him down. A lot of folks were counting on me to continue my work, and he didn't need me hanging around his house, taking up space.

"Gotta get back out there," I said gruffly, willing him to disagree, but he didn't.

"Yep." He nodded sharply. "But maybe not today? Looks like more spring rain is on the way. How about you make your call, and we go home and fix some lunch?"

*Home.* It wasn't, but he said it so naturally that I wanted it to be true in the worst way.

"How about a nap?" I gave him a heated look. I might not be the best flirt, but I knew how to get my point across.

"You sleepy?"

"Not a bit." I forced a smile.

"Well then. By all means. Let's go." Rolling ahead, he led the way out of the building to his car. The air around us was heavy and humid. Rain was on the way. Time to find shelter, however temporary.

# Chapter Twenty-Five

*Holden*

"Naptime." My voice sounded too jolly even to my own ears as we entered the quiet house. All morning Cal had slipped away from me, and this was my chance to yank him back, press him to me, pretend time wasn't short and slippery. "Bedroom okay? You sounded like you might have a particular...request back at the community center."

"Bed's fine." Cal followed me to the rear hallway. "You can make requests too, you know."

"I know." It was a half-truth because, of course, I *could* initiate, but something usually held me back, had me waiting for Cal's signal. "I try not to put pressure on you though, or make you feel obligated."

"If messing around with you is an obligation, please, obligate me more." Cal leered at me as we reached the doorway to my bedroom. He'd slept in here with me for over a week now, had a book and phone charger on the nightstand, had helped me change the sheets, and his toothbrush was snuggled up next to mine in the attached bathroom. "And yeah, I might have had an idea of how to pass the time."

"Oh? Want to get the rope?"

"Nah." He stripped off his shirt, revealing those muscles I loved so much. His complete ease with nudity around me was a huge turn-on, making my cock fill even before he dropped his dress pants. "Getting tied up is always hot, but right now, I want to get fucked."

"Yeah?" I tried not to sound too eager. We hadn't done that yet, and for all Cal's talk about obligation, I didn't want to push him into something he didn't truly desire. "You've been thinking about that?"

"Only every single day since you brought it up. Never really craved it before, but now I can't get the image out of my head."

"Tell me about the image," I ordered as I took care of my own clothing and reclined naked on my side of the bed, resisting the urge to groan as he stalked toward me, crawling across the bed to straddle me. "How does your fantasy go?"

"I'm not sure I'd call it a fantasy. Not that imaginative."

I snorted. "Says the guy who rigs himself up like a holiday turkey on a timer for funsies."

"That's logistics. This is..." His expression turned thoughtful. "More about a feeling? Not sure if that makes sense. Like, when I think about it, it's not about what you're doing to me but how it makes me feel. I want to feel... connected."

He tapped his heart, and I reached to frame his face with my hands. "I get it. You want the closeness. Not that two people have to fuck to make love, but—"

"Yeah. That." He interrupted me, surprising me with

his ready nod. "Not fucking. Making love. Leave it to you to bring the poetry."

"Oh, I'm not a writer." I stroked his jaw. "Just a podcasting professor who really wants to make you feel good, Cal."

"You do. Always." His expression turned sentimental, a level of softness I hadn't seen on his chiseled features before. "Kink. No kink. Just sleeping. It's all good."

"Cal..." I wasn't sure how to finish the thought, so I pulled him down for a kiss. The brush of lips turned hot and searing the moment his mouth opened with a gasp. He tasted like coffee and cheap, powdery cookies and mine. He tasted like *mine*.

"Mine," I growled. It wasn't everything I wanted to say, but it was for damn sure a start.

"I'm yours," he breathed against my lips. Cal rocked against my erection, a subtle motion, but one that had me moaning nevertheless. "Make love to me."

"Absolutely." I kissed him again, hands on his shoulders, holding him flush to my chest. "I want to do it just like this. You on top."

"It won't hurt you? I want what's best for you." He looked so earnest that I had to give him another slow kiss.

"You. You are what's best for me." It was as close as I could come to saying what was truly in my heart. "And you never hurt me."

A small lie. His leaving was going to gut me. But physically, I trusted him completely.

"You'll have to tell me what to do." Cal offered me a rueful smile.

"Don't I always?" I chuckled. "Position doesn't change who's in charge. I'll take care of you, baby. Promise."

"I meant more because I haven't done this before. But thank you."

"Thank me after." I leered at him until he also laughed.

"Oh, I plan to." Still smiling, he let me pull him close for another soft, slow kiss that had him grinding more purposefully against me.

"Careful, baby. Don't come yet." I moved my hands to his ass, staying his motions. Reaching over to the nightstand, I groped around until I came up with the tube of lube I kept in the nightstand, but I had to curse when my fingers failed to locate the box I sought.

"Heck. Condoms."

"Do we need them?" Cal didn't seem particularly concerned. "I'm the virgin here, remember?"

"Trust me that I'm not forgetting that detail." I gave a strained laugh. "And I'm tested on the regular. Haven't done anything other than with you since my last physical. But I've never skipped the rubber before."

"Do it with me. Then I'm not the only first-timer." Cal winked at me.

"Yeah, but going bare might make this the world's quickest first time."

"Let's find out." He waggled his eyebrows at me.

"Always such a risk taker." I shook my head fondly, not sure there was room in my chest for everything this man made me feel.

"Oh, you're not that big of a risk." Dipping his head, Cal kissed me so sweetly I trembled under him. "Feel free to give me a thrill though."

"Consider me your personal amusement park." I joked, but there was nothing I wouldn't offer Cal. I wanted to be the only thrill he ever needed, the safest risk he ever took, the answer to the adrenaline he craved, and the anchor holding him in place.

"Keep arms and legs inside the ride at all times." His blue, blue eyes sparkled. Emphasizing his point, he sat up, bracing his hands against my chest, wrists touching like they were held by invisible cuffs.

"Now there's an idea." I reached back to the nightstand to get the small hank of rope that had conveniently ended up there after a previous playtime. I held it up to show Cal. "You want?"

"Hell yes." He held out his hands for me to bind. I used a secure hold but made sure to position his hands in such a way that he could still brace himself with them for balance.

"Lift up," I ordered, readying my fingers with the lube. Slowly, I circled Cal's rim, little teases that gradually increased the pressure. I watched his face the whole time, the way his jaw went slack and his eyes glassy. Once he was relaxed and rocking down to meet my fingers, I pressed in, letting his body adjust to the invasion.

"Oh." Cal shut his eyes, mouth parting on a soft gasp.

"Good *oh*?" I needed to hear him say it.

"Yeah." He gave a breathy moan as he leaned forward, giving me even more access. "I kind of love that I can't stop you. Have to take it."

"You do." If this was the game he wanted, I was more than happy to play along. Using my free hand, I ran my fingers across his bound hands. "Have to let me get you ready for me."

"Because you're so big." He groaned, rocking like he was seeking out my cock right that damn minute. His hard cock bobbed in front of him, shiny precome glistening in the afternoon sunlight.

"Uh-huh. And I don't want to hurt you."

"You won't." He pushed down against my fingers, taking them deeper, setting his own pace. "Want to feel it."

I had to groan right along with him. "Oh, you will."

The next time Cal rocked downward, I curved my fingers, pressing both into his prostate.

"Wow." Shuddering, he took several sharp breaths. "What...?"

"You've never felt that before?" I worked the spot over, finding the angle and pressure that had him moaning.

"More lack of imagination." He chuckled and then groaned as I retreated. "Again. Harder."

"Thrill seeker." I responded with featherlight brushes of my fingers across his gland and shallow thrusts. "I decide how hard."

"Holden." Cal's voice came out as a whine. I rewarded his raw emotion with a harder, deeper pass that set him to trembling and gasping. "Now. Please now."

No way could I resist any longer myself. I reached down and generously slicked my cock. Not using a condom made me feel strangely exposed and raw like every nerve ending was right there for Cal to stomp on. Not that he would, but my abs still fluttered.

"Sit back." Using one hand to steady my cock, I placed the other on his hip to guide him. "Lower down. Easy."

"Ah." Cal made a noise somewhere between discomfort, frustration, and need. For my part, I tensed my muscles, using all my willpower to hold still and not thrust.

"Go as slow as you need," I gritted out.

"Need this." Cal moaned, pushing down to take more of my cock, broad head pushing past his tight ring of muscles to slip deeper. I moaned too, especially when he started to rock, taking a little more with each pass. Greedy little sounds escaped his throat. "*More*. Oh God."

My cock pulsed, possibly its hardest ever, and his slick, hot, tight ass brought me ever closer to climax. I clamped down around the urge to come, though, and stroked his side and stomach before grasping his cock. "Move however you want, baby. Make it good."

"Want to make it good for you too." His breath came in little huffs.

"Trust me, if it gets any *more* good, I will come right now."

"Oh?" Cal seemed determined to test that theory, rocking harder and faster. And then he went for bonus points, clenching his inner muscles.

I groaned, the pain of not coming a real thing. "Damn. You're amazing, Cal."

"Good." He rode me more urgently, each pass bringing more moans from both of us. His cock slid through my grip, his copious precome slicking my palm. "Please," he demanded. "Please."

Any determination I'd had of holding out fled in the face of his begging, his clear need, the evidence of how much he loved this, and the intensity of doing it bare. I'd never felt closer to another human, and it wasn't simply the skin-to-skin contact. It was the raw emotions flickering on Cal's face, the way his eyes kept fluttering shut only to open and bore into my soul, a connection unlike any other.

"Do it, baby. Get both of us there." With my other hand, I yanked the binding around his wrists. As I'd expected, Cal moaned louder at the reminder of the restraint, flexing his arms to intensify the stretch. I stroked his cock faster, knowing the sort of friction Cal loved, and he arched his back, whole body bowing.

"Don't stop," he gasped like that was an actual option.

"Never. Come on, Cal. Come all over me." I barely got

the request out before he was coming, long spurts that painted both our hands, my chest, and, amazingly, my jaw.

"Holden." He said my name like a dying prayer, and that did it for me even more than the erotic sight of him coming.

"Say my name again," I demanded, finally giving in to the urge to rock myself, thrusting up hard and fast.

"Holden. Holden, please come in me." He trembled, shuddering harder as I came, the reminder that we were doing this bare making every sensation that much sharper. I could feel his heat, how my cock slid easier as I came, the clench of his muscles, his pulse, and every harsh breath. My heightened awareness extended to the pleasure itself, each cell having an unrivaled experience from my pinkie toe to the top of my head, like my body was suddenly vibrating on a higher frequency.

"Fuck, yeah." Cal celebrated my orgasm even more than his own, groaning along with me and grinning down at me as I floated back to earth.

"I'll say." I was beyond dazed, leaving him to pepper my face with kisses until I remembered I was supposed to be untying his wrists. I gave him a lopsided grin as I did just that. "Oops. Sorry."

"Hell, promise me we can do that again, and you can leave me tied." He laughed then sobered.

Was there going to be an again? God, I hoped so, but Cal's darkened expression was far from a guarantee.

"Don't go making offers," I joked roughly. "Might keep you tied up in here forever."

He shrugged. "As long as you feed me. Probably wouldn't be terrible."

"So much enthusiasm." I tried to keep the gag going, but my heart wasn't up to the task.

"Hey." Cal stroked my jaw. "For you? Always."

*Always.* God. The only word I wanted more than *again.* *Again and again and always and forever.* I let him kiss me, knowing full well the difference between wanting and having.

# Chapter Twenty-Six

## *Holden*

Cal was a fun date. Even with everything swirling between us, our trip into Portland to retrieve his new scuba suit was enjoyable. Gorgeous spring day with light traffic and perfect driving weather. Cal handled his business at the scuba shop quickly enough that we were able to head to one of my favorite neighborhoods for lunch, followed by braving the long line for a nearby touristy ice cream place.

"I think I like Safe Harbor's ice cream better than Portland's offering." Cal smiled at me around a lick of his waffle cone. We were sitting at a wrought-iron picnic table, a jaunty red umbrella shading us from the afternoon sun.

"Blasphemy. Don't tell my Portland friends, but I might agree with you." Watching Cal eat ice cream was torture, and it took all my willpower not to lean over and kiss him. "This is still tasty. And lunch was good. Loved the chance to get Greek."

Small talk. My usual superpower saved us from another awkward silence. Because the list of topics we couldn't discuss was ever-growing. But weather and food could always be counted on to fill the space in the divide.

"Yeah, I'll take those gyros anytime. And thanks again for the ride. It's nice to have the suit squared away." Cal skirted perilously close to one of those dangerous topics as he took the last bite of his cone. The dry suit taking up the backseat of my car felt like a giant strobe light announcing Cal's availability to move on any time now. "And nice as it is letting you play taxi for me, I better hope I remember how to drive."

"Oh?" My heart knocked like an idling diesel engine, that departure getting ever closer.

"Since I took that offer on my old rig, the RV dealer friend of Earl's wants me to stop by in the morning, test drive a motorhome he has for a decent price."

"You should." I managed to keep my voice level, helpful even. "Let me know if you need help freeing the electronic funds."

"Will do. I should check the current amount." He pulled out his phone only for it to buzz with an incoming call. "Huh. I should get this."

Eyes narrowing, Cal pushed away from the table, pacing down the sidewalk. His frown deepened the more he listened, and I was hardly reassured by the way he kept nodding, posture military perfect. Whatever he was agreeing to, I wasn't going to like it.

"That was a SEAL contact." Pocketing his phone, Cal returned to the chair beside me. "Thought he'd probably lost my number, same as others. But he heard about my work doing recovery dives and visited my revamped website. Apparently, all those testimonials are the gift that keeps giving."

Cal offered a twisted smile, but I didn't laugh, instead gesturing for him to continue.

"Anyway, this buddy has been involved with a missing person's case down near Lake Tahoe in Nevada. Fellow Spec Ops warrior who checked himself out of a treatment program. Clues point to a particular small but deep lake near Tahoe. The family just wants some closure."

"Understandable." I tilted my head, trying to keep a neutral expression. It was a given where Cal was heading with this story, and that revving engine in my chest became louder, more insistent.

"Others have been refusing to dive the area the guy was last spotted because it's..." Cal trailed off, mouth pursing, undoubtedly trying to think of a way to minimize the potential hazards in his explanation. "It's a challenge. Not impossible. But definitely tricky, and better to do it now than try to wrangle the gear in the dead of summer. Also, changing weather and water conditions could influence the chances of a recovery."

"But you're going to do it?" I managed to phrase it as a question like there was any chance he'd said no.

Cal shrugged. "I've got my suit now. About to have an RV. Have funds for travel. No reason not to."

*No. Reason. Not. To.* Each word pierced my flesh, pointy and final. "What about...never mind."

"What?" Cal wrinkled his nose, either confused or frustrated, and I wasn't sure which would be worse.

"Are you going to dive solo?" I asked instead. If he'd wanted to count me, to count *us,* as a reason to stay, he would have done so.

"Always do. You know that." His eyes were sharp, more steel than sky, daring me to be stupid enough to try to tell him no. "I've dived worse. My buddy knows my skill set. He trusts me to get the job done."

There was a message there. A warning.

"I believe in your skills too, Cal." I reached for his hand, which he let me take, but his grip was anything but sure. "It's because I know you have the skills that I don't understand. Why take stupid risks? Take a crew down with you. A spotter at least."

"And add to the risks?" He shook his head. "No, thank you. The only one I want to be responsible for is me."

Well. If I wanted proof that Cal's go-it-alone attitude hadn't changed one bit, there it was.

"Mutual interdependence. Being part of a team isn't the worst thing in the world. Having others who have your back and care about your safety is smart."

"For whom?" Cal scoffed, gaze softening, going distant. To him, teamwork was a source of pain, but to me, it was my best shot at keeping the guy I cared about safe.

"For you. For them. Everyone benefits." My tone became more desperate by the minute, but hell if I could rein it in. "Humans have a need for connection."

"Others sticking out their necks for me is hardly something to encourage."

"Okay then." Done with my ice cream and the conversation, I rolled away from the table, heading toward where I'd parked the car along the urban street.

"I didn't mean all friendship is bad." Cal tagged along behind me. *Friendship.* Was that all this was? A single chapter in a buddy-roommate comedy?

"Good to know." I huffed a breath, hot and sticky. I wasn't intending to leave him in Portland, so I slowed for him to catch up and unlocked both doors.

"Friends are...okay. But I dive alone. I work alone. I don't put others in harm's way."

*Okay.* Every damning word made my stomach that much sourer, ice cream curdling, all the sweetness fading.

"What if they want to take the risk themselves? What if others *want* to help you?" Beyond frustrated, I got in the car and stowed my chair with jerky movements before resting my head on the steering wheel. "Why can't you value your own safety the way I do?"

My raw admission pulled a hurt noise out of Cal. I'd crossed a line, undoubtedly, by admitting I cared. I'd been so careful for weeks, afraid to startle him into bolting. But here he was, on the verge of leaving anyway. So what if my caring was too much for him? At least this way, he knew.

"I think you overvalue my skin." He stared stonily ahead at the SUV parked in front of us.

"Priceless. Your safety is priceless to me." Reaching over, I made him turn to look at me, so he could see my sincerity and so I had a reason to touch him. I wanted to memorize the warmth of his skin, the rasp of his jaw stubble, the spiciness of his scent.

"Holden." Cal leaned into my touch, resting his head against my palm. His tone was scolding, tinged by decades of hurt. "Don't put me on a pedestal or try to make me out to be something I'm not."

"Mine." I wanted to saw through all the layers of defense he kept erecting, make him see how wanted, how *necessary* he and his safety were to me. "I want you to be *mine*."

"But only if I stop diving?"

"I didn't say that." I made a frustrated noise, fingers tightening against his jaw. I wanted to kiss some sense into him, but I settled for resting my forehead against his. "If I asked, specifically *asked* you to take a spotter and not endanger yourself unnecessarily, would you?"

"Not sure if that makes a difference." He squished his eyes shut.

"Not sure?" I moved my hand to the back of his neck, anchoring him to me. "You alive and safe makes all the difference."

"Still same outcome for us." He shrugged out of my grasp, that much further away as he rearranged himself into the passenger seat and buckled his seatbelt. "I need to get back out there."

"Because the mission is everything." Bitterness laced my every word, poison darts, damning us even more than Cal's stubbornness.

"It's all I have."

I flopped back against my seat as if he'd shoved me. And he might as well have. "You could have me."

"At what price?" Cal leaned forward, studying the floor mats, looking seconds from hurling. Hell if I could manage much sympathy because his rejection felt like a buzzsaw to my core.

"I'd pay it," I gritted out.

"Maybe I don't want to let you. I don't mean the price for me. I'm trying to save you here too. I'm a bad bet for a relationship. Inevitably, I'm gonna disappoint you, not be what—*who*—you need."

"I refuse to believe that." I didn't reach for him because I couldn't handle it if he flinched away. Instead, I let my conviction do the reaching. When he stayed impassive, anger bubbled up, making my tone more strident. "But asking me to stand by while you take crazy risks? That's a disappointment."

"See?" Cal gave me a pointed stare like he'd been expecting me to reach that point the whole conversation.

"I simply don't understand why you're so willing to dismiss what we have."

"I'm not. It's...everything," he whispered, voice broken.

"But not enough." That much was only too clear.

"We should get back to Safe Harbor." He pointed at the busy street out the car windows as if he could will us there, away from this conversation and heartache. That he didn't want to fight for us was the biggest disappointment of all.

"You could be happy in Safe Harbor." If he could be stubborn, so could I.

"Not sure I fit in that box." He shook his head before yawning and stretching. "I'm gonna rest. No point in going round and round."

"Yeah." To me, there was all the point in the world, but I also didn't want to cross from frustration and hurt into the ocean of anger that kept threatening to swamp me. "Don't want to spoil what time we have left."

Even as I said it, I knew it was too late for that.

# Chapter Twenty-Seven

*Cal*

Monday dawned ominously, all the clear skies and perfect Sunday weather swept out by my argument with Holden and replaced by an unseasonable chill and damp wind. I'd slept in the guestroom last night and had seriously considered leaving the house after we returned from Portland, but I'd decided flouncing out with nowhere to go was a level of drama neither of us needed. Instead, I'd retreated to my room, shut the door, turned up the music in my headphones like I was sixteen and stuck at my grandparents, and proceeded to not sleep until my morning appointment at the RV dealer.

Crisp red and blue flags with white lettering fluttered in the stiff breeze, proudly proclaiming that Bud's RVs was the place to be for deals and five-star service. Various models were adorned with helium balloons and extra signage, giving the whole place a gaudy carnival air.

I couldn't get out of there fast enough.

"You chose well." Bud nodded up and down, heavy

jowls jiggling with the effort. In truth, I'd selected the first model I'd test-driven after pointing at the nearest motorhome that looked to have sufficient storage for my gear. But if Bud wanted to believe I was a savvy customer, I wasn't about to stop him. I let him prattle on in his tiny office inside the travel trailer that doubled as the business's headquarters while I tried to remember how to write a paper check. "Can't go wrong with this brand. Can't beat the low mileage either."

"Thanks for the deal." I signed the check, hoping my seldom-used writing was close enough to the signature on my license. Weird, writing out that many zeros. Made me edgy. We'd quickly come to terms for the RV, a number that wouldn't entirely deplete my reserves. I'd figured out how to transfer the donations to my checking account, and I was fairly certain the big check wouldn't bounce.

"What's next for you?" Bud asked, all smiles as I handed over the check. And wasn't that the million-dollar question. I'd walked from Holden's place rather than beg for a ride, and Knox had already insisted I take the day off to settle the RV purchase. Plumbing contractors were working on the Stapleton house this morning, so it made sense for me to stay away, even if the free time made me itchy as hell, especially with not wanting to stick around Holden's place.

"Not sure. Guess the first stop is finding an RV park." Actually, my first stop would be Holden's house to collect my gear and things, but Bud didn't need to know that. I pasted on a paper smile, brittle as ancient newsprint, not that Bud seemed to notice or care. "It'll be nice to try it out. Having more choices of where to stay is gonna take some getting used to."

"Head to Happy Village." Bud gestured vaguely west of downtown Safe Harbor. "Tell them Bud sent you."

"Sure thing." Of course I was anything but happy by the time I rolled into Happy Village RV Resort, a few miles outside of town. Holden's house had been blessedly empty when I'd pulled in with the RV, but the quiet had made transferring my belongings much more depressing. Funny how much space I seemed to occupy when we were both in the house, yet how little I actually had to leave with. A few bags plus my boxes of gear, and that was that.

Some of my rope-rigging supplies were still in Holden's bedroom, but I couldn't bring myself to even open the door. Besides, it wasn't like I'd need them anytime soon. Holden was it for me, and if I was going to stay and give up solo diving for anyone, it would be him, but I simply didn't trust myself to make him happy. Sooner or later, he'd get tired of me, and then where would I be?

Right back here, arriving at Happy Village, which featured a series of interlocking loops of RV spots and a cheerful manager who might as well be a cousin of Bud's right down to the heavy face and bushy salt-and-pepper mustache. I felt burned out inside, not empty but charred and full of soot and ash. The sign in the campground office over the manager proclaimed "Your home away from home" in a swirly font that made me nauseous.

*Home.* I'd never lived or stayed anywhere that had felt more like home than Holden's house. When he said, "Let's go home," the words rang right and true. It would be so damn easy to get cozy there, let my guard down, forget that I didn't want things like couch blankets and throw pillows and entanglements in my life.

*Would it be so bad?* a small voice inside my brain asked, and I had to gulp hard as the manager ran my debit card. Yes, yes, it would be that bad, and not just for me. I could weather the inevitable pain, but I'd already disappointed

Holden. How many more times could I let him down? He deserved way more of a sure thing than me. What did I really have to offer him?

"You want to upgrade to cable and full hookups?" the manager asked, thick finger hovering above the tablet used to process payments. "There's rain coming in again this week. Good time to catch up on some TV watching."

"No thanks." I winced like I'd been kicked in the ribs. TV time was for Holden, bad reality shows, side bets, boring documentaries that only he would sit through for me, time on the couch, a countdown to bedtime... No, I might never watch TV again.

But I regretted my refusal as soon as I was alone in my RV space, the rest of the day stretching out in front of me, no real plan other than trying not to think about Holden. Checking my email took a scant half-hour, enough time to type quick thank-you notes for a few more testimonials that had arrived, answer some questions from a recovery crew in Colorado, and open an email from the dive shop in Portland wanting to know if I'd be interested in teaching a few classes.

*Nope.* Me? In charge of a class? Holden I was not. I didn't have a natural gift for teaching. No one wanted to learn advanced diving techniques from my cranky ass. And I dove alone. If I couldn't handle a dive buddy, no way could I take responsibility for a whole class of newbies. *You trust someone else to do it?* Somewhere, Ev was laughing, pointing out the way I always checked gear myself, mine and everyone else's, the way I refused to trust a job unless I did it myself.

*It would tie you to the area.* That voice was my own, and it struck terror right in my gut, making my nonexistent breakfast and black coffee slosh around. Did I seriously want another reason to outstay my welcome? What if Holden got tired of me before the classes ended? Not that I was going to take the offer, but still. I needed to jot a quick email declining the job, but instead, I shut my laptop and retreated to the bedroom area of the motorhome, restless and at loose ends.

*You could always try...* Nope. Not only had I left the rigging supplies behind, but kink would forever be associated with Holden, with the way he could command and coax me, the way he always checked me afterward like I was precious and needed protecting.

*Why can't you value your own safety the way I do?* His question rang in my ears as I lay in the bed in the back of the RV, hands behind my head. What did he see that I couldn't? I wasn't all that—some muscles, a few cooking skills, a hard work ethic, and maybe some basic social graces if someone squinted. Kickass diver. Good with power tools. And...

"Now, Velma, mind the water hookup. Remember last time?" Voices filtered over from the campsite next to me. I looked out the small window on the side of my bed. Two older women had exited a large pickup towing a smaller trailer. The taller one with short gunmetal-gray hair struggled to unwind a hose for the water connection as a woman with a straw hat over a purple silk scarf hovered nearby.

Well, if nothing else, I could make myself useful.

"Need a hand?" Waving a greeting, I exited my motorhome.

"Yes," the short, plump woman answered for both of them. "Velma's knees just aren't up to the bending in this damp weather."

"I do fine, Martha." Nevertheless, Velma moved out of the way so I could crouch and take care of the hose and both connection points. "Thank you, young man. Where'd you serve?"

Velma nodded at my forearm tattoo, a familiar glint in her eyes, backed by the veteran license plates on the truck towing their RV.

"Spec Ops. Based out of Virginia mainly, but I did my time overseas." I regarded her levelly. After all my service, I recognized a fellow operator when I saw one.

"Good man. We lost my older brother to Nam, but that just pushed me to sign up as a nurse. Stayed as long as the navy let me, then worked at Walter Reed as a civilian till they too had enough of me, made me retire. These days, I'd have had more options to serve longer, go more places, I reckon."

"We could have used someone like you in the teams." I flashed a thin scar on my other arm. "Damn fine medic stitched this one up on an aircraft carrier in a location I'm not at liberty to reveal."

"Nice piece of work." She whistled through her front teeth. "Who did the one on your neck?"

"Army doctor, but the navy can't catch all the good ones." I forced myself to laugh along with the women.

"Camping alone?" Martha had the sort of pointed expression that had me bracing for a bevy of single relatives to be presented my way.

"At the moment." I added a vague gesture and immediately tried to focus the conversation back on them. "How long have y'all been traveling together?"

"Fifty years, if you can believe it." Velma chuckled before flipping over her long, bony hand to reveal a shiny wedding ring. "This here's my best friend. Only nowadays, I get to call her wife. Granddaughter Megan calls us ride-or-die besties. No one I'd rather see the country with."

"I bet." My breath caught in my chest. *Ride-or-die.* Holden didn't want me to die, didn't want to stick around for me to take risks, didn't want *me* as I was, risk-taking, diving and all. And I'd had a best friend once, lost him, found Holden, who wasn't my best friend, but also wasn't *not* my best friend either. *Besties.* The word wasn't nearly big enough for everything jostling around in my chest. "I better get back inside. I'll leave you two to your adventures."

"Ain't that the truth?" Velma smiled broadly. She had a long face and sharp eyes, and I could see how she'd managed to snare Martha for all these years. "Life's a grand adventure, better shared."

"She says that now." Martha gave Velma a tender look. "Wait till we're arguing over the remote later."

"Hey, you kick cancer's behind, and you can watch every darn dating show they make."

"Oh." I made an involuntary noise. The hat and scarf made more sense now.

"Don't you listen to her." Martha pursed her pale lips. "Lord, Velma, you make it sound like I'm out here on death's doorstep with a bucket list. Gonna send me sky diving next."

"I know some buddies who could make that happen."

"I bet you could." Martha shook her head, hat bobbling slightly. "I'm too ornery to kill."

But in that moment, she looked inescapably fragile, with small shoulders, thin hands, pale skin, and far, far too mortal. And Velma, well, I knew Velma's type, all bluster and business, routine and orders, cool as a cucumber under pressure. But if something happened to Martha, well, you might as well take Velma too.

*Ride-or-die besties.* Ah. I got it now, not the ride, but the until-the-end part. Perhaps my argument with Holden wasn't about whether he trusted me as a diver, was willing to risk others' safety to ensure my welfare, or even whether he desired my company enough to want me to stick around. He needed me safe because of what it would mean to *him* if something happened to me.

Damn. That was humbling.

As I made my way back to my motorhome, Velma retrieved a carved wooden walking stick from the side of their trailer, leaning on it as they set up camp. Martha bustled around, putting a red cloth on the picnic table and setting out a small portable grill. Standing on my RV steps, I tried to picture Martha without Velma, without that steadiness and balance. Would she wither away? I damn sure might if something ever happened to...

*Oh.* I stumbled into the small booth-style table in the motorhome's kitchenette area. A part of my soul had died right along with Ev, and nothing I'd done in the years since had managed to retrieve it. If I let myself have Holden—the way he seemed to be offering himself, the way he wanted to claim me—and lost him, well, my whole damn heart would go too. Choosing to ride with Holden was terrifying, but was there any alternative when the die part was a given?

*Fuck.* I didn't know. I scrubbed at my short hair.

*Buzz.* My phone vibrated its way across the table. I didn't recognize the number, but my back prickled, and I hit Talk.

"Phillips here."

"Cal? Rob Heinrich here, Safe Harbor chief of police. We met over the Stapleton evidence you found."

"I remember."

"Good, good. I've got a situation. Group of teens camping by the lake. Some of the group decided to dive at the old train wreck, and we've got reports of a missing diver.

Clock's ticking faster than I can get a rescue team together, and—"

"I'm on my way." Already swinging into action, I quickly disconnected my electricity and water, and I was underway while Rob continued to outline the plan.

"I've got a few amateur divers on the way. I'm inbound too, but you're the best."

"I..." I opened my mouth to say I dove alone, my constant refrain. But where every second counted, did I really want to pull rank? I shook my head as my motorhome rattled down the road at speeds more suitable to Holden's sports car. *Holden.* "Who do you have running command?"

"We're shorthanded. I'm not a diver, but I'll have to do."

"Call Holden," I ordered. "He can't dive with us, but he's got the search and rescue and prior dive experience we need. He can help get everyone organized and keep track of volunteers."

"Not a bad idea. Got some more calls to make. I'll see you at the lake." Rob ended the call, and I took the curving roads as fast as I dared, a million thoughts speeding through my brain. I hadn't had to think twice about demanding Rob call Holden in. I trusted him.

*I trust him.* The knowledge hit me like a boat anchor. If I could trust him with a life-or-death mission, if he was the one I wanted running my team, why couldn't I trust him with my heart?

# Chapter Twenty-Eight

*Holden*

Some stray impulse led me to come home for lunch. Wait, that was a lie. It'd been a rare morning without meetings or classes, and I'd been utterly useless, distracted by thoughts of Cal and how we'd left things.

And maybe I'd wanted to see for myself what I'd already suspected.

Cal was gone.

Bed in his room neatly made, no trace of his clothing or belongings, and the stack of boxes of gear in the garage was also gone. Well, at least he'd likely landed himself a new RV.

Bile rose in the back of my throat. No goodbye? Nothing? Was that how little this had been worth to him?

Wait. There was a note on the fridge, held in place by two superhero magnets.

*Thank you for everything. Got the new motorhome. Gonna stay a spell at Happy Village. I'm sorry.*

Somehow that was worse than no goodbye. He'd teased

me about love notes a few weeks ago only to leave me a goodbye worthy of a seldom-talked-to landlord. Cal was sorry? And grateful? Not enough. Not nearly enough. And certainly not the emotions I was hoping to inspire. That was the sort of note one left a distant acquaintance, not the man one...

*Gah.* I needed out of the house right this moment. I couldn't stay in the oppressive quiet and stuffy emptiness a moment longer.

I drove to Blessed Bean on autopilot, barely registering the familiar sights of Safe Harbor. Good thing my usual spot was empty because I parked in a fog and rolled into Blessed Bean in one hell of a funk.

"What can I get you?" Sam looked up from wiping down the counter. The clock over his head read a little later than I'd thought, past the usual lunch rush. A few patrons were scattered among side tables, but the place was otherwise quiet. Too quiet.

"Tell me something," I demanded. I needed noise way more than food or questionable coffee. "Anything."

"Ah. Distraction." Sam smiled slowly, giving me a knowing look. "What did you do to Cal?"

"Who says I did anything?" My voice came out too sharp, undoubtedly revealing how close to the truth he'd pricked.

"Holden." Sam arched an eyebrow, sounding for all the world like he was the older one, not five years my junior. "Tact is hardly your strong suit. And you tend to make jokes all the time. Even when maybe you shouldn't."

"I'm perfectly serious with Cal." Glancing down, I studied the rim of one of my wheels. At least Cal didn't reduce me to a comedian like the rest of my friends, assigning me the same role I'd had since middle school. And it wasn't that I hated that role. I loved my friends, loved being my natural extroverted self. But Cal gave me a chance to be *more*. With Cal, I could be deep, reflective, talk about what mattered. I could also be silly, but Cal seemed to know the difference. Cal took me seriously, especially in the bedroom, let me lead without question. And there was nothing jokey about my feelings for him either. "I'm serious *about* him too."

"I know." Sam sighed as he wrung out his rag into the sink at the end of the coffee bar.

"What's that sigh?"

"Nothing." Sam's weary and weighted voice called him a liar. "Just...don't go getting a hopeless crush on a guy who won't stick around."

My turn to give him a pointed look, complete with a tilt of my head and a slow eye blink.

"Ask me how I know." Sam dried his hands with brisk motions. "Not everyone is meant for the small-town life. Not everyone is going to want what you have to offer. You can keep reaching and reaching, but at a certain point, you have to accept it's not going to work."

Gah. The truth in those words *hurt*. Could I really keep reaching for Cal if he never reached back, if he never wanted to be the kind of team I wanted? And if he wasn't meant for staying, what was I really doing? But the last thing I wanted was to further discuss the state of my non-relationship with Cal, so I gave Sam another long look.

"I take it you haven't heard from Worth."

Sam snorted, seeing through me the way only a good friend could. "I thought we were talking about you and Cal."

"I don't want to talk about Cal."

"Uh-huh." Sam bit the inside of his cheek, released it.

He leaned against the bar. "Well, I don't want to talk about Worth. I heard one of the investigators flew down to ask him questions, but he was less than helpful."

"He's hurting. Maybe he's not ready to talk." I was talking about Worth, but my brain flashed to Cal. Maybe he wasn't ready to give up his solo diving crusade. Maybe he wasn't ready for what I had to offer. But not ready wasn't the same thing as never ever, and maybe I could have been more patient, more understanding in our discussion the day before.

"Hurt doesn't mean you get to treat people poorly. Or oneself." Sam gave a sharp nod as I made a strangled noise. "You okay? Still don't want to talk about Cal?"

*Why can't you care about your own safety?* Of course Cal wasn't going to value his own neck the way I did. He was hurting. But he'd never treated me poorly, never shut me out, never made promises he couldn't keep, never lashed out at me. No, Cal's favorite target was Cal, which was heartbreaking. I'd do battle with any number of demons for Cal to find real healing.

Perhaps the missing ingredient here was my patience. Maybe I'd asked for too much, too soon. However, it didn't matter how much room or space I gave Cal when the siren song of the open road was always going to win.

"No point in talking." Rubbing my temples, I glanced around, willing customers to appear to distract Sam from the conversation. When none appeared, I slumped further in my chair. "Like you said, he was always going to leave."

"I'm sorry." Sam came around the counter to lay a hand on my shoulder. "That had to be hard, asking him to stay and him choosing to leave anyway."

"I didn't exactly ask." The words slid out with a fair dose of recrimination. I was an idiot. All that talk yesterday, and none of the words that really mattered. And for what? Why had I held back my heart? Why not ask for what I wanted most? I'd hinted and tried to make it about Cal but never really shared my feelings. And why?

Fear. No. *Hurt.* All this time, I'd focused on Cal and his past hurts and wounds, but I had them too. Letting him go was easier than asking him point-blank to stay. And it was easier to tell him I wanted him in one piece than to say I wanted, needed, *required* him in my life, my bed, my heart.

I'd talked in half-truths and made demands for his safety, but I hadn't really offered him a reason to stay. And had he really *chosen* to leave? Or had I not stopped him? There was an important distinction there, one I was on the verge of grasping, and I made a frustrated noise.

*Buzz. Buzz.* My phone went off mid-contemplation, startling me into raising my gaze back to Sam. His narrowed-eyed expression was both concerned and slightly pitying, undoubtedly chalking up my failures with Cal to more of my usual antics. He was probably readying more good advice I wasn't particularly in the mood to hear, so I scooted away from the table to take the call.

"Cal said to call you." Rob barked a greeting that struck terror in my gut, a heavy sandbag of every awful possibility hitting all at once.

"Is he all right?" I gasped, each word a struggle. "Where is he?"

"Oh heck. I forgot you two are...a thing?" Rob's voice went up a notch as my heart rate refused to slow. "Think Knox mentioned that. Anyway, your guy is fine. Cal is on his way to the lake at my request. We've got reports of a missing diver."

My brain short-circuited on the word *fine.* Zip. Zap.

Done. I had to take several calming breaths before I could comprehend the rest of what Rob was saying.

"Missing diver? What do you need from me? I'm purely a recreational diver these days and can't dive without someone more experienced as a buddy diver. Damn it."

"Not asking you to dive. Need you to come work command with me." Rob's voice was clipped, and road noise filtered through the call. He was likely already en route. "We've got volunteers to organize, and Cal says you're the best at that, and God knows you know more dive lingo than me for keeping everyone in line."

"I'm on my way." I took a split second to wave at Sam before heading for the exit. "Tell...never mind."

I'd been about to ask Rob to relay a message to Cal, but that wouldn't be fair to any of us. Rob didn't need to be in the middle of my love life, nor was this the time to try to settle things with Cal. And a short message wasn't going to cut it. We needed a real talk, and I was simply going to have to hope we got the chance. No. Not hope. *Trust.* Trust that we *would* get the chance to work things out.

# Chapter Twenty-Nine

*Cal*

When I arrived at the lake, two officers were already there, talking with a distraught group of young people, all of whom were speaking over each other with much waving of hands and tearful expressions. My mind flashed back to Velma and Martha at the campsite. Fifty years of adventures. God, I hoped none of these kids ended up broken-hearted today, but the reality was they very well might.

"Are you Phillips?" The taller of the two officers, a woman with dark hair, approached me. "The chief said to expect you. A couple of other divers arrived a few minutes ago. They're prepping over there."

She pointed to a spot near a few badly parked cars. I recognized both divers from the Stapleton recovery, the ever-chipper Heidi from Washington and a younger man with a shaved head and closely trimmed goatee who let Heidi do all the talking.

I managed something of a greeting as I started organizing my gear on the side of my RV. Others arrived on the scene—more cops, a couple of civilians who were likely divers, but I didn't pay much attention until Rob arrived in an official Safe Harbor Police Department SUV, followed quickly by Holden. For once, I was thrilled with his bat-out-of-hell driving habits.

Forcing myself to breathe deeply and not run to him like a bad rom-com reunion, I took a moment to check over my gear once more and collect myself before Holden rolled over to me.

"You came." I licked my suddenly parched lips.

"Of course." He held my gaze with steady hazel eyes that saw and said way too much. "You asked."

"Knew I could count on you. You're the best." My voice came out in measured tones, simply stating the bald truth. He *was* the best, and I'd known he'd come, regardless of where our relationship stood. He was a far better friend than I deserved, a better man than most people gave him credit for.

"I try," he said levelly, but I wasn't sure he believed his own words. He tried. And succeeded. And the cost of that trying was something a lot of people would never see, but I had. He was a good person, almost effortlessly so, but he also put the work in where it counted.

Including with me.

He'd been so patient, asked for so little, and here he was, where he didn't have to be, simply because I'd asked. My heart swelled, pushing against my ribs, tightening my throat.

"Holden—"

"We have a job to do." He glanced over at the other divers and Rob. He was right, but damn it, my chest ached with everything that had to wait.

"We'll talk after. Please..." His eyes narrowed as he

inhaled sharply and then shook his head. "Never mind. Let's get to work."

"What were you going to say?" I demanded, voice harsh because we were running out of seconds.

"I trust you to come back to me."

"Oh." I swallowed hard. He'd been about to phrase it as a request, but he'd found his way to the trust I hadn't felt from him the day before when we'd argued. He sounded utterly sure, and his conviction bore into my soul, soothing rough spots and scars both. "I will."

This wasn't a moment for *I'll try*. There was only one response, one promise, and I intended to keep it.

"So what's the plan for the volunteers?" Rob strode over.

"Uh..." *Oh crap.* We should have been talking logistics, but where my mouth flopped open like a fish, Holden nodded confidently.

"We'll do a standard jackstay search grid pattern with teams of two volunteers, other than Cal, who dives alone."

"You can assign me a buddy." The words came out quickly but not without certainty. I'd just promised Holden I'd come back. And it wasn't an empty promise. I meant to do everything in my power to keep it, and that meant accepting that there were limits to my skill set. And that the comfort and feelings of others I cared about mattered.

"You don't have to prove a point," Holden said in a low voice as Rob summoned the other volunteers over. "Not to me."

"Maybe I'm proving one to me," I whispered back. My gaze shifted to the missing diver's tearful friend group. They hadn't followed good diving protocols, and they'd have to live with that if the worst happened. I wasn't about to make

Holden live with what-ifs and might-have-beens. "Assign me someone experienced, please. Let's bring this kid home."

"Absolutely." Holden nodded sharply, and we all spent the next few minutes hammering out a plan and a search grid as dive boats were readied. Holden scrawled volunteer info on a notebook he'd retrieved from his car before handing out assignments. Coming over to me, he pointed at the closest boat. "I'm sending you out on the first boat. And I'm giving you Heidi." He held up a hand when I would have groaned. "She's got certifications several of the more recreational divers don't. And she's ready to go, while others are still gearing up."

"Let's do it." I forced a bare smile as Heidi strode over. We had no time to waste. By all calculations, the missing diver would be well into his emergency air supply, and if Holden trusted Heidi, that was good enough for me.

As we descended near the submerged train engine, the deepest part of the lake, the water grew murkier, visibility at a premium. I used both hand signals and the com set to talk with Heidi as we worked the search area we'd been assigned.

"Whoa." She narrowly avoided snagging her suit on a jagged piece of the engine's smokestack. I stifled a curse. I'd agreed to a buddy for Holden's sake, but keeping Heidi safe was one more thing to keep track of while also battling pea-soup visibility levels.

"Careful. Go slow." I kept my voice as even as my breathing. I didn't want to waste any of my own air supply or our precious seconds.

"Cal. Go low." Heidi barked a sharp, surprisingly authoritative command, narrowly saving me from an over-hang of twisted metal and debris.

"Thanks." Okay. Maybe there were advantages to a dive

buddy. I tried to keep my mind on the search, but images of Ev kept flashing in my brain, all the countless times we'd saved each other, over and over, until the one time I couldn't. Did that one awful ending negate all the times we'd had each other's backs? All the good I'd found in team-work? The family I'd found in the SEALs? Had I really needed to dismiss all of that, erase all the benefits simply because...

*I hurt.*

I'd been wounded, laid low, like an injured wolf, deter-mined to heal my pain alone.

And then I met Holden.

He'd seen my pain, fought his way past it. Now, for the first time in five long years, I wanted to be part of a team again. *A family.* And I wanted to be a leader again, trust that part of my skills as well. I'd been a damn fine chief. I summoned those long-shelved commands and let my instincts guide Heidi and me.

And then we spotted him.

The diver was caught in a fine mesh metal net near the engineer's compartment, hopelessly entangled.

"Found him. Stand by for injuries." I relayed our coordi-nates back to command before Heidi and I worked in quiet, efficient tandem to free the diver with our dive knives. His body was distressingly unresponsive, but I detected the barest hints of pulse and respiration.

*Alive.* I had to cling to that chance as we prepped him to ascend with us.

"Thanks," I mouthed to Heidi. And I meant it. Her presence and ability to follow my lead had bought us precious minutes, quite possibly making the difference between a rescue and a recovery.

As soon as we were on the boat, Heidi and I continued

our joint efforts, stripping back the diver's gear to better assess his vitals. Biting her lip, Heidi shook her head.

"I felt something below. I did." My voice scraped against my sandpapery throat. "Start CPR."

"Absolutely." To her credit, Heidi didn't waste a second arguing with me, even though her eyes said she'd already called it.

We started CPR together, her on rescue breaths, me on chest compressions.

"Switch," Heidi ordered as we sped to the shore. The man piloting the boat kept glancing back at us over his shoulders, expression grim.

*Trust.* I had to trust she could do compressions as well as me. My exhausting myself served no one. There was nothing to be gained by being a martyr, a lesson I could have used dozens of dives ago, but here we were, held together by trust and hope and sheer determination to help this young man cheat death.

"Pulse. I think. Faint." I met Heidi's troubled gaze as I checked the diver's vitals again. An EMT crew was waiting on the shore, but they seemed miles away, the drumbeat of too far, too late pounding in my ears.

*Come on, come on.*

"Switch." We counted out another round of CPR, and the diver stayed still, skin pasty.

"Live, damn it." I made a frustrated noise, raising my voice for the first time all dive, the noise startling Heidi and the boat captain.

"Cal..."

"Keep going." I was not the one who needed sympathy here. I wasn't the one...

*I wasn't the one who died.* Tears started streaming down my face as I continued chest compressions, big heaving sobs.

*Cough. Cough.*

Heidi pulled back with a start as the diver coughed.

"Yes!" I couldn't remember a sound as welcome as those weak hacks.

"We've got respiration," Heidi reported into the comms shortly before we reached the shore. As soon as we were at the dock, the EMT crew took over, a familiar face hovering nearby.

"Doc Washington?" Remaining a bit dazed, I greeted the same ER doctor who had stitched my neck wound.

"It's my day off, but I heard the reports, came to lend a hand in case the EMTs couldn't make it here in time." She gave a curt nod. *Small towns.* Maybe gossip traveling like wildfire wasn't always such a terrible thing. And neither was caring about each other and strangers as well. "And at least it's not you I'll be stitching up this time, Phillips. Good work out there."

"Couldn't have done it without my dive buddy." I shot Heidi a look I hoped conveyed a fraction of my gratitude.

"*Cal.*" And then Holden was there, waiting, always waiting, at the top of the boat ramp, near my RV. His face was pale. "Thought for a moment that was you being hauled out."

"Me? I'm tougher than that." I crouched to put a hand on his shoulder and look him in the eye. "And I promised? Remember? I promised I'd come back to you."

"You did." Holden's lower lip wobbled, and I hugged him close. Or he hugged me close. One or the other, didn't much matter which. We were holding each other, and I was crying again.

"I didn't die," I murmured.

"You didn't." He tipped my head up with his thumb. "You lived."

"I did." I exhaled the weight of five damn years of guilt and grief and loss. "I lived."

"And that diver's going to live too, thanks to you and Heidi."

"Yeah." Utterly exhausted, I rested my head against him, welcomed the weight of his hand on the back of my neck, and didn't give a crap who saw or what they thought. "Take me home?"

"You have to ask?" Holden's voice was as tender as I'd heard it. "Of course. Come home, Cal."

# Chapter Thirty

## *Holden*

Cal's RV looked strange in my driveway, but the familiar sounds of him in my house were comforting, a stark contrast to the quiet earlier in the day. As I assembled a purely comfort-food dinner, I kept grinning at the little reminders Cal was here, like his shoes in the mud room, the beat of the water running in the shower, the hum of his electric razor after.

"You cooked?" Cal wandered into the kitchen in nothing but jeans, bare chest, bare feet, and my chest expanded three sizes, simply staring at how cozy he looked. Like he truly belonged here. He helped himself to one of the baby carrots on a plate I'd been nibbling from while cooking. "After a day like today?"

"Especially after a day like today." I grinned at him. The last forty-eight hours had been like flying through turbulent skies, and now that things had smoothed out, relief kept making me giddy. "It's practically therapy. Also, it's another ridiculously easy weeknight teacher special of my mom's. Taco casserole. You're not allowed to laugh at the tater tots on top."

I opened the oven to reveal the nearly-done casserole, and Cal's mouth twitched. "I wouldn't dream of laughing."

"I've been thinking..." I tried to play it casual, but my question was anything but. "Would you like to meet her?"

"The legendary Mrs. Justice? The one who strikes fear in high schoolers looking to pass physics? Your mom?" Cal looked somewhere between ill and intrigued, complexion going paler while his sharp gaze revealed interest.

"Can't believe it, but Greg and Kathleen's baby is likely arriving next week or so. Kathleen has rocked bed rest like a champ, and Mom's pushing for me to drive up when Marley flies in to meet our nephew." I kept my voice as upbeat as possible. Cal didn't seem like a baby person and had been wary the few times we'd run into a young family when out together, but perhaps if I made the road trip sound fun enough, he'd overlook the reason. "Mom will stick around a couple of weeks to help them get settled, so it would be a chance for you to meet everyone before summer truly gets underway."

"You want me to meet your family?" Cal's voice went from interested to truly alarmed on the word *family*.

"That is a traditional dating activity." As always, I defaulted to humor to defuse Cal's horror. This didn't need to be a huge deal. "You met the friend group. Now you brave the family."

"I'm not sure..." Mouth twisting, Cal trailed off. He busied himself retrieving two plates and silverware, setting them on the counter with a too-forceful clatter.

"It's okay. Forget I said anything." Luckily, I had tons of

practice not letting my smile dip. "Mom will be back in town eventually, and Marley flits through from time to time."

"I'm scared." Cal's harsh whisper cut through the room and my increasingly fake good mood.

"Oh. Baby, they'll love you." I rolled over to where he stood, putting a hand on his back. "You and Greg can hunker in the introvert's corner and let my mom feed you and—"

"What if they do like me? And if I like them? Then what?"

I had to struggle not to laugh. This was serious business to Cal. He'd lost Ev and Ev's family. The risk of caring for new people was one he didn't take lightly, and I wished I had a magic solution to make things easier for him.

"You said you want me to trust you. Well, this is where you trust me. I'm planning to keep you around a good long time, in whatever capacity you'll let me." Under my palm, Cal's back muscles tensed, so I started a gentle massage. "If you and the other most important people in my life get along, that's easier on everyone."

"Whatever capacity?" Pulling away from my touch, Cal sidestepped to turn and lean against the fridge. He grimaced, sucking in his cheeks and furrowing his forehead. "That doesn't seem fair to you."

"Help me understand. Do you not want to try dating again?" I softened my tone, trying not to let my hurt seep through. Cal stayed quiet, the sound of his breathing his only reply. *Fuck.* Maybe I'd read the situation all wrong. "I guess I assumed when you asked me to take you home that you meant..."

Cal shook his head. His expression was utter agony like

he was in the middle of a field amputation. Only it was me losing a vital organ. I stared at him for several long moments, willing him to speak. But he didn't, and the oven timer dinged.

"Guess that's what I get for assuming." I had to whisper to keep my voice light and steady. Rolling away from him, I grabbed the potholders, happy to shift my attention to the chiming oven. "Here. Let me at least rescue the food."

"I'll do it." Cal plucked the potholders from my hands and removed the casserole in a single smooth motion.

"I could have done it. I'm used to cooking on my own." My voice came out far too petulant, but I had a point. And I better get used to being solo again in a hurry. "Anyway, hand me those plates."

"Holden. Stop." Cal hugged the plates to himself like a shield.

"What?" Sometimes playing dumb was the only real option. "We still need to eat."

"I don't know how to love you like you deserve to be loved."

"Ah." The spatula I'd held clattered to the stovetop next to the steaming casserole. "It's okay. You don't have to love me. Not yet, especially." Somehow dealing with Cal's commitment-adverse mindset hurt far less than him stating the obvious. Of course he didn't love me. It was too much, too soon, and if dating and meeting mothers struck terror in his heart, love was likely to cause a cardiac event. "I'm happy to just spend time together, whatever you're comfortable with—"

Cal cut me off with a loud, frustrated huff. "Quit making excuses for me. Quit settling for less than you deserve." Setting the plates next to the casserole, he waved a hand at me. "God, look at you, so willing to throw your own wants and happiness away. I never said I didn't love you."

"Oh." I made a noise not unlike a balloon releasing all its air in a single gust, mouth remaining in perfect O long after the exhale. "You love me?"

"Yeah. Pretty sure I do. Never been in love before. And, like I said, I have no clue how to do it right. Heck, I even told you all wrong."

"Not so wrong," I whispered, but Cal was mid word spew.

"You deserve so much more than someone to spend time with." Frowning, he pointed at me, and I could see a glimmer of the chief he'd been in the SEALs. Scary. Not someone to argue with.

"Why don't you tell me then?" I was no green recruit, and Chief Phillips didn't scare me near as much as the thought of losing Cal, the guy who meant damn near everything to me. "What do I deserve?"

"You deserve someone who isn't afraid, first off. Someone who can love you and be excited, not terrified of meeting your family. Someone who won't constantly worry they're about to disappoint you."

"You're not going to let me down. I know that." Moving closer, I reached for his hand. When he let me hold it, my chest relaxed, and I took my first full inhale in several minutes. "And if you think I'm not scared..."

"Of course you are." Cal's voice had so much self-blame that I had to squeeze his hand even as he continued, "You're scared because you know I have to leave. You deserve someone who sticks around. Someone who loves this town as much as you do. Someone who wants to put down roots, carve a whole new branch of the family tree."

"I don't want to give you roots." I swung his hand lightly, trying to show him that there was plenty of give in our connection. "I want to give you *wings*. I'm not offering a choice between going and staying. That's where I went wrong yesterday. I'm sorry for acting like it was a choice between me and your work. You need to keep diving. You do. It's in your blood, and it's your mission. You do amazing work, Cal. Go forth. Bring that missing sailor in Tahoe home to rest with his family. I don't want to tie you down—"

Cal interrupted me with a loud snort.

"Other than when you ask nicely. What I mean is I can't stop you from going. I only want to be the place you return to after the job is done. When you asked me to take you home today, that's what I was hoping you meant. That this could be your *home*. The place you come back to."

"You want to be my home?" he asked softly, a lot of the fight finally leaving his voice.

"Yes." Testing my luck, I pulled him onto my lap, making a happy noise when he settled in and didn't pull away. "You seem to think I'm settling by choosing you, but I'm winning. I'm winning big. All this talk of what I deserve. How about you ask me what I *want*?"

"What do you want?" Tipping his head back, he leaned his forehead onto my cheek.

"I want a person who's loyal. Who loves me even though it scares them. Who loves me even when it's hard. Even when I don't entirely deserve it—"

"You always deserve it." His breath slid across my skin, as warm and welcome as his words.

"Again with the loyal. A person who will stick up for me, even when I won't do it for myself. I want the sexiest, kinkiest, cuddliest—"

"I'm cuddly?" he scoffed.

"You sleep like a baby koala. You can keep working on your awake cuddling game, but you give amazing massages, kiss like a dream, let me tie you up and have my way with you."

"Can we do that now?" His eyes sparkled and the corners of his mouth lifted, but I faked a stern head shake in response.

"I think you want to escape hearing all the nice things I have to say about you. You're the one I want. Period. You're who I deserve, who I need, who I love."

"You love me?" The brightness faded from his expression. "You don't have to say it back simply because I said it."

"Cal." I groaned and squeezed him tightly against me. "You make me want *everything*. I want to be here when you come back. I want to hear about your recovery missions. Heck, I want to go along on some of your dives when my schedule allows, be there to support you. I want to watch and help you grow your foundation. I want you to let me help. I want to run podcast ideas by you. I want to grade papers in front of bad reality TV with you. You make my whole world brighter, better. Of course I love you. You make me want everything from the super boring TV—"

"Hey now, Timber's dating adventures are not boring." Cal snuffled into my neck. His eyelashes were suspiciously damp, but I knew better than to try to dry them.

"I want every damn dating show on repeat. Just for you. You make me want all the once-in-a-lifetime special, totally ordinary moments." I tipped his head up so I could kiss him lightly. "Let me be your return address. That's what I want."

"Okay."

"Okay?" I blinked at him. After all that, he was going to agree that easily? I waited for the catch.

"You can be my return address, but I'm going to be your passport. Heck yes, you can come with me, but I'm taking you places. Hawaii. The Maldives. Maybe even Australia."

"How about the couch?" I suggested, glancing toward the living room. There was only so much kissing we could do sharing my chair.

"And let the casserole get cold?" He clutched a hand to his chest in mock horror even as he scrambled off my lap to allow me to wheel toward the couch.

"You don't have to take me anywhere, Cal." I flopped onto the chaise portion of the couch and motioned for him to join me. "Just keep coming home to me. That's all I need."

"Too bad." Cupping my face in his hands, he gave me a sound kiss. "I want to give you the whole damn world. And since I can't do that, I can at least give you back diving. We'll do it safely. With experienced operators. Add more pictures to your bedroom walls."

"But you dive alone." I wasn't convinced that his accepting the buddy diver on the rescue mission was anything other than a one-time exception.

"Turns out I don't. Or at least not well." He glanced down at his forearm and the naval tattoo there. "I'm better with a team. I want to be on *your* team, Holden. But you have to let me in. This can't be all you helping me. You've got to let me be a part of your team too."

"You want to start grading papers?" I cracked, only to earn myself a swift elbow in my ribs, light but effective.

"Sorry. Bad timing." I made my tone suitably apologetic. "I'll try...I *will*." I smiled because I already knew Cal's opinions on the word try. "I'll let you help. You're not the only one struggling with trust here."

"I know. But you're going to have to trust me. Trust that

I want to return. That I want to be a real partner to you. That I want to see your good days and your not-so-good days. Trust that I love you." He looked deep into my eyes, gaze brimming with so many emotions that my stomach clenched hard and my arm tightened around Cal.

There was truly only one possible answer. "Show me."

# Chapter Thirty-One

*Cal*

"Gladly." Smiling, I swung a leg over Holden to straddle him. Showing him how I felt was far, far easier than finding the right words. Usually, even if I started a kiss, Holden took ownership of it quickly, but this time, he seemed content to follow wherever I wanted to go.

Which was everywhere.

Holden said he wanted everything, all the tangible and intangible benefits of a partnership. He held me like that as well, loose but firm, hands roving up and down my bare back muscles. And I wanted *everything* too, but I also wanted to *go*, to travel, to explore, to visit all the places Holden had dreamed of returning to, places neither of us had been. I wanted to uncover new vistas on his body, his soul, carve my name into his heart until everywhere he went, I went too.

I kissed him as if I could tattoo my initials on him through sheer force of will. *Mine, mine, mine.* Or rather, *Cal was here. And here. And here too.* I wanted to ruin him for anyone who might come after, wanted every kiss to remind him of this one, the one where I said I loved him, the one where we both went all in.

My heart clattered like I'd leaped off the high dive, water rushing up alarmingly fast, but for the first time, I had a hand to hold on to. I'd told him I was terrified, and I was, but somehow it was way more bearable knowing he was in this too. Desperate for the connection, I linked our left hands together, holding him as tightly as he held me.

*Of course I love you.* His words rang in my ears, infusing my kiss with new meaning and purpose as I delved deep into Holden's mouth. My arm hair prickled as he sucked on my tongue, pleasure zooming to every cold and lonely spot the hot shower hadn't managed to reach.

But Holden had.

Warmed me up right through my core. Held me close with a firm hand on my ass.

"Cal." There it was, the moment he groaned my name and took over the kiss, lips rewarding my patience with the possessiveness that never failed to make my toes curl. I'd been dead set against being claimed, but then I'd experienced my first Holden Justice kiss, and I'd put my heart right up on the auction block, his for the taking.

*Own me.* I went pliant in his arms, releasing my usual iron grip on my strength. With Holden, I didn't have to be Cal, the SEAL. I could simply be Cal, the man. I let him have his way with my mouth as I started a slow grind, trying to find relief for my aching cock. However, Holden was warm and hard and subtly rocking up to meet me, and all I could do was get harder and moan louder.

"Easy, baby." Holden pulled back to chuckle against my cheek. "Don't want to come too fast."

"Maybe a quickie is what we need," I countered, not

really caring about duration as long as I got more of him right that second. "Besides, I feel bad letting your casserole get cold."

"It'll keep." Holden winked at me as he groped my ass. "This won't."

Eyes wide open, I drank him in, a picture slowly coming into sharp focus. Like a kaleidoscope or puzzle. Dark hair. Broad shoulders, rumpled dress shirt, stubble along his neck and jaw. Familiar sights, but somehow also brand new.

"You're so fucking hot," I marveled as I started undoing the rest of his shirt buttons. "Feel like I'm seeing you for the first time."

"Um. Thanks?" He cocked his head as he rolled his shoulders to help me slide his shirt off.

"Sorry. It's like...accepting my feelings, saying them aloud...has made everything more vivid. More magical." I gave a self-conscious chuckle, fully aware of how fanciful and unlike myself I sounded.

"Well, you've always been magical to me, but I really do love you, Cal." Cupping my face, Holden offered a tender kiss on my mouth before pressing one to my forehead. "What do you want, baby? Anything at all."

"You." I gave him a fast, fleeting impish kiss. "But since you're taking requests, be right back."

I scrambled off his lap to race to his room to retrieve what I needed, loving how his hot gaze locked on me upon my return, tracking my every stride.

"Lube? Not rope?" he asked as I tossed the bottle next to him on the chaise before stripping off my jeans. "Could do both..."

"Nah." I helped him out of his dress pants which were as rumpled as his shirt. "I feel like being free to touch you if I want."

"Or I want." Holden grinned wickedly, clearly confident about who was in charge with or without the rope.

"If we're handing out requests and all..." Wanting to shake up his cockiness a bit, I dropped to my knees on the floor on the side of the chaise and sucked his cock deep with no preamble.

"Holy hell." Holden cursed low as he shuddered, hips bucking upward. Making his usual control snap like a fishing line had my own cock throbbing as he stroked my head. "Warn a dude."

"You like?" I didn't wait for a reply, going right back to sucking him deep, going for the rhythm I knew he liked best, the one that had him groaning and cursing some more before shoving at my shoulder.

"I like it anymore, and you're not going to get the ride you're aiming for."

"Oh, I'm getting it all, all right." Much as I loved his taste, the weight on my tongue, and the stretch of my jaw, I wanted him in me even more. Craving to be fucked was still a strange, potent sensation, the way my cock pulsed and my ass tensed from merely thinking about how good the last time had felt. I loved the physical sensation, but there was an emotional component, not unlike bondage, welcoming him inside me, accepting it in the same way I relaxed into the freedom the rope allowed me. Straddling him again, I grabbed the lube, intending to prep myself.

"Let me?" Holden held out a hand, and I happily gave over the lube. For all that I'd been a virgin our first time, he'd made an instant convert of me. I loved everything about him, fingers absolutely included. Bracing my knees on either side of him, I raised up to allow him better access.

"Fuck. I've been thinking about this..." I trailed off on a low moan as he penetrated me exactly how I loved, slow but deliberate with consistent pressure. Hell, merely the sensation of his knuckles against my rim was enough to tease out another moan. "How is reality so much better?"

"Maybe you lack imagination?" he teased, continuing to light me up.

"Maybe you're that good?" I countered as I started to rock on his fingers, the craving turning to an all-out hunger, every brush of his thick fingertips against my gland both too much and not nearly enough.

"Fuck." Holden cursed as I fucked myself on his fingers, and he did that trick I loved where he scissored them open, stretching me more. "You're so hot with how much you love this."

"More. Want more." Eyes fluttering shut, I gave myself over to the experience, letting the pleasure wash over me in waves. I was vaguely aware when he started teasing a third finger. Knowing his cock was thicker, I bore down to take all three fingers deep, and Holden cursed again.

I opened my eyes to find him staring intently at me, watching my every reaction as I rode his fingers. His pinky was right there, resting against my stretched skin.

"Please. Do it." I wiggled my ass, encouraging him to try for a fourth, but he stayed my motions with his free hand.

"Let's not get ahead of ourselves..." He licked his lips, but the desire was readily apparent in his heated gaze. Gently, very gently, he splayed his three fingers, working me more open. "Think you could take four?"

"Yes. Please." I made a needy noise that wasn't entirely human. And hell, with him looking at me with that much wonder, I could climb the damn Himalayas. "For you. Could take all of them."

"Fuck." He cursed like I was tempting the last of his

control but then lightly slapped my ass. "If you're very, very good, I'll read up on fisting techniques and safety."

I gave a pained chuckle. "Only you could make kinky research sound so damn sexy."

"Because it is." Holden's eyes sparkled. "Research, then I'll truss you all up. Frog tie, maybe. Sit next to you on the bed, make you take my hand."

"Holden." I did my level best to get him to give me that fourth finger, so close to climaxing that precome was rolling down my tip. And the evil bastard had the gall to chuckle, dipping his head to lick across my cockhead.

"Don't come." He grinned wolfishly. "You wanted a ride, right?"

"Now." My voice was pure whine, but fuck if I cared.

"So demanding." Removing his fingers, he guided me back and down with his other hand. "Slow."

"Yes. Yes." My head fell back as he filled me, a thick and overwhelming pressure, exactly how I liked it. "Fuck. Even better than fingers."

"Well, my dick agrees." Holden's laugh had a strained edge as he let me set my rhythm.

Wanting to snap his control again, I put a foot on the floor, bracing myself with a hand on the back of the couch, riding him hard and fast. He slowed me with his hands on my hips, so I responded by working my inner muscles, tensing on the upstroke, loving his answering curse.

"Holy fuck. Where do you get these tricks?"

"Maybe you're not the only one who can do research." I preened simply to get another chuckle from him.

"As long as I'm the only one you practice with," he growled.

"Always." I dipped my head to claim a soft kiss. "Always. I'm yours."

"Mine." He tapped my heart, then his own. "Mine."

"I love you." The words sprung from my chest, as much a surprise as the feeling itself, and awe laced my tone. I'd said it earlier, but it felt way more real this way, joined together, bodies and hearts both. "Never thought...never knew...never expected you."

"Yeah, well, I didn't exactly expect you either, baby."

"Hot-headed speed demon." I rolled my eyes, flashing back to that first day. God, how entirely I'd misjudged him. Thank God, he'd kept hammering at my resistance until he won me over because I wouldn't trade a minute of the last few weeks.

"Salty old dive master." He kissed me back firmly. "I love you, Cal. Every cranky, prickly inch of you."

"Thank you." Gratitude came in waves, along with pleasure. Grateful for him. Grateful for this body. Grateful for how he filled me, for the sensations, for being right here to experience it all. I rode him harder, faster, hand tensing on the back of the couch, pushing against it so the pressure on my gland was much more intense. "Fuck. Might...wanna come."

"Then come." Holden didn't reach for my cock.

"Please." A frustrated noise escaped my throat.

"You're the one with the bag of tricks," he chided lightly. "Come on. Try to get yourself off. Come."

"Hold me tighter," I begged as I moved more urgently.

"I will. I'll never stop holding you," he promised, his expression so intent his features might as well be etched on granite. "Always."

His mouth twitched, cock going harder inside me, back stiffening, and that was it, the sight of him holding back climax. Boom. Done.

"Coming," I gasped, spurting between us like a hose, completely untouched, just coming and coming in huge waves that left me shuddering and shaking in his arms.

"Oh fuck." Holden thrust up to meet me. Once, twice, then he too was coming with a shout.

"Wow." Making a happy sound, I petted his shoulder as he trembled. I could *feel* him inside me, hard and slippery, and fuck if that wasn't the sexiest damn thing, knowing he'd come inside me. "Wow."

"Me too." He held me close against his chest. "And God damn, you were amazing, coming like that."

"I know." Shaking my head, I chuckled. "I had no idea that was a thing."

"Coming hands-free? Can't say if I've seen it outside of porn, but damn, it was hot."

"You're hot." I brushed a kiss along his stubbly jaw. "And dinner's cold."

"Stay." He gripped me securely, sealing us together, him still inside me. "Stay a little longer. We'll microwave the dinner. Right now, I just want you."

His eyes were as soft as his mouth against mine, and I kissed him again, long and slow, pulling back to whisper, "I'll stay. I will."

Returning to the kiss, I tried to tell him I meant so much more than simply in that afterglow moment. I was going to *stay*.

"And I'll come back, over and over." For the first time, I could picture it, me out on a dive, a long drive back to Safe Harbor, Holden's voice in my ear on his latest podcast, Holden the man waiting at home. *Home.* I couldn't help it. I had to laugh.

"What?" Holden wrinkled his forehead.

"Been a long damn time since I had a home address."

"You've got more than an address." He nuzzled my neck. "You've got me."

"I've got you," I agreed happily. "And you're home."

"So are you."

"Me?" I peered down at him through narrowed eyes. "I'm a salty old nomad diver. Isn't that what you called me?"

"Yeah, but you're my salty diver. What's home if not a place you can be yourself?" Holden stroked my face with his thumb. "That's what you are to me, Cal. Home. A place to relax. With you, I don't have to be funny. Or the extroverted friend. Hell, I don't even have to talk. I can have a bad day. Or three. And if I want to talk, I can talk about anything, about the hard stuff, the stuff that sucks, the stuff that doesn't seem fair."

"Always. You can always talk to me."

"Because you get it." He nodded. "You've done battle in the dark. Me whining isn't going to scare you away."

"It's not whining. It's just life. Sometimes good, sometimes bad." I cupped his face, willing him to see my truth. "And I want to be here for all of it."

"Good." His eyes looked suspiciously damp, so I took a page from his playbook and laughed.

"Guess you better start researching Seattle hotel rooms to visit your brother. See if you can work the visit to your family around my trip to Tahoe."

"You'll come?" His pleased expression was worth whatever discomfort the visit might cause me.

Wanting another laugh, I hummed an oldie, one my mom had sung all the time. "...I will follow..."

"No more cheesy TV for you. You're cut off."

We laughed and laughed until we were sticky and cold

and in extreme need of a shower. And I was still scared, more than a little. Terrified of meeting Holden's family and the possibility of messing everything up, but at that moment, all I could do was cling to Holden.

# Chapter Thirty-Two

*Holden*

"Everything okay?" my mom called out from Greg and Kathleen's kitchen. Ever the one in charge, she'd sent the new parents off to nap, Marley to the store, and put Cal and me on baby duty in the living room while she assembled lasagna for dinner for all of us.

"We've got this," I yelled back before she could come check. Casserole assembly was her happy place, and she'd been doing almost as much baby care as Greg and Kathleen. Mom had some murderous TV drama playing softly on her tablet in the kitchen as good smells wafted our way, and I was hoping she'd sneak off for a nap of her own while the lasagna baked.

"Do we have this?" Cal whispered to me as Mom flitted away from the kitchen doorway.

"It's one teeny baby." I shifted Charlie from my right to my left shoulder. He had jet-black hair like his mother, dark expressive eyes, part of my dad's name, and Greg's unrepentant night owl tendencies. He still looked suspiciously wide awake. And angry. Charlie had enjoyed rocking in my chair with me, wheeling back and forth, but apparently, the novelty had worn off. "He's been fed, diapered, and should be sleeping."

"Should being the operative word." Cal eyed the baby like a grenade. We'd arrived the day before, and he'd handled the onslaught of family and hugs like a champ, but he continued to give the baby a wide berth. Seeming to sense Cal's distrust, Charlie let out another unhappy squawk, and Cal peered over my shoulder. "Lungs like those, he'll make a hell of a diver."

"You planning to stick around long enough to teach him?" I teased, but internally, I cheered. The drive from Safe Harbor had been gorgeous, spring giving way to the early signs of summer. Soon it would be time to think about backyard barbecues and summer trivia-night league. The idea of Cal and me making it through another season and enough years to watch Charlie learn to dive made me ridiculously giddy.

"Someone's gotta." Cal's tone was pragmatic but not without enthusiasm. "Start with some toddler swim classes. Then we show him some easy snorkeling when he's bigger." Pausing, Cal narrowed his eyes at me. "Whatcha grinning at?"

"You said *we*."

"Hell, you think I'm funding swim classes on my own?" Cal raised both eyebrows at me, and I only grinned wider.

"Nope. We'll do it together."

"We will." Cal nodded decisively, money as good as spent. When that man made a promise, he kept it, and Charlie better learn to love swimming because I was going to hold Cal to however many years of lessons kept him right where he belonged. Cal dropped a kiss on the top of my head, a rare tender moment from him, and I tipped my head back, trying to catch a kiss.

*Baawaaaah.* Charlie took that moment to register his profound disapproval of romance.

"Need me?" Mom called.

"Nope." I waved her away, then thrust Charlie at Cal, careful to keep supporting the baby's head. "Quick. You try."

"Me?" Cal looked like I was offering him overcooked brussels sprouts. "Lord, I don't know..." Not taking no for an answer, I transferred over my squirming burden, and Cal instinctively cradled him in both big hands. "Oh hey, little angry sailor. You need to sleep now."

"Negotiation hasn't worked so far." I laughed because Charlie really did look a bit like a new recruit in a fuzzy white and blue sleeper with a little ship anchor detail.

"Who said negotiate? When cranky recruits mouth off, we march them around." Cal started a deliberate pace with the baby, who, miraculously, stopped crying. Smiling softly, Cal put more effort into marching, singing a jaunty tune. "I don't know, but it's been said, air force wings are made of lead. I don't know, but I've been told, navy wings are made of gold..."

"You can't sing him a navy cadence as a lullaby." I knew better than to whip out my phone, but this seriously was the cutest thing I'd ever seen.

"Says who?" Cal scoffed and kept right on singing. "He-ey Coast Guard. Pud-dle pirate Coast Guard. Get in your boats and follow me."

"Oh my God, it might be working," I whispered as Charlie shut his eyes and relaxed into Cal's chest. He let out a baby snuffle as Cal finished the cadence and moved to humming something I couldn't quite place.

"That's not a navy tune."

"Smart man, your uncle," Cal whispered to the baby before turning back my way. "It's a hymn."

"Sam's going to make a choir boy of you yet."

"They can stick me in back." Cal yawned, but he kept on marching the baby around.

"That wasn't a no."

"Nope." Cal's grin was a thing of absolute beauty. "But don't tell Sam that. He thinks we gotta win the summer trivia-night league to get my ass in a pew."

"You bet Sam church attendance?" I blinked. And blinked again. Maybe Cal really was thinking of sticking around a good long time. Forever might be a decent start.

"Was I supposed to bet cash?" Cal teased, then glanced at the baby snoring softly against his chest. "Well, would you look at that? Charlie's all tuckered out. Guess I can set him down—"

"The he—heck you can." I raised a hand before Cal could set him in the portable bassinet. "You know what happened last time we tried."

"Fine." Continuing to hold the baby, Cal plopped down on the sofa and put his feet up on the padded ottoman, arranging himself and Charlie into a comfortable recline before reaching for the remote. "Junior's gonna chill to the History channel."

A scant five minutes later, both Charlie and Cal were dozing, Cal's exhales matching Charlie's little huffs. Rolling as quietly as I could, I made my way into the kitchen to check on Mom. I put a finger to my lips as she turned around, eyes narrowing.

"Where'd you leave Cal and the baby?" she whispered.

"Look." I pointed back at the living room, smiling along

with her as she took in the photography contest-worthy picture the two of them made.

"Oh my word. That's adorable." She chuckled quietly. "He's so darn cute."

"Yeah, he's a good baby."

"I meant Cal." Gaze fond, she waved a spatula at me. "You really do know how to pick them."

"More like he picked me." I wheeled to the table, where a cutting board and some broccoli awaited me.

"As long as he makes you happy."

"He does." Keeping my voice low, I beckoned her closer. "I'm going to marry him someday. He doesn't know, of course. But someday."

Her eyes went wider than the dish of cheese on the counter. She opened her mouth, closed it, then nodded. "Good plan. I'll da—be at your wedding. With bells on."

"You can say dance, Mom. Really." Tilting my head, I gave her a pointed look. It had been years, but she could still be overly cautious about my disability. A counselor I'd had after my injury had explained that my family had their own journey of grief and acceptance and changed expectations. And she would always be such a mom, trying to spare my feelings, even when it did the opposite.

"I know." Reaching down, she patted my face. "Love you so much. Yes, I'll dance."

"Good. Because I'm planning to dance." I popped a wheelie in my chair and spun around, making both of us laugh before I sobered. "But seriously. I need to ask you for something."

"Anything." Yep, always a mom.

"If something ever happens to me—"

"Which it won't." She cut me off, exactly as I expected.

Given our family history, the topic was understandably dicey, but I needed to say this.

"But it could. I'm not trying to make you anxious. I'm fine. Healthy. It's about Cal. Promise that if anything ever happens to me, you'll keep Cal around. Don't let him pull away."

"Oh." Her face softened. "If ever there was someone who needed a family..." She nodded sharply before crouching to kiss my cheek. "I can do that. But you're not going anywhere."

"Nope." Chuckling, I waggled my eyebrows at her. "I've got a boyfriend who doesn't know it yet, but he's totally taking me on a honeymoon to the Maldives."

"Wouldn't Hawaii be safer?" She met my eyebrow waggle with a coy batting of her eyes.

"And where's the fun in that?"

"Holden. Look." Turning slightly, she pointed back at the living room. Cal was awake, baby stretched across his long thighs, alert and cooing, the two of them having some sort of serious discussion.

"Hey, Holden? Is there another bottle?" Cal called out. "The new recruit wants chow, and I don't think we need to wake Kathleen yet."

"We're keeping that man," Mom said decisively, patting my shoulder on her way to grab a bottle and a plate of cookies for Cal. "Don't you worry."

I did worry. Because I wanted this so damn bad, and despite everything, trust was hard. But it didn't matter how hard or how much I needed to work on trust. I was keeping Cal, and I was going to do my damnedest to give him the family he deserved.

# Chapter Thirty-Three

*Cal*

A slightly off-kilter Holden was freaking adorable, and I had to stop myself from bouncing in the passenger seat like a little kid.

"I don't understand why I can't use GPS for this," he complained, not for the first time that afternoon. He hadn't been entirely thrilled with the spontaneous Portland trip, but he was a good sport. It was the end of the Spring term, and he was busier than ever, but he'd want to make time for this.

If he knew. Which he didn't because, for once, I was determined to be the one surprising him. He did so many little gestures for me that I really wanted the chance to spoil him.

"Because you can't." I gave a long-suffering sigh, then pointed to the street coming up on the left. "Turn here. And then pull into the third parking lot on the right."

"SCUBA School?" Holden frowned at the low-slung,

blue industrial building with the friendly ocean-themed signage. "Are you diving?"

"Half right. *We're* diving." I grinned at him, nerves and excitement mingling into a giddy ball of energy in the center of my chest. "My new side hustle—"

"Your what?" He made a comical face as he finished parking.

"Side hustle. Obviously, the foundation is my main work. And then working for Knox when I'm in town, but I finally let this Portland scuba shop talk me into doing classes."

"That's awesome." Holden grinned wide enough to encompass the whole damn parking lot. Of course he was all in favor of anything that kept me local for a time. But instead of feeling like an unwelcome chain, his enthusiasm was an anchor, a reminder that this was my home and he loved having me here. He wanted me safe and by his side. I'd finally reached a place of understanding where his concern no longer chafed but instead felt like a rubdown from a warm towel. "I'm so proud of you."

"Eh. It's extra cash." The concern I could handle. Pride, though, pride still made me antsy. I wasn't all that. "I gotta put away for Charlie's swimming lessons and all that."

"Cal." Holden put his hands over mine, expression serious. "You could never bring in income again, and I'd still consider this an equal partnership and a damn bargain."

"I know." Unable to meet his warm gaze, I stared at our linked hands. Mine was tanner from my time outdoors in Tahoe, with a scratch across the back of my left one. Bare fingers. Holden wanting to eventually put a ring on my left hand was the world's worst-kept secret. The better secret? I was going to let him. Oh, I'd still be terrified of fucking this thing up, but I could be scared with a ring on if it made him that happy. "I want cash for other stuff too. I really do want to travel on your winter break this year. I've been researching more accessible dive outfits. Paying my own way feels good."

"Fair enough." He nodded before sitting up straighter, eyes going wider. "That's...wait. You said *we* earlier? *We're* diving?"

"Thought you might pick up on your favorite word." Grinning, I cackled at him. "Yes, my new employer, Rafe, is a great guy. He's worked with divers of various ability levels for years. I want to gauge your needs before we tackle Hawaii or Cancun this winter. And besides, I owe you a dive. I know it's just a pool—"

"It's everything." Holden took on a dreamy expression, and I rolled my eyes at him.

"It's a start. And these are skills I want too. I watched a video of Rafe diving with an eighty-year-old with arthritis the other day. I want to be able to give people those sorts of experiences."

"You do? Chief Solo Diver?" Clearly amazed, Holden shook his head. "Look at you."

"I'm still me." Cheeks heating, I shrugged. "It's...a different kind of service. Like, the recovery work is one way to pay it forward, but the teaching is another."

"You don't owe the world anything." Holden squeezed my hands. "There's no debt you need to pay off."

"I understand that." Understand was perhaps over-stating things a bit, but I was trying to get there for my sake as well as Holden's. "And I know I don't *need* to do something and still want to do it. Survivor's guilt is a real thing. A big part of my PTSD. And doing things like teaching and the recovery dives helps."

"Wow. I've never heard you talk about PTSD so directly."

"Well, that group Doc Washington has been dragging me to, they say when we label things, we give them less power over us." I quirked my mouth because I was still sorting out how I felt about going to a support group. Army. Navy. A couple of marines and some air force personnel to make nice with. All reserves or vets. Just trying to get through. "And it's funny, but it's working. Admitting my sleep issues are PTSD has made it easier to tackle them."

"And here I thought sleeping next to me was the cure." Holden winked before bumping my shoulder. "I'm joking. I know it's a multipronged attack. I don't have a magic dick."

"Oh, it's magical, all right." I gave a happy sigh at the memory of my homecoming a few nights prior. True to his word, he'd tied me up, a complicated new position to boot, showing off his latest research, and he'd worked me open slowly until I took four fingers easily and the tease of a thumb. Not quite fisting, but we had plenty of time to get there, and the trying was damn fun. And hot as fuck. Unsurprisingly, after two giant orgasms, I'd slept like a log. "Nothing wears me out like you."

"I'm so glad the group is helping." Holden ignored my compliment in favor of rubbing my hand.

"Bringing home that sailor, that helped too," I whispered. I hadn't talked much about my trip yet. I loved how Holden gave me space to come around to opening up on my own. Space where I could process and make sense of things. "All his friends were waiting on shore. Good-sized crowd." I wasn't doing justice to the somber sight of at least a dozen personnel, all respectfully standing at attention as my team and I brought up the remains. The missing sailor had had a hero's send-off, and I hoped like hell he'd found the peace he hadn't here on earth. Also, seeing so many former contacts among those on the shore reminded me of the kinship all service people shared. I hadn't stopped being a part of that even during the years I'd lost sight of the deep connection. "Friends like those, it's a family. Forgot how I have that too."

"You do." Holden leaned in, brushing a kiss across my forehead. "And you're always going to have a family with me."

"Hope—*Know* so. And ditto." I put conviction into my voice. Holden deserved better than *wish* or *try* or *hope*. What we had was the real deal, and while both of us were working on trust, I didn't doubt that Holden wanted to be my family. "I don't have any ready-made relatives for you, but I've got me."

"And that's more than enough." He kissed me then, deep and true, and it was almost enough to make me forget why we were at the scuba facility.

But right as I pulled back from the kiss, Rafe pulled into the lot in a shiny black half-ton truck, and I shifted my attention to prepping for Holden to dive.

Because it was a temperature-controlled pool, we didn't need full dry suits, enabling us to use the far-easier-to-fit wet suits and gear more appropriate to warmer water. I'd had to guess at Holden's size, but seeing as how his every muscle was seared into my memory, I'd done a good enough estimate. Together, we wrestled him into his suit in the pool's locker room before I pulled mine on.

Out on the pool deck, I moved slower than usual, hyper-aware of potential hazards for Holden's chair. The pool featured a hoist lift, but Holden had enough mobility to lower to a seated position on the side of the pool, allowing him to gear up with Rafe and me.

"Can't believe I really get to dive," he marveled, shifting his weight from side to side. He was antsy to get in the water, but I made him suffer through multiple rounds of equipment checks, practicing how I'd check the students in my class. And ever the patient one, Holden kept right on smiling. "You're going to make a great instructor."

"He is," Rafe agreed. He was a tall, skinny man with a shaved head and closely trimmed dark goatee. "Glad we finally convinced Phillips here to teach. No one better to teach advanced techniques and rescue and recovery. Going to make it safer for divers all over the region if we have more certified in rescue operations."

"I already signed the contract." I shook my head at both of them.

"It's not flattery if it's truth, Phillips."

"Listen to the man." Holden chuckled. "Everything locked and loaded?"

"Yeah." My heart started hammering, and I had to suck in a quick breath. Holden's eyes widened with sympathy, but I held up a hand. "I'm all right." I let myself do one final check of Holden's tanks and masks. "There. Let's do this."

Under the water was where the magic always happened for me, the calm, controlled descent to the bottom of the pool. Colorful tiles and fish decals added interest for the diving classes, but all my attention was on Holden and his unrestrained joy.

He swam easily and freely, the buoyancy of the water and suit giving him a fluidity he didn't have on land. And proving yet again that he was my perfect match. He was a natural diver, easily regulating his breathing, more of that joy infusing his every movement. Like me, he was the type of diver who'd stay down as long as practical, enjoying every moment of the experience.

And he was a good sport about the experiments Rafe and I wanted him to do, swimming through underwater hoops, testing his flexibility, and checking his endurance. He kept grinning under his mask, eyes crinkling, his whole body alive with a potent energy that made me want to give him every damn reef in the world.

As Holden navigated one of the underwater obstacles, we came face to face, eyes meeting. He always said how he wanted everything with me. Well, with him, I felt everything. All the emotions I'd run from for years, coupled with brand-new feels that I was still learning names for.

*I love you,* he signed with his hand. I felt it, a current through the water, a tangible certainty. I could doubt my own worth or curse the unpredictability of fate, but I couldn't question his love.

*Me too.* I returned the sign as a flash came from the side. Sneaky. Rafe had an underwater camera, and he was only too happy to show us the picture when we were all back out of the pool, lounging on the side.

"That's one for the wall." Rafe laughed. "Y'all are adorable. I'll message you the file so you can get prints."

"Deal." I didn't mind the teasing or being adorable if it meant getting to capture such a special moment.

*Oh.* For the first time in my whole damn life, I understood why people had weddings. Those rings Holden wanted? Totally happening. And I was ordering dozens of pictures. Moments we could look back on again and again, proof positive of what we shared. And why wouldn't I want to show him off, celebrate what we had?

Not now, but someday in the not-so-distant future, we were having a big damn party. I smiled, gaze catching Holden's again. He slowly nodded, expression intent. Yeah, he was thinking it too. None too subtle, he rubbed my knuckles with his thumb. I flexed my hand back into the *I love you* sign, and his answering grin lit up the whole darn facility.

"That was incredible." He kept grinning even in the locker room as we changed back into street clothes.

"Want ice cream on our way home?" My stomach rumbled. Technically, it was closer to dinner time than dessert, but life was sweeter with Holden. Why the hell not have dessert first?

"Only thing I like more than the ice cream idea is a double scoop of you saying *home*." He gave me a quick pat on the ass before transferring back to his chair.

"It is my home." I wasn't agreeing simply to make him happy either. It was the address on all my bills and checks. It was the place I'd finally unpacked all my bags and things, keeping only the necessary gear in travel boxes. It was where I put my feet up, where I laid my head, and where I wanted to be. "Driving back from Tahoe, listening to you and Monroe on the pod, I kept smiling."

"It was a good pod. God, I hope Monroe gets that confession." Holden sighed. Things were finally progressing in the Stapleton case again, and Monroe had been granted another interview with the convicted killer suspected of the crime. The task-force investigators were hopeful that a confession might be forthcoming that they could leverage for a plea deal of sorts, avoid a lengthy trial. "And for what it's worth, I smiled every time I thought about you the whole week you were away."

"Good. And as soon as I passed the Safe Harbor sign, the RV seemed to move faster. Lighter. Couldn't get home fast enough."

"I love that." He grabbed my hand and swung it lightly. "Love you."

"I'm going to keep coming home to you, Holden," I

promised, willing him to believe me, to trust me that much more. "There's no place else I'd rather be."

"Thank—"

Pulling my hand loose, I held it up. "You don't get to thank me for loving you."

"Yes, Chief." He pasted a suitably humble expression on his face. It wasn't gratitude I wanted from this man or praise. It was *him*. His heart. Him in my life. Him at the center of everything. I stared at him, trying to beam that fact into his thick skull, until he nodded. "I'll always be waiting. How's that?"

"Perfect."

And it was. I wouldn't always make him wait. I'd take him with me when I could, make good on my promise to give him the world. I wouldn't make him wait too long on those rings either. Life was short, and we had each other. Neither of us was perfect, but we were perfect for each other. Even this cranky old SEAL chief divemaster could see how that was damn worth celebrating.

# Epilogue

## Sam

I arrived at Holden and Cal's house with a fake smile and my mom's famous oatmeal-cranberry cookies, hoping one would make up for the other. Funny how it had been Holden's house alone for close to a decade, and then Cal rolled into town, and now it was Holden and Cal for everything. House. Car. Their dopey looks. The side of the table they sat on for trivia night. I didn't see one without asking about the other, and indeed, Holden looked darn near half-naked without Cal hovering nearby as he let me into the house.

"Is Cal back yet?" I asked Holden as he wheeled ahead of me, taking a moment to wipe the sweat from my forehead. I'd walked despite the July heat because trying to find parking on a holiday weekend in Holden's neighborhood was no joke. I'd passed no less than a dozen barbecues on my walk over.

"No." Holden harrumphed his way into the house, where Knox and Monroe were waiting in the living room.

"Ix-nay on the ask-kay," Knox joked, standing to greet me with a back-slapping hug and taking the plate of cookies. He glanced pointedly at Holden. "Someone's a bit cranky."

"Good." I laughed.

"Good?" Monroe frowned, studying me closely.

"I'm not being mean." I held up my hands. "It's been nice, the past few months, seeing another side of Holden."

I probably wasn't explaining it well, but Holden had been my friend for years, always occupying a particular slot, quick with a joke, loyal to a fault, ready to help, but lacking the emotional depth that made true communication possible.

Not that I was opening up to many these days, but for the first time, Holden was on the list of those I might talk with if I could figure out what the heck I wanted to say.

"Maybe that side's always been there." Knox shrugged. He didn't know Holden as well as Monroe and I did, so, undoubtedly, Holden's transformation was less dramatic for him. However, to me, love had sculpted Holden, revealing layers and edges.

He was a lucky, lucky man, being cared about the way Cal loved him. Not that Cal wasn't lucky too, and watching the two of them was so beautiful it *hurt*. Some days more than others.

"You're right." Monroe crossed over to Holden, set a hand on his shoulder. "I'm sorry."

"Thanks, but you didn't miss anything." Holden quirked his mouth, waving away all our concerns. "It was... easier, being the comedian. The funny friend."

"Well, I like you better this way, my friend." I nodded at him, trying to tell him with my eyes how happy I was for him.

"And you're still funny." Monroe chuckled as Holden

276

glanced again at the door. "Cute how you keep checking the window."

"It's holiday weekend traffic." Knox straightened his messy man bun before giving Holden a reassuring smile. "He'll be here."

"I know he's coming." Holden exhaled hard. "And I've kept busy with summer classes and the pod. I've just missed my guy."

There was a group *awwww* as Holden spared a last look at the driveway before leading us toward the back of the house. "Let's fire up the grill. My mom's in the kitchen, video chatting Greg and Kathleen."

"Video chatting Charlie, you mean." Like all of us, Knox had heard all about Holden's new nephew over the last few months. And like Knox's new baby brother across town, Charlie was apparently the most brilliant of infants. Luckily, both babies produced super cute pictures for us to admire.

"Charlie needs to come down and meet baby Keller," I suggested, summoning enthusiasm I didn't much feel. Although Holden's younger brother was closer in age to me, I'd always connected more with Holden and his friend group for *worthy* reasons I refused to think about right then. "It would be nice to see Greg again."

"Ha. I'll remind him Safe Harbor also has coffee now." Holden chuckled.

"Who's hungry?" Holden's mother swooped out of the kitchen, and the next hour or so was a flurry of food prep and getting the grill ready on Holden's patio. Cold beverages flowed as smoothly as the small talk, and I let the afternoon swirl around me, the nearness of my friends as restorative as ever.

By the time I spied Cal creeping through the glass patio

doors, I was in a far better mood and not about to ruin his surprise, so I hung back, waiting for the moment Holden spotted his guy.

And it didn't disappoint. Cal came up behind Holden, putting his hands on Holden's shoulders, and the way joy washed over his every chiseled feature was a thing of true beauty and hope.

Everyone should find someone to look at them the way Holden gazed up at Cal, head tipping back. "You made it."

"Told you I would, *baby*." Cal bent to give Holden a sound kiss before holding up a bulging white paper sack. "Picked up some ice cream on my way into town. The line was ridiculous but worth it for the Fourth of July flavors."

"How was the...trip?" Holden's mom asked delicately as she brought him a big glass of iced tea.

"The recovery went well." Cal gave her an indulgent smile. He loved Holden, that much was clear, but he absolutely doted on Holden's mom, going along to fetch her home a few weeks back and helping reopen her house, putting in hours of yard work so everything was just-so for her return to Safe Harbor. "Police department in rural Idaho trying to crack a cold case. Low on funds and leads. We used lift bags to turn and bring up a car. Always exciting to recover a whole vehicle. And a lot of valuable evidence for the investigation. Can't wait to explain it all on the next episode of Holden's podcast. My team did good."

"You're getting a regular little crew now." Holden's mom busied herself fixing Cal a plate. "Tell Heidi to come around next time Marley's in town."

"Matchmaking?" Holden chuckled before shifting his attention back to Cal, so much pride and love in his eyes. "Good work. I'm so proud of you. Mom's getting you some food. What else do you need?"

"You." Setting the ice cream on the picnic table, Cal plopped himself down on Holden's lap as the group gave another collective *awwww*. "Are we celebrating?" Cal asked Monroe from his perch on Holden's lap. He took a sip of tea, apparently in no rush to find an actual chair. "Holden told me about the book deal on the phone the other night."

"We're celebrating," Knox answered for Monroe, as proud of his guy as Holden was of Cal. With good reason too. Monroe now had a fancy literary agent, one who specialized in true crime and thrillers. And as of a few days ago, he now had a big book deal for his work on the Stapleton case.

"My book deal is good news. As is the confession, but it feels weird being happy." Monroe sighed, crinkles appearing around his striking eyes. He'd earned that deal, being the only one to get the serial killer to talk, breaking his cryptic movie quote code, and gathering enough information for the task force to bring the case to a close with a whimper of a plea deal, not the bang of a conviction or drama of a big trial.

"Yeah," I echoed weakly. If any other friend had sold a book deal, I would have arrived with a cake or some small gift, but like Monroe himself, I hadn't been sure how to celebrate this development. "Not sure what to feel."

"Life is complicated," Cal said pragmatically, leaning back against Holden, who held him fast. "We can be happy for you and relieved at the resolution for the case and still sad for the loss."

"Not sure on resolved." I studied my half-eaten veggie burger as if it might yield more answers than my troubled brain. Ordinarily, I'd totally agree with Cal on the complexity of life, beautiful and terrible all at once, but this matter was different. "I see your point, but..."

"It's hard." Monroe finished my thought for me. "You haven't heard—"

"Where do you keep your ice cream bowls?" Knox cut him off brightly, bouncing toward the house, saving me from answering the inevitable question of whether I'd heard from Worth. That I was still texting him was a given. Couldn't lie to my friends, and I was damn grateful to be spared the conversation.

"Thanks," I whispered to Knox when he returned with an ice cream scoop and passed out small bowls.

"Anytime." He grinned at me. "And any time now to get your sparkle back, sunshine. We miss our optimistic friend."

*I miss me too.* But all I did was nod. It wasn't any of their faults or problem that I was so wrapped up in my decades-old crush on Worth Stapleton that I lived from emoji to emoji and worried nonstop about how he was coping with all the news about his mother's case. For someone I hadn't laid eyes on in almost twenty years, the man occupied so much free real estate in my head that he might as well have his own skyscraper.

Sighing at my ridiculousness, I distracted myself by helping serve up the ice cream, making sure everyone had some of the various imaginative flavors. We voted on favorites and toasted Monroe's success and lingered until an evening breeze swept through.

"Guess we should head back before downtown clogs with all the people going to the town fireworks show." Knox stretched as he stood up from the picnic table.

"You gonna be okay tonight with all the firecracker noise?" Monroe asked Cal. It wasn't an idle question. The holiday was difficult for all service people, especially those struggling with PTSD. The noise could sound eerily like gunfire, and indeed, both Cal and Monroe had startled at the few stray fireworks neighbors had sent up earlier in the day. "Call us if you need anything."

"We have a plan." Cal glanced at Holden. They'd moved to snuggling in a glider on the patio. The heat in his gaze said the plan was something other than earplugs, and Knox snorted.

"Doubt it involves trying to sleep through the noise."

"Hush." Monroe shot him a look. "You're embarrassing Sam."

"He's not," I protested, not that anyone seemed to hear me. That I was blushing was a given, but not for the reason Monroe assumed. I was Sam, the good guy, preacher's kid, someone to protect from dirty jokes and innuendo. Some nights, I got really darn tired of being that guy.

"You hush." Knox shot back lovingly at Monroe, voice firm and unmistakenly sexy. "Maybe we need a *plan* too."

"Please." Monroe mouthed at him before turning back to us, all but dragging Knox toward the house. "Night, all."

"Night." I said my own goodbyes as quickly as I could. "See you Wednesday for choir practice, Cal?"

"I'm trying to tell y'all I can't really sing."

"A bet is a bet." I slapped his shoulder, managing a hearty chuckle. "And you wouldn't be the first choir member who can't carry a tune in a bucket, but I've heard you, buddy. The secret's out."

"Yeah, it is." Holden cuddled Cal closer, sniffing his short hair and looking for all the world like he was seconds from making out with him right then and there.

Perfect time for me to escape, and I headed out in the night air. Not quite twilight yet, but the sound of fireworks was already echoing through the neighborhood. The smell of charred meat hung in the air, and all around me, laughter filtered out of backyards, snippets of conversations that only made me feel that much more alone.

The last single friend.

It was so darn easy to feel sorry for myself. And deep in my pity party, I almost tripped over a small dog, some sort of sheltie, hunkering under a bush, half on the grass and half on the sidewalk. She was doing that little kid and scared animal thing of pretending like if she couldn't see me, I couldn't see her.

"Hey, girl, how'd you get here?" I stroked her cautiously as I felt for a collar or tag. Nope. And when another firework explosion erupted, she leaped into my arms, every furry, smelly inch of her. She sure was scroungy. Likely a stray, not an escapee from one of the neighboring houses.

I listened to see if people were calling for a dog, but all I heard was more fireworks and laughter. The dog huddled closer into my lap. Well, I guessed I'd wanted someone to cuddle with. God sure did have a sense of humor.

Scooping the dog up, I petted her more. "Guess you're coming with me."

The local shelter was closed for the holiday weekend, and the dog wasn't exactly a police emergency, but I also couldn't leave her where she was, alone and scared and hungry. I'd take her home, check the town app for lost dog reports, and decide which vet friend I could call for advice.

Focused solely on the dog, I turned onto my street. Funny how I'd owned the Stapleton house for months and months but had only been moved in for weeks. And it was still the Stapleton house to me, though things were gradually becoming mine. My street. My yard. My bedroom on the third floor.

Maybe with time, the whole place would feel like home and mine. And maybe I could figure out how to not think of Worth every other minute. Put myself on a phone diet. Silence the text notifications. Stop hunting memes to share.

And with time, perhaps—

I pulled up short, clutching the dog tighter. Inside the low white fence, a stranger sat under the big tree in my front yard. "What the...?"

I took a cautious step forward. The light-haired man appeared to be possibly sleeping or deep in thought. He wore a wrinkled suit, a three-day beard, and an air of despair. For all her earlier fear, the dog didn't bark, but like me, she was on red alert for trouble.

Debating whether I needed to call someone about the trespasser, I shifted the dog to one arm and patted my pocket for my phone, only to drop the thing as the stranger blinked his eyes open.

This was no stranger.

I'd know those haunted eyes anywhere. Dark alley. Siberia. Anchorage. There was nowhere I could escape to and not know exactly who this was and what his presence meant: Worth Stapleton had come home at long last to Safe Harbor.

\* \* \*

Find out what happens when Worth and Sam reunite, the Stapleton cold case is solved, and all our Safe Harbor men have finally found peace, love, and happiness. *Find Me Worthy* is the final book in the Safe Harbor series and is currently at Amazon and in Kindle Unlimited. You can turn the page for a sneak peek of chapter one.

Thank you, readers, for loving my Safe Harbor family as much as I have. They wouldn't exist if it wasn't for your support.

<3 Annabeth

# Sneak Peek of Find Me Worthy

## *Worth*

This was still my tree.

I had no clue what I was doing in Safe Harbor on the Fourth of July, a town I hadn't been to in nearly twenty years, sitting in front of a house that hadn't belonged to me in almost as long. My back was pressed against the same massive Oregon white oak where I'd spent many an hour sitting and thinking as a kid. It'd been from here that I could watch the neighborhood, especially on nights like this, when the sounds of barbecues and gatherings filtered all down the block. And here where I could think.

I wasn't a kid anymore, wasn't that same person—hadn't been in forever—but here I was, sitting under the same tree. A little wider now, both me and the tree, a little more gnarly with age, wild branches, and rumpled leaves. We both needed a good trim.

The ground under me was mossy and soft, years of shade from the dense leaf canopy keeping the grass at bay. The ground stayed cool and damp even in the middle of summer. The evening air brought a chill as well, not uncommon for the mercurial Oregon summer weather.

Or maybe that was the cold in my soul: icy and directionless. August would be far warmer, but I wouldn't be here then. Heck, I didn't fully believe I was here now.

I stared at the house, but it had nary an answer. Darkness had started to fall, and with it, the sound of fireworks and backyard celebrations picked up, making me more aware of how very alone I was. My gaze turned inward, unfocused, the last forty-eight hours—okay, the last forty damn years—catching up with me.

"Worth?" The sound of my name snapped me alert. A younger guy holding the scroungiest, ugliest sheltie mix stood in front of me and my tree. The white wooden front gate hung open.

"Who are you?" I demanded. The guy was younger than me, probably early to mid-thirties, with darkish hair and lighter eyes. It was hard to determine color at night, but he was slim with a strong bone structure. No one I recognized, although clearly, he knew me.

"You don't know?" The guy sounded disappointed as he bent to retrieve a phone from the ground, and if I had any more self-recrimination in me, I might feel bad.

"Sorry, man. Been a lot of years since I was back around these parts."

"I know." His voice was flat as he shifted the scraggly dog to his other side. "I'm Sam."

*Oh, Sam.* This was *Sam.* And if I'd checked social media anytime in the last decade, I might have known that.

"Sam Bookman? But you're..." I trailed off because both *you turned out hot* and *you're supposed to still be a kid* were wildly inappropriate. "What are you doing here?" I asked instead. "Don't you live on the other side of town?"

"I live here." Sam's tone was somewhere between patient and irritated. "This is my house. You're on my front lawn."

He gave me one hell of a pointed look. The Sam I'd known once upon a time was endlessly chipper and never got irritated, but perhaps I was to blame there. I seemed to try everyone's patience lately, including my own.

"Oh." I scrubbed my hair, suddenly aware of exactly how many hours it had been since my last shower. "That's right. You bought the place. I heard that. Forget from who."

The house and my tree had been through one bad owner after another. It was a wonder both were still standing. My stomach gnawed at itself, empty but angry, and the longer Sam stared at me, the more I had to fight the urge to rub my middle.

"Worth, why are you here?" A bottle rocket whistled, a pink firework bursting over Sam's head. The light revealed his auburn hair, a deeper shade than the candy-apple red it had been as a kid. "Why now? You didn't come for your mom's memorial."

"I didn't." Nothing to do but agree. Sam didn't need to know I'd had a ticket to Portland, a hotel reservation too. In fact, despite shaking hands and a queasy stomach, I'd been debating which suit to pack when the feds had shown up at my high-rise condo, and that had been that. No doing the right thing, the expected thing. Story of my whole damn life.

*Memorial.* I hated that word. It sounded so...tidy. Serene and peaceful almost. Unlike the other M-word: *missing.* The word that had ridden shotgun with me ever since my mom's disappearance twenty years ago. And then the M-word I could barely wrap my brain around: *murder.* I hated that word most of all. Unlike memorial, it was a gory, messy word, bringing drama and chaos. Upending everything I thought I'd known, including the two decades I'd spent convinced my father was behind the disappearance. He wasn't. A serial killer was. The reopening of the cold case had proven that. And the truth was so much more complicated than any story I'd told myself to get through the long years of not knowing.

"You don't reply to my messages anymore either." Sam had been thirteen or fourteen the year I'd been eighteen. He'd had a young teen's voice and had always been popping up where I least wanted him. Some things apparently never changed. But other things were radically different, like Sam's melodic, radio-worthy voice having no trace of his bouncy teen mannerisms. And his adult voice was far harder to dismiss, the tone used by teachers everywhere, a scolding that wasn't easily ducked. "From what I hear, I'm not alone in getting ghosted. Should I call Holden or Monroe for you?"

"God, no." I couldn't have either of my oldest friends see me like this. And if I couldn't explain to myself why I was here, no way would I be able to answer the questions of two professional investigators. "And I...um...had to change numbers recently. Long story." I waved a hand. "But I did get your messages before that. I might have fallen behind on liking a few memes, but..."

"A few." Sam sighed, dog wriggling in his arms. About a year ago, messages had started appearing. First from Monroe and Holden, who were championing the re-opening of my mother's cold case, then from Sam, the kid from my past who'd always wanted to be the sidekick to our little group. Unlike Monroe and Holden, who wanted answers, Sam apparently wanted nothing more than to send me positive-thinking memes and funny cats. And he'd never know, but there were days—hell, weeks—where he'd been my only reason to crack a smile.

"Hey." I pointed at the dog. In all the memes, and there had likely been dozens, it was always cats doing silly things, never dogs. "Aren't you a cat person?"

*Ka-boom.* Another firework went off, and the dog leaped from Sam's arms to my lap.

"I am. Trust me that Delilah is not going to be amused, but I found this girl all alone and scared. I need to check my phone. Safe Harbor has an app now for used furniture, yard sales, and things like lost pets."

"This dog won't be on the app." Narrowing my eyes, I peered at the dog's ratty collar, almost hidden by her dense fur. The silver tag had been attacked with some sort of metal implement, the name and contact info scratched out. "Someone dumped her on purpose."

"In Safe Harbor?" Sam's frown deepened. "I found her in a nice neighborhood, over by Holden's house."

"Yes, Sam, in Safe Harbor." I mocked his horror. "Hard to imagine, but bad things happen here too."

"I know they do." Sam had a piercing gaze, seeing so much more than I wanted, even in the dark. And in his shrewd expression, I saw the last year play out—my mom's cold case getting resurrected, providing all the proof anyone needed that bad things happened in Safe Harbor. Even perfect small towns weren't immune from serial killers. Hell, I was undoubtedly now one of those terrible occurrences, the prodigal son who couldn't even make his own mother's memorial.

*The shame.* I could hear the pearl-clutchers. How much louder would they be if everyone here knew the truth? It was bound to come out. Only a matter of time. The heavy sense of doom that had plagued me for days intensified. *No way out.*

Looking away, I returned to the dog's collar. "No phone number. No address. Can't even make out the name anymore."

"Luckily, my understanding is that dogs are quick to learn new names. The animal shelter should be open tomorrow, and hopefully, she finds a new family and new name fast." Sam's tone was pragmatic, but something in his offhand tone pissed me off.

"So, what? She gets a place to stay for the night, then she's someone else's problem to solve?" I pet the dog's shuddering head. I wasn't being fair. Sam could have left the beast where he'd found her, but my rant kept gathering steam. "What if she's sick? Injured? Old? And she stinks. What if the shelter doesn't have time to make her presentable? Not all dogs get adopted, you know." My voice cracked on the word *adopted.*

"I do know a thing or two about strays," Sam said mildly. And oh, that was right, he ran some sort of charity for at-risk youth, putting them to work in a nonprofit coffee shop. Crouching, he lifted the quaking dog back off my lap. "It's okay, girl. The fireworks will be over soon. Not everyone likes the Fourth of July."

"I used to love it," I blurted. "Big stack of fireworks, Mom's potato salad, friends over for a big barbecue. Red-white-and-blue bunting on the front porch. Twinkling lights out on the back deck."

"I remember." Still kneeling, he petted the dog before standing and studying me closely. Too closely. "Come inside, Worth. Let's get your princess cleaned up and see what we're dealing with here."

"You can't call her princess. That's like the most cliché

dog name of all time." I ignored the hand he offered to help me up. I was staying right where I was.

"And yet, you seem determined to be her white knight." Finally dropping his hand, Sam looked down at the dog. "Okay, Buttercup. Let's see if we can sneak you past Queen Delilah."

"Buttercup is hardly..." I paused, another tendril of a memory snaking its way through my brain. Movie night. Youth group at church. Old movie, everyone quoting parts they'd long since memorized. Sam's laughing face popping up over the back of a couch where I sat with some girl. Late night. Hide and seek. Sam raiding the junk food with Holden and me.

*What are you going to do after graduation, Worth?*
*Take on the world.*

God, if I could only go back. My voice dropped to a hoarse whisper. "Okay. We can call her Buttercup."

"We? Are you coming in to help then?"

Another firework sounded, and the dog whimpered pitifully. "You want me to come inside? The house?"

"That is where the shower is," Sam said mildly. "Were you planning to spend all night under this tree?"

"Not sure I had a plan." Understatement of the fucking century. I closed my eyes. "Just wanted to find my tree—"

"My tree." Sam was quick to correct me. Not mean, just accurate, but damn, that stung.

"You know what I mean." I pursed my lips.

"I do." He pursed his right back. A stalemate.

"Anyway, I thought if I could just sit here long enough, I might find... God, I don't even know." I hefted myself to my feet, irritated at my own ridiculousness. "A reason? Sounds stupid saying it aloud."

"No, it doesn't." Sam exhaled hard, voice gentling. "But

I have to say, you look pretty rough. Did you sleep on the plane?"

"No plane. I drove." I pointed at his driveway. I'd parked in the back like I always used to. I was surprised he hadn't noticed my Beemer, but maybe I was surprise enough. "The car pointed itself north, and well, here I am."

"Sounds like quite the plan."

"Plan A, B, C, and D have all failed." My voice was as caustic as my stomach. Fuck it. "No more plans."

"What happened?" Sam's voice wasn't unkind, but the way he shifted the dog and glanced at the front porch said he was quickly losing patience with my delay tactics.

"Guess you'll find out soon enough." No more eager to enter the house, I relieved him of the dog, who cuddled her damp self right into my dress shirt. Oh well. I'd seen worse. "Surprised the gossip hasn't arrived ahead of me, actually."

"Why don't you tell me?" Sighing, Sam perched on the top step. I half expected him to break out treats next, to lure me up the steps like a lost puppy.

"You already know the start of my story. Local boy makes good. Standford MBA, cushy investment banker job, high-rise condo, living the life." I paused for dramatic effect, waiting for Sam to nod. "And then...it all crumbles. Perry & Ellis is no more—"

Sam narrowed his eyes. "You worked for Perry & Ellis?"

"Ah. He does know my story," I said to the dog before returning my attention to Sam. "Yep, the same investment firm making headlines for duping customers, embezzling funds, and a pretty sweet Ponzi scheme. And me? I was their star associate on an inside partnership track. I was Perry's right-hand man up until the feds hauled him away, and he squawked like an angry parrot to anyone who would listen about how Ellis masterminded the scheme."

"So you lost your job?" Sam asked when I paused for a breath. "The scandal broke months ago, I thought."

"Oh, it gets better. No job, and not much savings because I was strung-out on credit, waiting for the partnership offer to come, trying to keep up with a high-dollar lifestyle. Thank God I paid for my car with my last big bonus, or else I guess I'd be on a bus to nowhere tonight. My condo foreclosed because, silly me, I kept waiting for everything to blow over. Except it didn't. I've got no hope of a new job because the whole damn world, including every last friend and contact in the financial world, thinks I was in on it."

"Were you?" Sam asked as casually as if he were inquiring if I preferred fries or tots with my burger.

"How can you ask me that?"

"Because your answer matters." He shrugged. "If you say you didn't do it, you didn't."

"You can't just take someone's word for something like that, Sam. Geez." If only life were that damn easy. Sam might be all grown up now, but I seriously worried about his naivete.

"Well, did you?" He sounded fully prepared to believe me either way, which was all kinds of disconcerting. First, the kid had had a serious case of hero worship for me way back when, which seemed to have all but evaporated. Also, even without the blind adoration, Sam seemed willing to believe the best of me at a time when no one else was, not even me.

"Nope. I wish." I gave a bitter laugh. "I'd be on an island somewhere drinking away the money I'd stashed in offshore accounts. But no, I'm Worth Stapleton, local golden boy and village idiot who didn't know a damn thing until the feds showed up on my doorstep. I defended Perry, not that it did any good because he'd already talked, making me look even worse."

"I'm sorry." Wonder of wonders, Sam actually sounded like he meant it. "If it matters, I believe you."

I made a distressed noise. My stomach burned like hot ashes had landed with Sam's every word. He believed me. Wow. The surprise might be enough to lift my bleak mood if I were still capable of hope and wonder. However, like my stomach, I'd taken up permanent residence in a fiery hell.

"No one else does. And unless you've got a Fortune 500 company hiring, I'm not sure it makes a hell of a lot of difference."

"Nope," he way-too-readily agreed with me. "No job offer. Just a smelly dog who needs a shower and a couch you can crash on." Standing back up, he approached the front door. "Coming?"

# Also By Annabeth Albert

**Amazon Author Page**
Many titles also in audio and available from other retailers!

## Mount Hope Series

- Up All Night
- Off the Clock
- On the Edge

## Safe Harbor Series

- Bring Me Home
- Make Me Stay
- Find Me Worthy

## A-List Security Series

- Tough Luck
- Hard Job
- Bad Deal

- Hard Job

## Rainbow Cove Series

- Trust with a Chaser
- Tender with a Twist
- Lumber Jacked
- Hope on the Rocks

## #Gaymers Series

- Status Update
- Beta Test
- Connection Error

## Out of Uniform Series

- Off Base
- At Attention
- On Point
- Wheels Up
- Squared Away
- Tight Quarters
- Rough Terrain

## Frozen Hearts Series

- Arctic Sun
- Arctic Wild
- Arctic Heat

## Hotshots Series

- Burn Zone
- High Heat
- Feel the Fire
- Up in Smoke

## Shore Leave Series

- Sailor Proof
- Sink or Swim

## Perfect Harmony Series

- Treble Maker
- Love Me Tenor
- All Note Long

## Portland Heat Series

- Served Hot
- Baked Fresh
- Delivered Fast
- Knit Tight
- Wrapped Together
- Danced Close

## True Colors Series

- Conventionally Yours
- Out of Character

## Other Stand-Alone Titles

- Resilient Heart

- Winning Bracket
- Save the Date
- Level Up
- Sergeant Delicious
- Cup of Joe
- Featherbed

## **Stand-Alone Holiday Titles**

- Better Not Pout
- Mr. Right Now
- The Geek Who Saved Christmas
- Catered All the Way

# About Annabeth Albert

Annabeth Albert grew up sneaking romance novels under
the bed covers. Now, she devours all subgenres of romance
out in the open—no flashlights required! When she's not
adding to her keeper shelf, she's a multi-published Pacific
Northwest romance writer.

Emotionally complex, sexy, and funny stories are her
favorites both to read and to write. Fans of quirky, Oregon-
set books as well as those who enjoy heroes in uniform will
want to check out her many fan-favorite and critically
acclaimed series. Many titles are also in audio! Her fan
group Annabeth Albert's Angels on Facebook or Patreon
are the best places for bonus content and more!

Website: www.annabethalbert.com

## Contact & Media Info:

patreon.com/AnnabethAlbert

facebook.com/annabethalbert

x.com/AnnabethAlbert

instagram.com/annabeth_albert

amazon.com/Annabeth/e/BooLYFFAZK

bookbub.com/authors/annabeth-albert

# Acknowledgments

For twenty years, I have dreamed of writing a romance novel with a hot, handsome, sexy man on the cover who happens to be a wheelchair user. Reese Dante made my vision possible with her cover wizardry. This series was inspired in part by Wander Aguiar's Black Friday photo sale, but it's Reese who transformed the picture into the sort of representation I've wanted for years. Thank you to Reese for always going above and beyond.

Reviews, ratings, likes, mentions, comments, and shares are the lifeblood of the modern author, now more than ever. Thank you to every reader who makes what I do possible. If you loved this book, please tell a friend! And thank you simply for reading my work. You make it all worth it.

All my literary roads lead through Abbie Nicole, and this new series is no exception. I told her last fall that I wanted to write a series centered around unexpected roommate situations, and she was as supportive as ever. Her cheerleading, plot sounding board, editing, and promo savvy are the motor that keeps my business humming. Louise Auty beta read an early version of this book, and her comments made my representation stronger. I couldn't have finished this book without my writing sprint buddies, my author friends, my beloved readers, and the cheering squad pushing me on.

A huge thank you as well to Lori at Jan's Paperbacks. She makes providing signed copies to my readers so painless, and she's an amazing beacon in the romance community to boot! Her tireless advocacy for romance, queer fiction, and small businesses inspires me.

Deidre Knight, Elaine Spencer, and Tantor came together to make audio for this series possible. I so appreciate everyone at the Knight Agency, which handles my foreign rights as well.

Lastly, this series is about change. Coming home. Finding home. Discovering oneself and sense of place. Found family. MAKE ME STAY is the story of finding a family for Cal, and I have to shout out my own found family. Thank you to everyone who makes up my family of choice, the family of my heart. To my kids, I'd choose you a million times over. To my friends, I wouldn't be here without you in my circle. And I mean that on so many levels. Thank you to everyone who enriches my life.

Made in the USA
Las Vegas, NV
15 December 2024

14296337R00184